THE TYCOON TAKES A WIFE

BY

CATHERINE MANN

AND

HIS ROYAL PRIZE

BY

KATHERINE GARBERA

D0865856

MILLS & BOON

"I thought you wanted a divorce."

"I do." He secured the lily behind her ear, his knuckles caressing her neck for a second too long to be accidental. "But first, I want the honeymoon we never had."

She gasped in surprise, followed by anger...then suspicion. "You're just trying to shock me."

"How do you know I'm not serious?" His blue eyes burned with unmistakable, unsettling—irresistible?—desire.

She'd barely survived their last encounter with her heart intact. No way in hell was she dipping her toes into those fiery waters again. "You can't really believe I'll just crawl into bed with you."

"Why not? It isn't like we haven't already slept together."

Not that they'd slept much. "That night was a mistake." One with heartbreaking consequences.

THE TYCOON
TAKES A WIFE

BY
CATHERINE MANN

© Catherine Mann 2010

Published in Great Britain 2011
by Mills & Boon, an imprint of Harlequin (UK) Limited,
Eton House, 18-24 Paradise Road, Richmond, Surrey TW9 1SR

... ers that are natural, ... ewable and
... products and made from wood grown in sustain... ble forests. The
... facturing processes conform to the leg... environmental
regulations ...

To my intrepid traveler and oldest daughter, Haley.
Congrats on taking the world by storm!
You'll always be our princess.

RITA® Award winner **Catherine Mann** resides on a sunny Florida beach with her military flyboy husband and their four children. Although after nine moves in twenty years, she hasn't given away her winter gear! With over a million books in print in fifteen countries, she has also celebrated five RITA® Award finals, three Maggie Award of Excellence finals and a Booksellers' Best win. A former theater school director and university teacher, she graduated with a master's degree in theater from UNC-Greensboro and a bachelor's degree in fine arts from the College of Charleston. Catherine enjoys hearing from readers and chatting on her message board—thanks to the wonders of the wireless internet that allows her to cyber-network with her laptop by the water! To learn more about her work, visit her website, www.CatherineMann.com, or reach her by snail mail at PO Box 6065, Navarre, FL 32566, USA.

Dear Reader,

Wow, I can hardly believe it's already time to introduce you to the last Landis brother! What a delightful journey it has been for me sharing the stories of Matthew, Sebastian and Kyle Landis. Now in *The Tycoon Takes a Wife*, we learn what really happened to Jonah when he traveled to Europe. If you're new to THE LANDIS BROTHERS, no worries! I've penned the tale so you can dive right into this delicious family packed with powerful men.

I do so enjoy connected stories, especially family sagas, so it came as no surprise to me when my interest was piqued by the royal family of Jonah's wife, Eloisa. Stay tuned for more on those intriguing Medina monarchs later this year.

Thank you again for all your e-mails and letters about THE LANDIS BROTHERS as well as my other books! I love hearing from readers, so please feel free to contact me through my new website: www.catherinemann.com or write to me at PO Box 6065, Navarre, FL 32566, USA.

Happy reading!

Catherine Mann

Prologue

Madrid, Spain: One Year Ago

He wanted to drape her in jewels.

Jonah Landis skimmed his fingers along the bare arm of the woman sleeping next to him and imagined which of the family heirlooms would look best with her dark hair. Rubies? Emeralds? Or perhaps even a string of fat freshwater pearls. His knuckles grazed from her shoulder to her collarbone, his five-o'clock shadow having left a light rasp along her creamy flesh.

He usually didn't dip into the family treasure trove. He preferred to live off the money he'd made with his own investments. But for Eloisa, he would make an exception.

Early morning light streaked through the wrought-iron window grilles in the seventeenth-century manor home he'd rented for the summer. A gentle breeze rustled the linen draping over the bed. At first he hadn't even realized she was American, she'd looked so at home walking among the Spanish castle ruins. And exotic. And hot as hell. While she'd picked her way through the scaffolding making notes, he'd lost track of his conversation with fellow investors.

Most labeled him the impulsive one in his family, not that he cared much what others thought of him. Sure he took risks on a regular basis in his work realm and private life, but he always had a plan. And it had always paid off.

So far.

Last night, for the first time, he hadn't planned a damn thing. He'd simply jumped right in with both feet with this coolly intriguing woman. He wasn't sure how the decision would pan out in the long run, but he knew they were going to have one helluva summer.

The rest? They could take a day at a time.

"Uhmmm," she sighed, rolling to her side and draping her arm over his hip. "Did I oversleep?"

Her eyes were still closed but their dark, rich color had cloaked the hauteur of an Ottoman empress. He'd lost plenty of time wondering about the woman behind them during historical reconstruction meetings.

He checked the digital clock resting on a carved walnut end table. "It's only six. We still have a couple of hours before breakfast."

Eloisa burrowed her head deeper in the feather pillow, her black hair fanning a tempting contrast across white cotton. "Am still so sleepy."

She should be. They'd stayed up most of the night having sex…catnapping…showering…and ending up tangled together all over again. It didn't help that they'd had a few drinks.

He'd limited himself to a couple, but those two seemed to hit her harder than him. He stroked back her long black hair, so smooth it glided through his fingers now as it had when she'd been over him, under him.

He throbbed from wanting her all over again when he should be down for the count for a while yet. She needed the rest more.

Jonah eased from the bed, fresh morning air from outside whispering over his skin. "I'll call down and have someone from the kitchen send breakfast up here. If you have any preferences, speak now."

She flipped to her back, eyes still closed as she stretched, her perfectly rounded breasts on amazing display as the comforter slipped to her waist. "Hmmm, anything is fine with me." Her words were slurred with sleep. "I'm having the most wonderful dream—"

Eloisa paused, scrunching her forehead. She peeked through barely open inky lashes. "Jonah?"

"Yeah, that would be me." He stepped into his silk boxers and reached for the phone.

Her gaze darted around his room quickly, orienting. She grasped the comforter and yanked it up, bringing her hand closer to her face. Suddenly she went stock-still and frowned.

"What's the matter?"

She couldn't possibly be shy after last night. It wasn't as if they'd kept the lights off.

"Uh, Jonah?" Her voice squeaked up a notch.

He sank to the edge of the bed and waited, already thinking through at least five different ways he could distract her throughout the summer.

She extended her arm, splaying her fingers wide. Sunshine through the window glinted off the simple gold wedding band he'd placed there last night. Eloisa blinked fast, her eyes going wide with horror.

"Oh my God," she gasped, thumbing the shiny new ring around and around. "What have we done?"

One

"Congratulations to the bride to be, my little princess!"

The toast from the father of the bride drifted from the deck of the paddleboat, carried by the muggy Pensacola breeze to Eloisa Taylor back on the dock. Eloisa sat dipping her aching feet in the Florida Gulf waters, tired to the roots of her ponytail from helping plan her half sister's engagement party. Her stepfather had gone all out for Audrey, far more than a tax collector in a cubicle could afford, but nothing was too good for his "little princess." Still he'd had to settle for a Monday night booking to make the gala affordable.

The echo of clinking glasses mingled with the lap of waves against her feet. Dinner was done, the crowd so well fed no one would miss her. She was good at that, helping people and keeping a low profile.

Putting together this engagement party had been bittersweet, forcing her to think about her own vows. Uncelebrated. Unknown even to her family. Thank God for the quickie divorce that had extracted her from her impulsive midnight marriage almost as fast as she'd entered it.

Usually she managed to smother those recollections, but how could she not think about it now with Audrey's happily-ever-after tossed in her face 24/7? Not to mention the cryptic voice message she'd received this morning with *his* voice. Jonah. Even a year after hearing it last, she still recognized the sexy bass.

Eloisa. It's me. We have to talk.

She swept her wind-whipped ponytail from her face, shivering from the phantom feel of *his* hand stroking her face. A year ago, she'd indulged herself in checking out the heritage of her real father. A summer indulgence had led her to one totally wrong man with a high-profile life that threatened her carefully protected world. Threatened secrets she held close and deep.

Eloisa blinked back the memories of Jonah, too many given how little time she'd spent with him. They were history now since she'd divorced him. Not that their twenty-four-hour marriage counted in her mind. She should ignore the call and block his number. Or at least wait until after her sister's "I do" was in the past before contacting him again.

A fish plopped in the distance, sailboat lines clinking against masts. The rhythmic, familiar sounds soothed her. She soaked up the other sounds of home, greedily gathering every bit of comfort she could find. Emerald-green waters reflected a pregnant moon. Wind rustled through palm trees.

An engine growled softly in the distance.

So much for a late-night solitary moment. She shook dry one foot, then the other and glanced over her shoulder. A limo rolled closer. Late arriving guests? Really late since after-dinner dancing was well underway.

Reaching for her sandals she watched the long black stretch of machine inching beside the waterway. The shape of the sleek vehicle wasn't your average wedding limo. The distinctive grille glinted in the moonlight, advertising the approach of an exclusive Rolls-Royce. Tinted windows sealed off the passengers from view, but left her feeling like a butterfly pinned to the board of a science project. The private area should be safe. Yet, was anywhere totally secure, especially in the dark?

Goose bumps stung along her skin and her mouth went dry. She yanked on her shoes, chiding herself for being silly. But still, Audrey's fiancé was reputed to have some shady connections. Her stepdad could only see power and dollar signs, apparently unconcerned with the crooked path that money took.

Not that any of those questionable contacts had cause to hurt her. All the same, she should return to the floating party barge.

Eloisa jumped to her feet.

The limo sped up.

She swallowed hard, wishing she'd taken a self-defense class along the way to earning her library studies degree.

Okay, no need to go all paranoid. She forced her hands to stay loose and started walking. Only about thirty yards ahead, and she would alert the crew member at the gangway. Then she could lose herself in the crowd of dancers under the strings of white lights. The engine grew louder behind her. Eloisa strode longer, faster.

Each breath felt heavier, the salt in the air stinging her over-sensitive pores. Her low heel caught between planks on the boardwalk. She lurched forward just as the car stopped in front of her.

A back door swung wide—not even waiting for the chauffeur—and blocked her getaway. She couldn't continue ahead, only sideways into the car or into the water. Or she could back up, which would take her farther from the boat. Frantically she searched for help. Would any of those seventy-five potential witnesses in party finery whooping it up to an old Kool and the Gang song notice or hear her?

One black-clad leg swung out of the limo, the rest of the man still hidden. However that Ferragamo python loafer was enough to send her heart skittering. She'd only met one man who favored those, and she hated how she still remembered the look and brand.

She backed away, one plank at a time, assessing the man as he angled out. She hoped, prayed for some sign to let her off the hook. Gray hair? A beer belly?

Anything non-Jonah.

But no such luck. The hard-muscled guy wore all black, a dark suit jacket, the top button of his shirt undone and tie loose. He wore his brown hair almost shoulder length and swept back from his face to reveal a strong, square jaw.

A jaw far more familiar than any shoes. Nerves danced in her stomach far faster than even the partiers gyrating to the live band on the boat.

He pivoted on his heel, facing her full on, the moonlight glinting off the chestnut hints in his wavy hair. Sunglasses shielded his eyes from her. Shades at night? For a low profile or ego?

Regardless, she knew. Her ex-husband wasn't content with just calling and leaving a message. No, not Jonah. The powerful international scion she'd divorced a year ago had returned.

Jonah Landis whipped off his sunglasses, glanced at his watch and grinned. "Sorry I'm late. Have we missed the party?"

To hell with any party. Jonah Landis wanted to find out why Eloisa hadn't told him the entire truth when she'd demanded a divorce a year ago. He also wanted to know why his passionate lover had so dispassionately cut him off.

The stunned look on Eloisa's face as she stopped cold on the dock would have been priceless if he wasn't so damn mad over the secret she'd kept from him, a secret that he'd only just found out was gumming up the works on their divorce decree.

Of course when he'd met her in Madrid a year ago, he'd been distracted by the instantaneous, mind-blowing chemistry between them. And looking at her now, seeing her quiet elegance, he figured he could cut himself some slack on missing details that could have clued him in—like how much she'd fit into her Spanish surroundings.

The woman was a walking distraction.

Wind molded her tan silk dress around her body. The dimly lit night played tricks with his vision until she looked nearly naked, clothed only in shifting shadows.

Had she known that when she chose the dress? Likely not. Eloisa seemed oblivious to her allure, which only served to enhance her appeal.

Her sleek dark hair was slicked back in a severe ponytail that gave her already exotic brown eyes a tug. Without so much as lip gloss, she relegated most models to the shadows.

Once he had her name on the dotted line of divorce papers—official ones this time—he would have nothing to do with her ever again. That had been the plan anyway. He didn't need round two of her hot-cold treatment. So he'd misread the signs, hadn't realized she was drunk during the "I do" part. That didn't mean she had to slap his face and fall off the planet. He was over Eloisa.

Or so he'd thought. Then he'd seen her and felt that impact all over again, that kick-in-the-gut effect he'd thought must have been exaggerated by his memory.

He tamped back the attraction and focused on seeing this through. He needed her signature and for some reason he refused to leave it up to lawyers. Maybe it had something to do with closure.

Eloisa inched her heel from between the planks and set both feet as firmly as her delicate jaw. "What are you doing here?"

"I came to accompany you to your sister's engagement party." He hooked an elbow on the open limo door, the chauffeur waiting up front as he'd been instructed earlier. "Can't have my wife going stag."

"Shhh!" Lurching toward him, she patted the air in front of his face, stopping just shy of touching his mouth. "I am not your wife."

He clasped her hand, thumb rubbing over her bare

ring finger. "Damn, I must have hallucinated that whole wedding ceremony in Madrid."

Eloisa yanked her hand away and rubbed her palm against her leg. "You're arguing semantics."

"If you would prefer to skip the party, we could grab a bite to eat and talk about those semantics." He watched the glide of her hand up and down her thigh, remembering well the creamy, soft texture under his mouth as he'd tasted his way up.

She stared at him silently until he met her eyes again. "You're kidding, right?"

"Climb into the car and see."

She glanced back at the boat, then at him again, her long ponytail fanning to rest along her shoulder. "I'm not so sure that's a good idea."

"Afraid I'll kidnap you?"

"Don't be ridiculous." She laughed nervously as if she'd considered just that.

"Then what's holding you back? Unless you want to continue this conversation right here." He nodded toward the boat full of partyers. "I thought you wanted me to be quiet."

She looked back over her shoulder again, and while it appeared no one noticed them, who knew how long that would hold? Not that he gave a damn what anyone thought, unlike his enigmatic wife. He'd learned a long time ago he had two choices in this world. Let others rule his life or take charge.

The second option won hands down.

He cocked an eyebrow and waited.

"Fine," she bit out between gritted teeth.

She eyed him angrily as she angled past and slid into

the car without even brushing against him. Eloisa settled into the leather seat.

Jonah tucked himself inside next her, closed the door and tapped the glass window between them and the chauffeur, signaling him to drive. Just drive. He would issue a destination later.

"Where are we going?" she asked as the limo eased into motion, the tinted windows closing them in their own private capsule.

"Where do you want to go? I have a penthouse suite farther down on Pensacola Beach."

"Of course you do." Her gaze flicked around the small space, lingering briefly on his computer workstation to her left before moving on to the minibar and the plasma screen TV.

"I see you haven't changed." He'd forgotten how prickly she could be about money. Still, it had been refreshing. He'd had plenty of women chase him because of the Landis portfolio and political influence.

He'd never had a female dump him because of it. Of course back then he hadn't known she had access to money and influence beyond even his family's reach. Mighty damn impressive.

And confusing since she hadn't bothered to share that even after they married.

He put a damper on the surge of anger, a dangerous emotion given the edge of desire searing his insides. To prove to himself he could stay in control, he slid two fingers down the length of a sleekly straight lock of her black hair.

Eloisa jerked her head away. "Stop that." She adjusted the air-conditioning vent nervously until the blast of air ruffled her ponytail. "Enough playing, although you certainly seem to be an expert at recreation. I just want to know why you're here, now."

With all he knew about her, she still understood so little about him. "What's wrong with wanting to see my wife?"

"Ex-wife. We got drunk and ended up married." She shrugged casually, too much so. "It happens to lots of folks, from pop stars to everyday Joes and Josephines. Just check out the marriage logs in Las Vegas. We made a mistake, but we took steps to fix it the morning after."

"Do you consider all of it a mistake? Even the part between 'I do' and waking up with a hangover?" He couldn't resist reminding her.

A whisper of attraction smoked through her dark eyes. "I don't remember."

"You're blushing," he noted with more than a little satisfaction, grateful for the soft glow of a muted overhead light. So he was smug. Sue him. "You remember the good parts all right."

"Sex is irrelevant." She sniffed primly.

"Sex? I was talking about the food." He turned the tables, enjoying the cat-and-mouse game between them. "The *mariscada en salsa verde* was amazing." And just that fast, he could all but taste the shellfish casserole in green sauce, the supper she'd shared with him before they had after-dinner drinks. Got hitched. Got naked.

He could see the same memory reflected in her eyes just before her mouth pursed tight.

"You're a jackass, Jonah."

"But I'm all yours." For now at least.

"Not anymore. Remember the morning-after 'fix'? You're my *ex*-jackass."

If only it were that simple to put this woman in his past. God knows, he'd tried hard enough over the past year to forget about Eloisa Taylor Landis.

Or rather Eloisa *Medina* Landis?

He'd stumbled upon the glitch in a church registry, a "minor" technicality she'd forgotten to mention, but one that had snarled up their paperwork in Spain. The sense of shock and yeah, even some bitter betrayal rocked through him again.

No question, he needed to put this woman in his past, but this time he would be the one to walk away.

"Now there you're wrong, Eloisa. That fix got broken along the way." He picked up a lock of her hair again, keeping his hand off her shoulder.

Lightly he tugged, making his presence felt. A spark of awareness flickered through her eyes, flaming an answering heat inside him. He looked at the simple gold chain around her neck and remembered the jewels he'd once pictured there while she'd slept. Then she woke up and made it clear there would be no summer together. She couldn't get out of his life fast enough.

Her breath hitched. He reminded himself of his reason for coming here, to end things and leave.

Now he wondered if it might be all the more satisfying to have one last time with Eloisa, to ensure she remembered all they could have had if only she'd been as upfront with him as he'd been with her.

He glided his knuckles up her ponytail to her cheek, gently urging her to face him more fully. "The paperwork never made it through. Something to do with you lying about your name."

Her eyes darted away. "I never lied about my name—" She sat up straighter, her gaze slamming back into his. "What do you mean the paperwork didn't go through?"

She seemed to be genuinely surprised, but he'd learned not to trust her. Still he would play this game out in order to achieve his ultimate goal—a final night in her bed before leaving her forever.

"The divorce wasn't finalized. You, my dear, are still Mrs. Jonah Landis."

Two

He had to be joking.

Eloisa dug her fingers into the leather seats, seriously considering making use of that bottle of bourbon in the limo's minibar. Except indulging in a few too many umbrella drinks had landed her in this mess in the first place.

She'd taken pains to cover her tracks. Her mother had warned her how important it was to be careful. Keep a low profile. Stay above reproach. And never, ever invite scrutiny.

Eloisa looked out the window to see where they were headed. They passed nail salons and T-shirt shops along the beachfront, nightlife in full swing on open-decked restaurant bars. The chauffeur truly seemed like he was simply driving around, not headed anywhere specific—such as Jonah's hotel.

She simply couldn't pay the price for being impulsive again. "We signed the divorce paperwork."

His blue eyes narrowed. "Apparently there's some–thing you neglected to tell me, a secret you've kept mighty close to the vest."

Eloisa bit her lip to hold back impulsive words while she gathered her thoughts and reminded herself to be grateful he hadn't stumbled upon her more recent secret. Her empty stomach gripped with nerves. She tried to draw in calming breaths, but had to face a truth learned long ago. Only when working at the library could she relax.

Best she could tell, there weren't any books conveniently tucked away in this superbly stocked luxury ride. Although the backseat area was packed with enough technology to provide a command central for a small army. Apparently Jonah preferred to have the world at his fingertips. Odd, but she didn't have time for distractions right now.

"What secret?" she asked out of a long-honed habit of denial. To date, no one had pressed the point so the strategy hadn't let her down yet. "I have no idea what you're talking about."

His jaw went tight with irritation. "That's the way you want to play this? Fine." He leaned in closer until she couldn't miss the musky scent of him mixed with his still-familiar aftershave. "You forgot to mention your father."

Her chest went tighter than her hands twisting in the skirt of her dress. "My dad's a tax collector in Pensacola, Florida. Speaking of which, why aren't you home in Hilton Head, South Carolina?"

He gripped her wrists to stop her nervous fidgeting. "Not your stepdad, your biological father."

Apparently, Jonah wasn't easily diverted tonight.

"I told you before about my biological father." A shiver passed over her at even the mention of the man who'd wrecked her mother's life, the man she lied about on a regular basis. "My mother was a single parent when I was born. My real father was a bum who wanted no part in my life." True enough.

Her dad—no more than a sperm donor as far as she was concerned—had broken her mother's heart then left her to raise their child alone. Her stepfather might not have been Prince Charming—wasn't that damn ironic?—but at least he'd been there for her and her mother.

"A bum? A royal bum." Jonah stretched a leg out in front of him, polished snakeskin loafer gleaming in the overhead lamp. "Interesting dichotomy."

She squeezed her eyes shut and wished it was that easy to shut out the repercussions of what he'd somehow discovered. Her mother had been emphatic about personal safety. Her biological father still had enemies back in San Rinaldo. She'd been foolish to tempt fate by going to Spain in hopes of unobtrusively learning about half her heritage on the small island country nearby. Damn it all, fear was a good thing when it kept a person safe.

She steadied her breath, if not her galloping heart rate. "Would you please not say that?"

"Say what?"

"The whole *royal* thing." While her stepfather frequently called Audrey his "little princess," he—and the rest of the world—didn't know that Eloisa was actually the one with royal blood singing through her veins, thanks to her biological father.

Nobody knew, except Eloisa, her deceased mother and a lawyer who conducted any communication with the deposed king. Eloisa's so-called real father. A man still hunted to this day by the rebel faction that had taken over his small island kingdom of San Rinaldo off the coast of Spain.

How had Jonah found out?

He tipped her chin with one knuckle as his driver slowed for jaywalking teens. "You may have been able to fool the world for a lot of years, but I've figured out your secret. You're the illegitimate daughter of deposed King Enrique Medina."

She stiffened defensively, then forced herself to relax nonchalantly. "That's ridiculous." Albeit true. If he could figure it out, how much longer until her secret was revealed to others? She needed to know, hopefully find some way to plug that leak and persuade him he was wrong.

Then she would decide what to do if his claim was actually true, a notion that could have her hyperventilating if she thought about it too long. "What makes you think something so outlandish?"

"I discovered the truth when I went back to Europe recently. My brother and his wife decided to renew their wedding vows and while I was in the area, I stopped by the chapel where we got married."

A bolt of surprise shot through her and she couldn't help but think back to that night. She'd been emotionally flattened by her mother's death and had only just returned to finish her studies in Europe. She'd shared some drinks with the guy she'd secretly had a crush on and the next thing she'd known, they were hunting for a preacher or a justice of the peace with the lights still on.

Visiting the place where they'd exchanged vows sounded sentimental. Like that day meant more to him than a drunken mistake.

She couldn't stop herself from asking, "You went back there?"

"I was in the neighborhood," he repeated, his jaw going tight, the first sign that the whole debacle may have upset him as much as it had her.

He'd let her go so easily, agreeing they'd made an impulsive mistake rather than asking her to crawl back in bed with him and discuss it later. A huge part of her had wanted him to sweep away rational concerns. But no. He'd let her leave, just as her father never claimed her mother.

Or her.

She tore her eyes away from the tempting curve of his mouth, a mouth that had brought such intense pleasure when he'd explored every patch of her skin later that night after their "I do." Except they'd exchanged vows in Spanish, which had seemed romantic at the time. Between her hiccups. "Everyone knows King Enrique doesn't live in San Rinaldo anymore. Nobody knows where he and his sons fled after they left. There are only rumors."

"Rumors that he's in Argentina." Jonah lounged back in the seat, seemingly lazy and relaxed, except for the coiled muscles she could see bunched under his black jacket.

She knew well he came by those muscles honestly. Her first memory of him was burned in her brain, the day she'd joined the restoration team on a graduate internship to assist with research. Jonah had been studying blueprints with another man on the construction site. She'd mistakenly thought Jonah worked on the crew, from his casual clothes and mud-stained boots. The guy was actually a couple of credits away from his PhD. He wasn't just an architect, he was a bit of an artist in his own right.

That had enticed her.

Only later, too late for her own good, had she discovered who he was. A Landis, a member of a financial and political dynasty.

Eloisa looked away from his too-perceptive eyes and swept her hem back over her knees. "I wouldn't know anything about that."

Lying came so easily after this long.

"It also appears that neither you nor your mother has been to Argentina, but that's not my point." His eyes drilled into her until she looked back at him. "I don't give a damn where your royal papa lives. I'm only concerned with the fact that you lied to me, which gummed up the works for our divorce."

"Okay, then." She met his gaze defiantly. "If what you say is true, maybe it means the marriage is void, too, so we don't need a divorce."

He shook his head. "No such luck. I checked. Believe me. We are totally and completely husband and wife."

Jonah slid his fingers down the length of her hair until his hand cupped her hip. His hand rested warm and familiar and tempting against her until she could swear she felt his calluses through her dress. She struggled not to squirm—or sway closer.

She clasped his wrist and set his hand back on his

knee. "File abandonment charges. Or I will. I don't care as long as this is taken care of quickly and quietly. No one here knows about my, uh, impetuosity."

"Don't you want to discuss who gets the china and who gets the monogrammed towels?"

Argh! She tapped on the window. "Driver? Driver?" She kept rapping until the window parted. "Take me back now, please."

The chauffeur glanced at Jonah who nodded curtly.

His autocratic demeanor made her want to scream out her frustration but she wouldn't cause a scene. Why did this man alone have the power to make her blood boil? She was a master of calm. Everyone said so, from the stodgiest of library board members to her sixth grade track coach who never had managed to coax her to full speed.

She waited until the window closed before turning to him again. "You can have every last bit of the nothing I own if you'll please just stop this madness now. Arguing isn't going to solve anything. I'll have my lawyer look into the divorce issue."

That was as close as she would come to admitting he'd stumbled on the truth. She certainly couldn't outright confirm it without seeing what proof he had and hopefully have time to take it to her attorney. Too many lives were at stake. There were still people out there tied to the group that tried to assassinate Enrique Medina, had in fact succeeded in killing his wife, the mother of his three legitimate heirs.

Enrique had been a widower when he met her mother in Florida, and still they hadn't gotten married. Her mom vowed she hadn't wanted any part of the royal lifestyle, but her jaw had always quivered when she said it. Right now Eloisa sympathized with her mother more than she could have ever imagined. Relationships were damn complicated—and painful.

Thank goodness the limo approached the paddleboat again because she didn't know how much more of this she could take tonight. The car stopped smoothly alongside the dock.

"Jonah, if that's all you have to say, I need to return to the party. My attorney will be in touch with you first thing next week."

Eloisa reached for the door.

His hand fell to rest on top of hers, his body pressing intimately against her as he stretched past.

"Hold on a minute. Do you really think I'm letting you out of my sight again that easily? Last time I did that, you ditched before lunch. I'm not wasting another year looking for you if you decide to bolt."

"I didn't run. I came home to Pensacola." She tried to inch free but he clasped her hands in his. "This is where you can find me."

Where he could have found her anytime over the past twelve months if he'd cared at all. In the first few weeks she'd waited, hoped, then the panic set in as she'd wrestled with contacting him.

Now, they had no reason to talk.

"I'm here now." His thumb stroked the inside of her wrist. "And we're going to fix this mess face-to-face rather than trusting the system again."

"No!" Already her skin tingled with awareness so much more intense than when he'd cupped her hip—and she'd been mighty aware.

Damn her traitorous body.

"Yes," he said, reaching past and throwing open the door.

He was letting her go after all? But hadn't he just said they were going to confront things face-to-face?

However, who was she to waste time questioning the reason he'd changed his mind? She rushed out of the limousine and turned at the last second to say goodbye to Jonah. Why was her gut clenching at the notion of never seeing him again?

She pivoted on her heel only to slam into his chest. Apparently he'd stepped out of the vehicle as well. Distant voices from her sister's party drifted on the wind, something she could barely register since his sun-bronzed face lowered toward hers.

Before she could breathe, much less protest, his mouth covered hers. His eyes stayed open, which she realized must mean hers were open, too. Just like a year ago, she stared at his eyes, the kind of blue poets wrote about. His wild and fresh nature scent was the same sort evoked by a literary walk through Thoreau's *Walden*.

And just that fast, her lashes fluttered closed. She savored the taste of him on her lips, her tongue again. Her hands slid up to splay on his chest, hard muscles rippling under her fingers.

Then unease niggled at the back of her brain, a sense of unrest. Something was off about this kiss. She remembered what it was like to be kissed by Jonah, and as nerve tingling as it felt to be pressed against him, to inhale the scent of him, this wasn't right.

She tried to gather her thoughts enough to think rationally rather than just languish in sensation. His broad hand moved along her waist, lightly, rhythmically.

Totally in control.

Where everyone could see.

He was putting on a display for the partyers on the boat, damn him. Indignation, anger and a hint of hurt smoked through her veins, chasing away desire. She started to pull back then reconsidered. The damage was already done. Everyone at the party had seen them kiss. They would assume the worst. She might as well take advantage of the opportunity to surprise Jonah for a change. And yes, even to extract a little revenge for how he'd staged this whole encounter tonight to knock her off balance rather than simply notifying her through their attorneys.

Eloisa slid her arms around his waist, not that anyone could see behind him. But what she was about to do wasn't for public viewing anyway.

It was all for Jonah.

Eloisa grabbed his butt.

Jonah blinked in surprise, her hand damn near searing through his pants. He started to pull away…then sensation steamrolled over him. This kiss wasn't going the way he'd planned. He certainly hadn't expected her to take control of the game he'd started.

Now that she had? Time to turn the tables again.

Gasps of surprise drifting on the wind from the boat, he cupped her neck and stroked his tongue along the seam of her lips, just once, but enough, if the hitch in her breathing was anything to judge by. Her body turned fluid as she pressed closer to him. Her hands skimmed up along his spine to his shoulders. Then she speared her fingers through his hair, sending his pulse spiking and placing his self-control on shaky ground.

Without question, he wanted to take this encounter

further, but not here. Not in public. And he knew if they moved to the limo, reason would pull her away again. So with more than a little regret, he ended the kiss. He'd made his point anyway.

Jonah eased away from her, still keeping his hands looped behind her back in case she decided to bolt—or slap him. "We'll finish this later, princess, when we don't have an audience."

When he could take this to the natural finish his body demanded. And when she was totally consenting rather than merely acting on impulse. The kiss may have started as a staged way to make her family aware of their connection, but halfway in, he'd realized his instincts were dead-on.

He couldn't walk away without one last time in her bed.

Her lips pursed tight as if holding back a retort, but her hands shook as she slid them from behind him to rest on his chest. He watched over her shoulder as a small group left the boat and started toward them on the boardwalk. A trio led the pack. Thanks to photos from an investigator, Jonah IDed the three right away. Her stepfather, Harry Taylor. Her half sister, Audrey Taylor. And Audrey's fiancé, Joey.

Eloisa leaned closer and whispered through tight teeth. "You are so going to pay for doing this."

"Shhh." He dropped a quick kiss on her forehead, liking the taste of his revenge so far. His appetite for it—for her—only increased the longer he spent by her side. "We don't want them to hear us fighting, do we, dear?"

Jonah slipped his arm around her shoulders and

tucked her by his side, her soft curves pressed enticingly against him.

She stiffened. "You can't be planning to tell them... uh..."

"About your father?"

Her brown eyes flashed with warring anger and fear. "About your theories. About you and me."

"My lips are sealed, princess."

"Stop calling me that," she said through gritted teeth as the footsteps thunked louder and closer.

"You and I both know it's true. There's no more denying it. The only question is, how far will you go to keep me quiet?"

She gasped. "You can't mean—"

"Too late to talk, Eloisa dear." He squeezed her lightly as the group closed in, her family leading. "Trust me or not."

The older man in the lead fanned a hand over his wind-blown blond hair, whisper thin along the top. His daughter—the bride to be—was an even paler version of her father. Even her hair seemed bleached white by the sun, yet she didn't sport even a hint of a tan. Her fiancé hovered behind, fists shoved in his pockets. He shuffled from foot to foot as if impatient to be anywhere but here. A small crowd gathered behind them while others watched from the deck railing.

Jonah extended his hand to Eloisa's stepfather. "Sorry I'm late, sir. I'm Eloisa's date for tonight's shindig. I'm Jonah Landis."

She wouldn't be able to dismiss him as easily this time.

Harry Taylor's eyes widened. "Landis? As in the Landises from Hilton Head, South Carolina?"

"Yes, sir, that would be my family."

"Uh, Harry Taylor, here. Eloisa's father."

The guy all but had dollar signs flashing in his pupils like some cartoon character.

Jonah stifled the irritation for Eloisa's sake. He appreciated the advantages his family's money had brought him, but he preferred to make his own way in the world.

Meanwhile, though, Jonah knew how to deal with money suck-ups like this. He'd been on guard against them since the sandbox. Even kids figured out fast whose dad had the biggest portfolio.

A photographer stepped from the back of the pack, lifting the lens to his eyes. Eloisa tucked behind his shoulder as flashes spiked through the night.

Smiling widely, Harry shuffled aside to clear the way for the photographer to get a better angle. The old guy all but offered to hold the photographer's camera bag.

Audrey elbowed her yawning fiancé, hooking arms with him and stepping closer. "When did you and Eloisa meet, Mr. Landis? I'm sure our guest—the editor of the local events section of our illustrious paper—will want plenty of deets for her column."

"Call me Jonah." He could feel Eloisa's heart beat faster against him.

He could claim her easily here, but then their separation would be out in the open as well. He intended to be much closer to her. "I met Eloisa during her study-abroad program last year. I found her impossible to forget and here I am."

Every word of that was true.

Eloisa's sigh of relief shuddered against him.

Audrey loosened her death grip on her fiancé's arm

long enough to sidle beside her sister for the next round of pictures. "Aren't you full of surprises?"

"Not by choice." Eloisa smiled tightly. "Besides, this is your night. I wouldn't want to do anything to detract from that."

Her stepsister winked, eying Jonah up and down. "Hey, if he were my date, I'd be lapping up all the media attention."

What the hell kind of family was this?

Jonah pulled Eloisa closer to his side, sending a clear "back-off" signal to Audrey. She simply smiled in return, tossing her hair over her shoulders playfully. Her fiancé seemed oblivious, poor bastard.

Eloisa buried her face against Jonah's shoulder and he started to reassure her—until he realized she wasn't upset or even seeking him out. She was just hiding from the clicking camera.

The photographer snap, snap, snapped away, the flashes damn near blinding in the dark night.

Audrey reached for her sister. "Come on. Just smile for the camera. You've been hiding out here all night and I could use some fun and interesting pictures to add to my wedding album."

Eloisa thumbed off the band from her ponytail. Her hair slid free in a silken sheet that flowed over her shoulders and down her back. She'd never seemed vain to him, but then most women he knew primped for the camera. Even his three sisters-in-law were known to slick on lipstick before a news conference.

Except as he watched her more closely he realized she used the hair as a curtain. The guy might be getting his photos—to deny them would have caused a scene with

Audrey—but there wasn't going to be a clear image of Eloisa's face.

Realization trickled through of a larger problem between them than even he had anticipated. He knew she wanted to keep her royal heritage a secret. That was obvious enough and he respected her right to live as she pleased. But until this moment he hadn't understood just how far she would go to protect her anonymity. A damned inconvenient problem.

Because as a Landis, he could always count on being stuck in the spotlight. Just by being with her, he'd cast her into the media's unrelenting glare.

He'd wanted revenge, but didn't need to unveil her secret to repay her for her betrayal. He had other, far more enticing ways of excising her from his mind.

Three

Eloisa wished that photographer would tone down the flash on his camera. Much more of his nonstop shutter bugging and she would have a headache. As if this evening wasn't already migraine material enough.

Thank God the party had finally all but ended, only a few stragglers hanging on and sidling into the photo ops. Jonah—the cause of her impending headache—stood off to the side with her stepfather. Determined to keep her cool, Eloisa stacked tiny crystal cake plates left haphazardly on the dessert table. Her sister watched from her perch, lounging against the end of the table.

Audrey balanced a plate with a wedge of the raspberry chocolate cake on one hand, swiping her finger through the frosting and licking it clean. "You should let the catering staff take care of that. It's what they're paid to do."

"I don't mind, really. Besides, the cleaning staff charges by the hour." She also needed a way to burn off her nervous energy from Jonah's staged kiss.

"That doesn't mean you need to work yourself to the bone. Go home."

She wasn't ready to be alone with Jonah. Not yet. Not with her feelings still so close to the surface. But judging from the stubborn set of his jaw as he stood under a string of white lights, he wasn't leaving her life anywhere anytime soon.

"I'm staying here with you." Eloisa sidestepped a band member carrying two guitar cases. "No arguments."

"At least have some cake. It's so amazing I almost don't care that I'll have to get my wedding gown resized." Audrey swiped up another gob of frosting, her blue eyes trekking over to Jonah, then sliding back. "You're just full of surprises, aren't you, sister dear?"

"So you said earlier." Eloisa placed the forks in a glass so all the plates stacked evenly and handed over the lot to a passing catering employee.

How rare that someone accused her of being full of surprises. She'd always been the steady one, tasked to smooth things over when her more-sensitive baby sister burst into tears.

"But it's true. What's the scoop with this Landis boyfriend?" Audrey gestured with her plate toward Jonah who looked at ease in his suit jacket, even in Florida's full-out May heat.

Eloisa had found his constant unconcern fascinating before. Now it was more than a little irritating, especially when she couldn't stop thinking about the feel of plunging her fingers into his thick hair when they'd kissed.

She forced her hands to stay steady as she clasped them in front of her, leaning against the table beside Audrey, her half sister topping her by five inches. Her willowy sister looked more like her blond father.

But they both had their mother's long fingers. What would it have been like to turn to her mother right now? And how much it must hurt Audrey not having their mother around to help plan the biggest day of her life.

Certainly their mother's shocking death from an allergic reaction to medication had stunned them all. Eloisa had been numb throughout the entire funeral, staying in the fugue state all the way back to Spain, to her study program.

And into Jonah's bed.

Waking up the morning after with that ring on her finger… She'd felt the first crack in the dam walling up her grief. She'd barely made it out of Jonah's rented manor home before the tears flowed.

Which brought her back to the dilemma of Jonah.

What was the scoop? Why had he shown up now when he could have sent a lawyer? It wasn't like he wanted to see her or he could have contacted her anytime in the past year. "His arrival tonight came as a total shocker to me."

Audrey set aside her plate, plucked a pink stargazer lily from the beach-themed centerpiece and skimmed it under her nose. "You never mentioned meeting him before."

She hadn't mentioned even the working relationship because she'd been afraid they would hear in her voice what she could barely admit to herself then, much less now. "Like I said earlier, this is your time, your wedding. I wouldn't want to do anything to distract from that."

Audrey bumped her waif-thin shoulder against Eloisa's. "Could you please drop the altruistic gig for just a few minutes while we squeal over this like real sisters? He's a Landis, for crying out loud. You're rubbing elbows with American royalty."

"Who wouldn't squeal over that?" She couldn't resist the tongue-in-cheek retort.

"You, apparently." Audrey twirled the lily stem between her fingers. "Heaven knows I would be calling a press conference."

Eloisa laughed, then laughed some more, so much better than crying, and let all the tension from the evening flow out of her. Audrey had her faults, but she never pretended to be anything other than who she was.

Which made Eloisa feel like a hypocrite since she hid from herself every damn day.

Her laughter faded. "Forget all about this evening and Jonah Landis. I meant it when I said these next couple of weeks are totally about you. This is the wedding you've been planning since you were a kid. Remember how we used to practice in the garden?"

"You were always the best maid of honor." She tucked the stargazer lily behind Eloisa's ear. "I wasn't always a nice bride."

"You were three years younger. You got frustrated when you couldn't keep up."

"I still do sometimes." Her smile faltered just a bit.

"Remember the time we picked all the roses off the bushes?" Eloisa steadied the lily behind her ear, the fragrance reminding her of their childhood raid on their mother's carefully tended yard. "You took the rap."

Audrey rolled her eyes and attacked her cake again

with her pointer finger. "No huge sacrifice. It's not like I ever got in trouble. I cried better than you did. You were always into being stoic."

"I'm not the weepy sort." Not in public anyway.

"Tears can be worth their weight in gold. I may be the youngest, but you should take my advice on this one." Audrey fixed her stare on her father, her fiancé and Jonah. "When it comes to men, you have to use whatever tools you have."

"Thanks for the advice." Not that she could see herself taking it even in a million years. "Now can we get back to focusing on your wedding? We have a lot to accomplish in the next couple of weeks."

She tried to stem her reservations about Audrey marrying a guy with questionable connections. Her little sister had ignored all the warnings, even threatening to elope if Eloisa didn't keep her opinions to herself.

Audrey pulled another flower from the centerpiece for herself. "And about Jonah Landis?"

Eloisa shrugged, suddenly hungry for the cake after all. "He's my date." She forked up a bite from the lone remaining slice on a plate the caterers hadn't yet cleared. "It's as simple as that."

"Guess you don't need a ride home tonight." Audrey needled with the same practiced teasing she'd used on her since the days of Eloisa's first boyfriend—the librarian's son who occasionally snitched the keys to the reference room so she could read the Oxford English Dictionary in total privacy after hours.

"I have my car here."

"One of Joey's brothers can drive it over for you." Audrey arched up on her toes. "Hey, Landis? My sister is ready to go. How about you get your chauffeur to pull up that Rolls Royce limo of yours. Eloisa's been on her feet all day."

Jonah's gaze slammed into hers, narrow and predatory. She'd seen that look before, right before she'd shimmied out of her dress and fallen into bed with him.

Shoveling a bite of cake into her mouth, Eloisa tried to tell herself it would be enough to stave off the deeper hunger gnawing through her tonight.

Eloisa shifted uneasily in the limo seat.

Climbing back into Jonah's car had seemed easier than discussing driving arrangements in front of the gossip rag reporter. Now that she was alone with Jonah, however, she questioned her decision. The drive to her town house felt hours away rather than a couple of miles.

Searching for something, *anything* to talk about other than each other, Eloisa touched the miniprinter and laptop computer beside her. She started to make a joke about checking Facebook from the road, but paused when her finger snagged on a printed-out page.

She looked closer before she could think to stop herself. It seemed like some kind of small blueprint—

Jonah pulled the paper from the printer and into a briefcase. "Why were you so camera shy at the party earlier?"

"I prefer to keep a low profile. Not everyone is hungry for a spot on the front page." Ouch. That sounded pretty crabby coming out, but Jonah had a way of agitating her every nerve.

"Do you avoid the press because of your father? You can't expect to stay under the radar forever."

Did he realize how intimately their thighs pressed

against one another? Eloisa slid her hand from the printer and scooted an inch of space between them. "My mother and I managed over the years. Do you intend to change that?"

She bit her lip, unable to stop from holding her breath after finally voicing the question that had chewed at her all night long. Her mother may have managed but it didn't escape Eloisa's notice that she'd screwed up mere days after the funeral. She waited through Jonah's assessing silence so long that dots began to spark in front of her eyes.

"Breathe," he commanded, holding her gaze until she exhaled then nodding curtly. "Of course I'll keep your secret. If anyone finds out, it won't be from me."

Sighing with relief she flopped back in her seat and fanned her face, relaxing for the first time since she'd heard his engine growl around the corner. That was one secret taken care of, and she had no reason to believe he could have found out her other. "You really could have saved me a lot of angst tonight if you'd told me that from the start."

"What kind of guy do you think I am?"

A rich one judging by his clothes, his lifestyle and famous surname? Yet all of those were superficial elements. She scoured her mind for things she'd learned about him a year ago...and most of it focused on attraction. She wasn't so sure she liked what that said about her. "I'm not really sure how well I know you."

"Then you'll have the next two weeks to figure me out."

"Two weeks?" Her muscles kinked all over again. "I thought you wanted a divorce."

"I do." He secured the lily behind her ear, his knuckles

caressing her neck for a second too long to be accidental. "But first, I want the honeymoon we never had."

She gasped in surprise, followed by anger…then suspicion. "You're just trying to shock me."

"How do you know I'm not serious?" His blue eyes burned with unmistakable, unsettling—irresistible?—desire.

She'd barely survived their last encounter with her heart intact. No way in hell was she dipping her toes into those fiery waters again. "You can't really believe I'll just crawl into bed with you."

"Why not?" He angled closer to her, so close she would only have to lean just a little to rest her cheek against his amazing hair. "It isn't like we haven't already slept together."

Not that they'd slept much. "That night was a mistake." One with heartbreaking consequences. "A mistake I do not intend to repeat, so get back on your side of the car."

"Fine then." He eased away, leather creaking at his every lazy, slow movement. "Whether or not we have sex will be your call."

"Thank you." She laced her fingers together on her lap to keep from hauling him over again. Why hadn't she eaten more cake?

"Just give me two weeks."

"What the hell?" The words slipped out of her mouth, startling her as much as it appeared she'd surprised him. "I can't deal with you right now." There. She'd actually been honest with him about how she felt. "My sister needs me."

And then she had to muck it up with a half truth to hide how much he tempted her.

"Doesn't she have a wedding planner or something?"

"Not everyone has unlimited funds."

"Your father doesn't send support?"

"That's none of your business, and regardless, it wouldn't have been Audrey's anyhow."

"Ah, but if you had a king's ransom tucked away, I am certain you would have shared it with sister dear. Am I wrong?"

His words stung and she hated how that hinted at his power over her. "I'm not a pushover."

Although Jonah was right, damn him, that if she did have money, she would have written her sister a big fat check to cover wedding expenses.

Regardless, she didn't want Enrique Medina's money. Her mother had insisted she didn't want it either, but she'd married another man for what appeared to be financial security. What a confusing tangle.

She knew one thing for sure. "I'm not a minor. I make my own way in the world. Besides, he's not a part of my life and I am not for sale."

She wouldn't allow herself to be dependent on any man. Even months after the fact, it scared her to her teeth to think of how close she'd come to mirroring her mother's past—alone, unloved.

And pregnant.

Four

Jonah told the driver to wait, then pivoted toward Eloisa as she raced toward her town house. Hopefully he would be sending the driver on his way soon, because quite frankly, he didn't trust Eloisa not to bolt the second he left.

Not that it was any great hardship to be with her. God, he could watch her walk all night long, the gentle sway of her hips and the swish of her ponytail illuminated by the street lamp.

He didn't expect to get any further than talking tonight. He needed to take his time with her now in a way he hadn't back in Spain.

Problem was? He could only afford to take these next two weeks off, then he needed to get back to work on his next restoration project. Working on architectural designs around the world fed his wanderer's spirit.

Next stop? Peru in two weeks.

And if he hadn't finished business with Eloisa by then? Could he just walk away?

He refused to consider failure. They would go to bed together again. And they would exorcise the mess from last year.

Hands stuffed in his pockets, he followed Eloisa along the walkway. Waves rolled and roared in the distance, the shore three streets away. She lived in a stucco town house, the fourth in the row. New, they'd been built to resemble older, turn-of-the-century construction. Each unit was painted a different beachy color—peach, blue, green and yellow.

She marched toward the yellow home, calling back over her shoulder. "Thank you for seeing me safely to my front stoop, but you're free to leave now."

"Not so fast, my dear wife." He stopped alongside Eloisa at her lime-green door. Keys dangled from between her fingers but he didn't take them from her. He wanted her to ask him inside of her own free will, no coercion. But that didn't exclude persuasion.

She faced him with a sigh. "You managed a whole year without speaking to me. I'm sure you'll do just fine without me for another night."

"Eloisa, just because I didn't contact you doesn't mean I stopped thinking about you." That was sure as hell the truth. "We left a lot unsaid. Is it so wrong for me to want these next couple of weeks to clear the air before we say goodbye?"

Eloisa studied her clunky key chain, a conglomeration of whistles, a lanyard from some children's festival and a metal touristy-looking token. "Why a couple of weeks?"

Damn. It wouldn't be that persuasive to say that was all the time he had available to pencil her into his work schedule. His brother Sebastian's marriage had fallen apart because of his insane hours at his law practice.

"That's how long my attorney says it will take to get the ball rolling." He'd asked for Sebastian's help this time, as he should have done a year ago. "You can't blame me for wondering if you will disappear again."

Sure the morning after their spur of the moment wedding, they'd both agreed it was a mistake. Okay, they'd both agreed after she'd slapped him. Then she'd gasped in horror and yanked on her clothes as she'd stumbled toward the door. He'd expected once she cooled down, they would at least talk about things, maybe take a step back—a few steps back.

Except once she'd left his place in Spain, she'd ignored any further communication other than mailing the paperwork his way. So actually, the crummy paperwork was her fault.

And his. He couldn't deny it. He shouldn't have been so damn proud he didn't show his lawyer brother Sebastian.

Jonah tugged the dangling keys from her loose grip, sifting the bulk in his hands. The touristy token caught his attention. He looked closer and found…an ironwork reproduction of the house he'd worked on restoring the previous summer. Interesting. Encouraging. "Nice key chain."

"I keep it as a reminder of the risks of impulsiveness." She tugged her keys back, gripping them so tightly her fingers turned bloodlessly white.

"Risks?" Anger kicked around in his gut. She was the one who'd walked out, after all. Not him. "Seems like you walked away mighty damn easily. If it wasn't for this inconvenient legal snafu—" not to mention her lies "—you would have gotten away scot-free."

"Scot-free?" Her face went pale in the moonlight. "You can't possibly think this didn't affect me. You have no idea how deeply I've wrestled with what we did, the mistake we made."

Confusion dulled the edge of his anger. She'd left. She'd never called. Why the hell had she been hiding out if their time together stayed with her this heavily?

"Well, Eloisa? What do you say we make every effort possible to put this to rest once and for all? For the next couple of weeks, you can just call me roomie."

She gasped. "You can't really expect to bunk at my place?"

"Of course not." Jonah focused on the little piece of memorabilia on her key chain, a sign that she'd remembered and even cared. He let her relax for a second before retorting, "I could phone the chauffeur and we could be taken to my beachside suite."

Shaking her head, she slid the key into the lock. "You're outrageous."

He clapped a hand over his chest with a half smile. "That hurt. I prefer to think I'm being considerate to my wife's needs."

"I'm just dying to hear how you reached that conclusion." Shaking her head, she pushed her front door open and stepped inside without giving him the boot.

He took that as an invitation and followed. Victory pulsing inside him, he checked out the space she called home for clues about her. The more he knew the better his chances. He wouldn't make the same mistake again of letting her keep him in the dark.

The living area was airy and open with high ceilings in keeping with the historic-reproduction feel. Her tastes ran to uncluttered, clean lines with a beach theme—white walls, wood floors and rattan furniture with cushions in a muted blue, tan and chocolate. And of course books—in end tables, shelves, curio cabinets. She'd always carried books in her purse in Spain, reading during breaks.

Her reed roll-up shades covered the windows from outdoor eyes. Only the French doors gave a glimpse to a garden patio with an Adirondack chair and ferns. Did she lounge there and read? Soak up the sun?

What he wouldn't give to take her to his penthouse suite with a rooftop pool and deck where they both could do away with restrictive bathing suits.

He slid his jacket off and hooked it on the coatrack made from a canoe paddle. "Nice place."

"I'm sure it's not near the luxury level you're used to, but I like it."

"It's lovely and you know it. Don't paint me as a bad guy here just to make it easier to dismiss me."

She glanced back over her shoulder, her purse sliding from her shoulder onto the island counter separating the kitchen from the living space. She tossed her keys beside the bag, the cluster jangling to rest. "Fair enough."

He'd spent more than a few nights in tents or trailers during the early, intense stages of a restoration project, but he didn't intend to make excuses to her. "Would you like more luxury in your life?"

His brothers showered their wives with pampering extras and while his sisters-in-law vowed they didn't need them, he'd noticed they always used those spa gifts.

He thumbed a thick silver binder with an engagement photo of Audrey Taylor and her fiancé. "You said earlier you're swamped with wedding plans." He tapped the three-ring binder. "If we stay at my suite, you won't have to cook or clean. You can indulge in the spa. A massage would take care of your stress at the end of the day. You and your sister and all the bridesmaids could avail yourselves of the salon the day of the wedding, my gift to the bride, of course."

She slid out of her gold strappy heels and lined them up side by side on the floor mat by the patio door. "You can't buy me off any more than my father could."

He took his cue from her and toed off his python loafers, nudging them near the coatrack. How much further could they take this undressing together? "I was brought up to believe it's not what a gift costs, it's whether or not the gift is thoughtful. Needed."

"That's nice." She relaxed a hip against a barstool.

"Then pack your bag and let's go to my penthouse."

She stiffened again. "I'm not leaving."

"Then I guess I'm bunking on your sofa." He stifled a wince at spending the night on the couch at least six inches too short.

"You can't tell me you actually wanted me to stay together?" Her eyes went wider with shock. "Every woman on that site in Madrid knew what a playboy you are."

"Were. I'm a married man now." He still had his ring and hers in a jeweler's box in his suite. He wasn't sure why he'd brought them.

She shook her head slowly with a weary sigh. "I'm too tired for this tonight, Jonah. Go back to your hotel. We'll talk tomorrow when we've both had a good night's sleep."

"Honestly? I don't trust you."

"Excuse me?" she gasped in outrage.

Then something else shadowed through her eyes. Guilt?

"You didn't tell me about your father, a pretty major part of your past. You may have done a damn fine job hiding the truth over the years. But when my divorce attorney compared the information you filed on our marriage license at the church registry with your passport information, he found a red flag in the slightly different way you listed your name and your parents. He dug deeper and found your birth certificate. The original one, not the one reissued when Harry Taylor adopted you." The shock he'd felt upon discovering the whole mess roared back to life inside him. "With a little help from a private detective, the rest of the pieces fell into place about your real father. I'm surprised you got away with it for this long."

"You had no right to send private detectives snooping into my private business."

Her words stoked his barely banked anger. "I'm your husband. I think that gives me a little latitude here. For God's sake, Eloisa, what if I'd gotten married again, thinking we were divorced?"

"Are you seeing someone else?" Wow, she sure had

that prim librarian gig down pat. She could have stared down an armed gang.

"Hell no, I'm not seeing anyone else." He couldn't keep himself from comparing other women to her and they all came up short. "Bottom line? Like I said, I don't trust you. You ran once before. I intend to stick close until we have this settled."

She pointed to the binder. "I have my sister's wedding. I'm not going anywhere."

"There are a lot of ways to lock a person out of your life." He'd seen his brother Sebastian and his wife put a massive chasm between each other while living in the same town.

"You can't really expect to stay here, in my town house."

He would have preferred they stay in his suite where he could have wooed her with all the resort offered, but sleeping under the same roof would suffice.

Jonah picked up her keys from the island and held them up so the Spanish charm caught the light. "We both have a lot of unresolved business to settle in two weeks. We should make the most of every minute."

She stared at the keys in his hand for so long he wondered if she was halfway hypnotized.

Finally, Eloisa pressed her fingers to her forehead. "Fine. I'm too tired to argue with you. You can stay, but—" she held up a finger, the stern glint in her eyes relaying loud and clear she was done compromising for the night "—you'll be sleeping on the sofa."

All the same he couldn't resist teasing her, suddenly needing to see if her smile was as blinding as he remembered. "No welcome-home nookie?"

She frowned. "Don't push your luck."

"A guy can still hope." He turned on a lamp, his gaze dropping to the glass paperweight sealing off a dried rose and seashell. He scooped it up, tossed it, caught it, tossed, caught…

"Could you put that down, please?" she snapped with an edge to her voice he hadn't heard since the morning she'd left.

He looked back at the paperweight in his hand. Was it something sentimental? A gift from another guy perhaps? He didn't like the swift kick of jealousy, but damn it all, she was his wife, for now at least. "Should I be worried about a boyfriend showing up to kick my ass?"

"Let's talk about you instead. What have you been up to over the past year, thinking you were a bachelor?"

"Jealous?" God knows he was because she hadn't answered his question. Except if there had been another guy, surely he would have been at the party with her tonight.

His conclusion wasn't proof positive, but he took comfort in it all the same.

She snatched the paperweight from his hand. "I am tired, *not* jealous."

Did he want her to be? No. He wanted honesty. So he settled for the same from himself. "I've spent the past twelve months pining for my ex-wife."

As much as he'd meant to be a sarcastic joke, it hadn't come out of his mouth the way he'd planned.

Confusion flickered through her dark eyes. "The way you say that, I can almost believe you. Of course I know better."

"I thought you said we barely knew each other. We only spent a month together. And we spent most of the time in bed." He sat on the sofa, stretching his arm along the back. "Let's talk now."

"You first." She perched on the edge of the chair beside the sofa.

"You already know plenty about me. My family's in the news and what you don't see there you can find on Wikipedia." He watched her chest rise and fall faster with nerves, lending further credence to his sense she disliked anything high profile.

"None of that information tells me anything reliable about who you are." She counted on her fingers. "I remember you were always on time for work. You never talked on your cell phone when you spoke with the foreman on the site. I liked that you gave people your full attention. I remember you downplayed the Landis connection so well I didn't even know you were related until three weeks into the job." She folded her fingers down again. "But Jonah, that's not enough reason to get married. Even with the divorce, we have a history now. We should know more about each other than our work habits."

"I know you like two sugars in your coffee," he offered with a half smile.

This didn't seem the right time to mention he knew her heart beat faster when he blew along the inside curve of her neck. The sex part would have to wait.

Talking appeared to be the only way to get closer to her, so he would talk. "You want to know more about me? Okay. My brother Kyle got married recently."

"You mentioned that already when you talked about their vows renewal."

"They went to Portugal, which is how I ended up in Spain again." Nostalgia had pulled him over there, the hope that if he revisited the places he'd been with Eloisa he could close the door on that chapter of his life. "The press doesn't know the reason they renewed their vows so soon after saying them in the first place. They got married to safeguard custody of my niece, my brother Kyle's daughter. Her biological mom dumped her on Phoebe, then disappeared." Anger chewed his gut all over again when he thought of how close his niece Nina had come to landing in foster care. "The whole mess really rocked our family. Thank God little Nina is safe."

"You love your niece?" she asked, her face inscrutable.

"Gotta confess, I'm a sucker for kids. I take pride in being the favorite uncle. Want to see pictures of the rug rats?"

"You carry family pictures?" she squeaked incredulously.

"Got a whole album on my iPhone." He unclipped the device from his belt and tapped the screen until pictures filled the display. He leaned closer to her. "My brother Sebastian and his wife remarried after divorcing each other. They have a son."

He brought up an image of his toddler nephew taking his first steps. Then clicked to an infant girl. "That's Sebastian and Marianna's daughter. They adopted her then her birth mother changed her mind."

He swallowed down a lump in his throat and kept his eyes averted until he could speak again. "Here's my brother Matthew—"

"The senator from South Carolina."

"Yes. This is him with his wife and their daughter at the beach." He shuffled to the next photo. "And this is a family portrait taken in Portugal. There's Mom with her husband, the General, his three kids with their spouses and children."

"Your family is huge."

Her family wasn't so small either, when taking into account her biological father and his three sons, but mentioning that didn't seem prudent. "Christmas can be rather noisy when we all get together at the family compound in Hilton Head."

"It's amazing you can gather everyone for any event with all the high-profile commitments."

"We make time for what's important." Would she see and understand that his family was about things more important than a press release or bank balance?

She leaned back in her chair, crossing her arms defensively. "Your brothers are happily married, which means your mother is probably riding your back to produce a happily-ever-after of your own with a wife and make chubby-cheeked cherubs, so you dig up me."

Not even close to what he'd intended. He placed his phone on the end table by the glass paperweight. "That's one helluva scenario to draw from a simple update on my brothers."

"You're not denying it."

He was losing ground here and he wasn't even sure why. "My mother may be a strong-willed politician in her own right, but I'm also very much her son, strong will and all. No one coerces me into anything."

"Unless that influence comes from the bottom of a bottle."

"I wasn't drunk the night we got married." He'd only had two of the local beers. "That was you."

"Are you saying you actually wanted to be married to me?"

"I thought so at the time."

Her mouth fell open, her eyes wide with horror. "You were in love with me?"

"The magnitude of your horror is positively ego deflating."

She shoved up to her feet. "You're playing with me." She walked across the room and opened a closet full of linens. "I don't appreciate your making fun of me."

The way she so easily dismissed what had happened between them a year ago really pissed him off. Okay, so their wedding had been an impulsive mistake. His brothers had been getting married. He'd had this idea that what he felt around Eloisa resembled what his brothers described about finding "the one." He may have been wrong about that. She may have had a couple of drinks, but she'd been clear about how much she wanted him, too, how much she'd needed him.

Need wasn't love. But they had felt something for each other, something strong and undeniable.

"I would never mock you." Frustration sliced through him with a razor-sharp edge. "There are far more interesting things I would like to do with you tonight. Let's back up to the part about sex."

She laughed. "At no time were we talking about sex."

"You mentioned making cherubs." Yeah, they were engaging in good old-fashioned bantering but damn, he found it arousing and a fine way to take the edge off his anger. "I'm sorry if your mother never got around to giving you the talk, but sex makes babies."

Her face closed up again. "You're not half as funny as you think you are."

"I'm halfway funny? Cool."

She dumped an armful of linens into his lap. "Make up your own bed on the sofa. I'm done here."

He watched her grab her purse before pounding up the steps to her bedroom, and he couldn't even rejoice over the fact she'd let him stay. Her door clicked shut behind her, the sound of a lock snicking a second later.

Somewhere along the line he'd misstepped. And he didn't have a clue what he'd done wrong now any more than before.

Upstairs in her room, Eloisa sunk to the edge of her bed, sliding down to the floor. She clutched her knees, tears making fast tracks down her face.

Seeing Jonah touch that glass paperweight had almost driven her to her knees earlier. After she'd lost the baby four months into her pregnancy, she'd had a private memorial service all her own for her child. She'd taken a tiny nosegay of white rosebuds to the beach and let waves carry them away as she'd prayed.

She'd kept one rose for herself. The bloom had dried far faster than her tears. Then she'd had the bud encased in glass along with a couple of tiny shells and some sand from that stretch of shoreline.

Jonah obviously loved children, evident not just from his words but from the way his eyes had gone soft over that family photo album. Each beautiful baby's face had torn a fresh hole in heart, tormenting her with what her child—hers and Jonah's—might have looked like.

The doctors had told her it was just one of those things. There was no reason why she couldn't have more children, but she couldn't see any way clear to having forever with any man, much less starting a family.

Between fears about threats from her father's enemies to even deeper fears about living out her mother's legacy... Eloisa swiped her eyes with her forearm.

God, she was mess.

What would Jonah say if he learned she'd kept the pregnancy a secret from him?

She still didn't understand why she'd delayed contacting him about the baby. She'd told herself she would let him know before their child was born. When she'd miscarried and her emotions had been such a turmoil of grief, contacting him seemed an overwhelming hurdle.

Every day that passed, it seemed easier to stay quiet. Telling him now wouldn't serve any purpose.

Her cell phone chimed from inside her purse, startling her midsob. She definitely didn't feel like speaking to anyone this late. Thank goodness the chimes indicated a text message.

She fished out her phone. Her sister's name scrolled across the screen. Eloisa thumbed View.

R U home? Worried about u.

Eloisa clutched the phone. She'd never shared her burdens with anyone before. The secrets were too big, too deep. Unburdening herself would be selfish. She stifled back the crazy notion of what it might feel like to spill her guts to her sibling.

Eloisa typed out, *Am home and ok. No worries.*

She sent the message and pushed to her feet. She needed to splash water on her eyes and go to sleep. Would that be possible with Jonah downstairs on the sofa?

Her phone chimed in her hand. Audrey again.

What about tycoon hunk? Is he there?

She set the cell on the bathroom counter next to the sink. Her fingers hovered over the keypad. What should she tell her sister?

He was most definitely bothering her by his mere presence so much more than she could have even expected. But if she wanted time to figure out what to do about him, her father, her biology, she needed to play along with his bizarre game a while longer.

Beyond that? What did she want?

Eloisa looked at herself in a mirror framed with seashells and sand dollars. She picked at a strand of hair that had slipped loose from her severe ponytail, her face devoid of makeup. But her cheeks were flushed in a way they'd never been before—except for that too-short month in Spain.

The truth settled inside her with a resounding thud. She couldn't be the sort of person who would walk into that living room, whip the covers off Jonah and say to hell with the consequences, she was making the most of her marital status. She'd gone that route before and it only led to their current mess.

A tempting alternative tickled at her brain. What if she did sleep with him again, but the next time was more about fun, with no ring? She'd let things get too serious before. That had obviously been a mistake on so many levels.

Could she forget the past and have an affair with her ex-husband?

Five

Eloisa made it through the night without a trip downstairs, although it had been rough going when she'd woken up at around four.

But finally the morning sun streaked through her reed roll-up blinds. She could leave her room without feeling she'd caved. Since it was only six-thirty, she might just get to watch him sleep, something she'd missed out on during their one night together.

She pulled on a white terry-cloth robe, securing it tight before leaving her bedroom. Halfway down the stairs she realized the sofa was empty. Well, empty other than the thin quilt straggling off the side. The pillow still bore the deep imprint of a head. Eloisa padded barefoot down the rest of the steps, her toes sinking into the carpet runner along the wood.

Where was Jonah? The spare bathroom downstairs

was silent, the door cracked open, steam still lightly fogging the mirror and a pale blue towel hung on the rack. Had he left as abruptly as he'd shown up, even after joking about wanting a final night together? Just the thought of being with him again sent a tingle along her skin, a tingle doused by the possibility he'd already left.

Her bare feet picked up speed along the hardwood floor, but the kitchen was empty, too.

"Uh-huh…" His voice drifted inside.

She spun around. The French doors were open an inch. She sagged back against the island counter and stared through to the patio. Jonah lounged in her Adirondack chair, cell phone pressed to his ear. Curiosity held her still and quiet when she probably should have done something to announce her presence, like slam a couple of cabinets open and closed.

His jean-clad legs stretched out long and so damn sexy, showcased by the morning sun. There was something hot and intimate about his bare feet and while she couldn't see his chest, his arms appeared bare as well.

Memories of making love in Spain flamed hotter in her mind after simmering below the surface all night long. She may have had a couple of drinks and lost some inhibitions, but she remembered the sex. Good sex. Amazing sex. She'd been so hungry for him as she'd torn away his shirt, popping buttons in her frenzy. His chest had captured her attention all by itself. She'd known he was muscular. The ripples under his shirt had been impossible to miss, but she hadn't been prepared for the intense definition, the unmistakable strength and power far more elemental than any money or prestige.

She'd always considered herself the cerebral sort, attracted to academic types. So it had totally knocked her off balance when she'd gone weak-kneed over a peek at Jonah's pecs.

"Right," he said to whoever was on the other end of the line. He thrust a hand through his still-damp hair, slicking it back. "I realize that cuts a week off our timeline. Go ahead and send me the new specs. I'll get back to you with an answer by the end of business today." He listened and nodded. "I can be reached at this number. Meanwhile, I'll be on the lookout for your fax."

He disconnected and didn't show signs of dialing again, apparently done with chitchatting for the moment. Any second now, he might stand and notice her. Eloisa looked around for some excuse to appear busy rather than to be eavesdropping. She snatched the empty coffeepot from the coffeemaker.

Jonah stood, stretching his arms overhead.

Her mouth went dry. His chest was everything she remembered and more. She'd forgotten about the deep tan. The honey-warm glow of his skin made her want to taste him all over.

She visually traced the cut of his six-pack lower, lower still down to…oh my…he'd left the top button of his jeans open.

No boxers.

Just a hint of a tan line.

Eloisa grabbed the counter for balance.

She tore her gaze off his bare stomach and brought it to his face. He was looking straight back at her as she stood in the kitchen, stock-still, holding on to the counter with one hand. Her other held a coffeepot dangling uselessly from between her fingers.

"Sorry, uh, Jonah," she babbled, startling into action and shoving the coffeepot under the faucet as he sauntered inside. "I didn't mean to interrupt your call."

"It's okay. We'd already wrapped up business." He tucked the phone half into his pocket, studying her as intently as she'd studied him. "Are you making coffee or tea?"

The intensity of his gaze made her edgy. Was her robe gaping? Her hair a mess?

She glanced at the pot.... Damn. She'd forgotten to turn on the faucet.

"Coffee." Eloisa turned her back to him and focused on making extra-strong java. Hopefully by the time the last drop dripped she would have scavenged some self-control and dignity. "Were you talking to your lawyer about moving forward on the divorce?"

"That was a work call." The heat of his voice and breath caressed her shoulder and she hadn't even heard him approach. He moved quietly for such a big man.

"You have a job?" she asked absently, setting the glass pot on the counter rather than risk dropping it. When had her fingers gone numb?

He flicked her ponytail forward over her shoulder. "I think I'm insulted you have to ask."

Ducking away, she opened the cabinet and foraged for her favorite hazelnut-cream-flavored beans. "Weren't you working on your grad studies like the others when we met?" She glanced back at him. "I assumed..."

He cocked an eyebrow. "You assumed that I was a perpetual student content to live off Mom and Pop's nickel? You sure painted quite a picture of me with very little info."

She finished pouring coffee beans into the coffeemaker, closed the lid and hit Start. The sound of the grinder grated along her already ragged nerves. "You made assumptions about me, too."

"Such as?" He leaned against the counter, dipping his head into her line of sight.

"I gave off the appearance of being someone different during those weeks in Madrid." She crossed her arms over her chest, keeping her robe closed and her hands off his chest. "That time of my life was very out of character for me."

"How so?"

"I'm a homebody, not a world traveler. I like my books and my Adirondack chair with a mug of coffee. That sort of exotic adventure was a onetime good deal. I lucked into a scholarship program that granted me the extra credits I needed. Bottom line, I'm a bookish librarian, not a party girl who gets drunk and impulsively marries some hot guy."

"You think I'm hot, huh?" His blue eyes twinkled as brightly as the rising sun glimmering through the sliding patio doors.

"You already know I find you physically attractive." She conjured her best "librarian" voice that put even the rowdiest of hoodlums in place. "But there are more important issues to address here."

"Of course." He selected an apple from her wicker fruit bowl on the counter. "I have a theory."

"What would that be?" They were nearly naked. He had an apple.

Where was the snake? Because she certainly was tempted.

He gestured with the fruit in his hand. "I think you *are* the sort of woman who travels the world and impulsively takes risks, even knowing sometimes those risks may not work out. Deep down you want to take more of those risks because you also know that sometimes things do work out."

"You seem to have decided a lot about me."

Without answering he crunched a big bite off the side. Why couldn't he have chosen one of the more innocent oranges or plums?

She watched his mouth work. She'd done that before, in Spain during a late-day picnic with the whole crew. Back then she'd only indulged in what-if fantasies about Jonah, never for a second thinking she would one day act on them.

And here she was daydreaming about the feel of his mouth moving along her skin...

Except his mouth was moving because he was talking and she didn't have a clue what he'd said.

"Pardon me?" She rearranged the plums until the fruit was balanced again.

He set aside his half-eaten apple. "Our time together was intense. You can learn a lot about a person in time-compressed moments."

What was he driving at? "But you agreed with me the morning after that we'd made a mistake."

"Did I?"

She stared back into his serious blue eyes and tried to understand him, understand this whole bizarre reunion. But he wasn't giving away anything in his expression. She wasn't so sure she could say the same for herself.

Eloisa touched his hand lightly. "Don't play mind games with me. I know what I heard. And it's not like you came after me."

"I'm here now."

What if he'd come after her right away? She would have told him about the baby. She wouldn't have been able to stay silent if face-to-face with him. How much different things might have been.

Or maybe not. Her mother certainly hadn't experienced a fairy-tale ending when she'd gotten pregnant.

Eloisa shook off the haze of what-ifs. "You've shown up for your one night of sex. Followed by a divorce."

"Who says we can't change our minds?" Before she could answer, he pitched his apple into the corner trash can. "I have to check on that fax."

Blinking fast, she watched him walk out the door shirtless, her head still spinning from his abrupt departure. The front door closed, but she could still see him through the skinny windows on either side of the door. The limo loomed conspicuously in the parking lot, idling alongside the curb. Jonah ducked his head and climbed inside and she remembered that mobile office/command center.

And she realized he'd never answered her question about his phone call or what he did with his life now. While Jonah seemed to have figured out so much about her, she had precious little other than Wikipedia information on him.

If she really wanted to move forward with her life, the time had come to quit drooling over the guy's body and start seriously looking at the man underneath.

* * *

He'd seen the desire in her eyes underneath her veneer of calm.

Jonah tugged on a black polo shirt while he waited for Eloisa to finish her shower upstairs. No amount of work in his fax machine could distract him from thoughts of her under the spray. In some ways he thought he remembered every nuance of her body. That night was burned in his memory.

Would his fascination with her ease if he had more time with her? He certainly hoped so because he didn't want another year like the one he'd just endured.

The sound of water faded, then ended. Silence echoed for what felt like forever before he heard the rustle of her upstairs in her bedroom. Getting dressed.

He'd never considered himself a masochist, but listening to her was serious torture. Jonah pivoted away from her door and opened cabinet after cabinet in search of a coffee mug. As he started drinking his second cup, he heard her door click and swing open.

Jonah poured some java for her, spooning two sugars in the way he remembered she preferred. And why he recalled that detail, he didn't know. He turned to face her.

He stopped short. Reality definitely beat the hell out of memories—and she wasn't even naked.

Eloisa stepped into the kitchen barefoot, wearing a simple blue sundress. The flowing lines clung subtly to her curves, and her skin glowed warm and pink from the shower. Her black hair was wet and pulled back in her signature ponytail, exposing her neck. He'd seen her arousal earlier when he'd hung up the phone and he could probably persuade her now....

But he didn't want to win in some all-out seduction. He wanted *her* to come to *him*.

Eloisa took the cup from his hand carefully, so carefully their fingers didn't even brush. "Did you get your paperwork?"

"Yes, I did." His next job didn't begin for another thirteen days. Most times, he would have headed out early. He was about to tell her about the nineteenth-century Peruvian hacienda he'd been hired to renovate and expand into a resort.

Then remembered she'd only asked because she thought he was contacting his attorney about the divorce.

She blew air across the top of the cup, watching him through upswept lashes. "I don't have much for breakfast, just some granola bars or toast and whatever's in the fruit basket. You're welcome to what's here."

If only she meant that the way he wanted her to. "I can feed myself."

"Good then." She nodded. "Tell me more about your job."

Hey, wait. "But I don't have one, remember? I'm just a lazy playboy."

She lowered her cup, genuine contrition lighting eyes as dark as her coffee. "I was wrong to make that assumption. I genuinely want to hear now."

He wasn't so sure he wanted to be in the hot seat, and definitely didn't know what had brought her to this about-face from pushing him away to shooting the breeze together. "Don't you have to get to work or help your sister with wedding plans?"

"Audrey's busy today, and I have a half hour before I have to leave for the library."

"I'll let the chauffeur know."

"No need." Turning away, she cradled her mug in both hands and walked to the sofa, her hips swaying gently, loose folds of the dress swishing a hypnotic *follow me*. "My sister's fiancé took care of returning my car. She already texted me that it's out in the parking lot."

"Then you're all set." He watched her place her coffee on the end table.

She pulled his blanket from the sofa and began to fold. "Tell me about your job."

He set his mug beside hers and reached for the end of the quilt trailing the ground. "What do you want to know?"

"Why do you hang around historic sites rather than slick new buildings?" She came closer, nearly chest to chest, and met his hands.

His eyes held hers and he considered kissing her right then and there, but he was determined for her to close that last gap. He knelt to sweep up the ends of the blanket and stood again. "I'm a history buff, always have been even when I was a kid, and my family traveled overseas a good bit."

Finishing the final fold, she clasped the quilt to her chest and sat on the sofa. "Tell me more."

She hadn't taken the chair this time and he wasn't missing the chance to get a little closer.

Jonah swept aside a couple of froufrou decorative pillows and sat beside her, keeping space between them. For now. "I'm an architect. I specialize in historic landmarks."

"That's why you were in Spain last year." She sagged back, her face relaxing into a smile for the first time since he'd seen her last night. "But you were also a student, right?"

He shifted uncomfortably. Couldn't he just give her a résumé? "I finished my dissertation."

"You completed your PhD? I'm impressed."

He winced. He hadn't shared that with her to wow her. He preferred not to talk about himself at all. "I enjoy the subject matter." He shrugged offhandedly. "I had the luxury of not worrying about school loans."

"But you were also in Spain in a more official capacity?"

"Yes, I was." What did she hope to accomplish by grilling him?

"Why did you keep it a secret?"

Was this a trap? "I didn't keep anything a secret."

He just didn't feel the need to relay everything to everyone.

"You're playing with words." She leaned closer, her shower-fresh scent, the tropical perfume of her shampoo, teasing him. "You can't blame me for making assumptions when you won't share. Well, tell me now. What else were you doing there?"

To hell with figuring out motives or playing games. He had her here. Talking to him. Not running. If he had to scavenge chitchat to make headway with her, then fine. Might as well dish up some information about his past. "When I turned eighteen, I decided I didn't want to live off my family. While I was in college, I started flipping houses."

"You worked construction in college?" She set aside the quilt and reached for her coffee.

Good. He had her relaxing bit by bit. "Is there something wrong with that?"

She paused midsip. "Of course not. I just… Okay, I made assumptions about your college years."

"I didn't have time for the frat-boy scene, princess." He'd worked his ass off, and considered the time well spent as it gave him real-world experience once he'd graduated. "So I flipped houses, made investments then took things to another level by underwriting renovations of historic manor homes and castles. I made more investments." He shrugged. "And here I am."

"What about your family's influence in world politics? What about your inheritance?"

Some of the women in his life had been sorely disappointed to hear about his lack of interest in being a part of the political world his family inhabited. "What about it?"

"Do you just leave the money sitting around?"

"Hell, no. I invest it. I expect to leave more for my kids."

"You want children?" She averted her eyes, setting her mug down.

"Damn straight, I do. A half dozen or so."

She pushed to her feet abruptly, backing away, nearly stumbling over her bare feet. Eloisa grabbed the chair for balance. "I need to finish getting ready for work."

What the hell had caused her quick turnaround? He'd been sure he was making headway and suddenly she was checking her watch, shoving on her shoes and scooping up her purse.

Maybe he'd hit a snag there by pushing too hard, too fast. But he wasn't one to admit defeat. It was all about building on the progress he'd made, one brick at a time. He watched her rush around the town house, gathering herself on her way out the door. And as she turned to wave goodbye, he realized.

She'd put on lip gloss.

He thought back to the evening before. She'd been stunning, silhouetted against the waterside, wind rippling her dress and lifting her hair. She had an unstated style and innate grace that proclaimed her timeless beauty regardless of what she wore.

And he was damn sure she hadn't worn makeup last night or a year ago. Yet for some reason, she'd slicked on gloss today. Sure, it was a minor detail, but he found himself curious about every detail surrounding the woman he'd married.

They'd made a decent start in getting to know each other better today. Although they'd mostly talked about his job. And now that he thought about it, he didn't know much about her career since she'd transitioned from being a student.

If he wanted to get closer to Eloisa, perhaps it was time to learn a little more about *her* workplace.

Six

Eloisa perched on the second-to-top step of the rolling ladder, replacing two copies of *The Scarlet Letter*. They'd been returned by a couple of high schoolers who'd lost their classroom edition and had to check it out from the library in a panic before the test. And while work usually calmed her, channeling peace through the quiet and rows of books… Today the familiar environment fell short of its normally calming effect.

She placed the blame squarely on her husband. Having Jonah show up in her life again so unexpectedly was unsettling on too many levels. No wonder she was having trouble finding her footing. She'd contacted her attorney and it appeared Jonah's claim was correct. The divorce hadn't gone through after all. Her lawyer had received the paperwork just this morning, although he vowed he had no idea how Jonah had learned of her Medina roots.

The lawyer had gone on to reassure her he would look into it further. In fact, he planned to go straight to the source and speak with her father and brothers directly. If they didn't have the information, they would need to be warned, as well.

She aligned the books and started back down the ladder. A hand clamped her calf. Gasping, she grabbed the railings to keep from pitching over backward. She looked down fast—

"Jonah," she whispered, her world righting and narrowing to just him, "you scared the hell out of me."

"Sorry about that. Wouldn't want you to fall." He kept his hand on her leg.

Eloisa continued down, his hand naturally sliding up for an inch, and another. Her heart triple-timed as she wondered how long he would keep up this game.

She descended another step.

His hand fell away. The heat of his palm remained.

Soft chitchat sounded from a couple of rows over, the air conditioner nearly as loud as the conversation. Otherwise, this section of the library was pretty much deserted this morning.

Eloisa gripped a shelf since the floor felt a little wobbly. "What are you doing here?"

"I came to take you out. Unless you have to do something with your sister's wedding plans, in which case, I'm here to supply lunch." He gripped the shelf just beside her, his body blocking the rest of the row from sight and creating a quiet—intimate—haven.

A lunch date? God, that sounded fun and wonderful

and more than a little impulsively romantic. *So* unwise if she wanted to keep her balance while finding out what made Jonah Landis tick. "I already bought a sandwich on my way in."

"Okay, then. Another time." He looked past her, then over his shoulder, a broad shoulder mouthwateringly encased in his black polo shirt. "Mind if I have a tour of the place before I leave?"

Her mouth went dry at the thought of more time with him. She eyed the water fountain. "It's a public library. As in open. To the public. Like you."

He traced down the binding of a misplaced Dickens book. "I was hoping for my own personal tour guide. I'm partial to sexy brunette librarians who wear their long hair slicked back in a ponytail. And if she had exotic brown eyes with—"

"I get the picture, you flirt." She held up her hand and stifled a laugh. "You want a tour?" She pulled *A Tale of Two Cities* from the shelf and tucked it under her arm. "Of a library?"

"I want a tour of *your* library. You saw my workplace in Spain." He propped a foot on the bottom step of the ladder. "Now I want to see yours."

Could he really be serious here? Could he perhaps, like her, need some additional insights in order to put the past behind him? The whole flirtation could just be his cover for a deeper confusion like she felt.

And she was probably overanalyzing. Didn't men say things were a lot simpler for them?

Regardless, what harm could there be in showing him around the library? She couldn't think of anywhere safer than here. Now where to start?

If she took him downstairs to the reception area, she

would face questions later from the rest of the staff. Better to go farther into the stacks.

She mentally clicked through other areas to avoid. A book-group discussion. A local artist in residence hanging her work. Eloisa discussed the facility's features by rote.

Jonah reached ahead to push open a doorway leading into a research area. "What made you decide on this career field?"

She looked around. Definitely secluded. She could talk without worrying about being overheard, but also she wouldn't have the same temptations of being alone in her town house with Jonah. "My mother spent a lot of time staying under the radar. I learned low-key at an early age. Novels were my..."

"Escape?" He gestured around the high-ceilinged space that smelled of books and air freshener.

"Entertainment." She shoved a chair under the computer desk. "Now they're my livelihood."

"What about after your mother married what's-his-name?" Jonah followed, palming her back as she rounded a corner.

"My mother still liked to keep things uncomplicated." How in the world had her mother ever fallen for a king? And a deposed king at that, with all sorts of drama surrounding his life? Enrique Medina seemed the antithesis of her stepfather, a man who might not be perfect, but at least had been a presence in her life. Loyalty spurred her to say, "His name is Harry Taylor."

"Yeah, what's-his-name."

Eloisa couldn't help grinning. Her stepfather wasn't a bad guy, if a bit pretentious and pompous.... And she knew in her heart he loved his biological daughter more than he loved her. It hurt a little to think about that, but not anywhere near as much as it used to. "While I appreciate your championing my cause, I truly can stand up for myself."

"Never doubted that for a second," Jonah answered without hesitation. "What's wrong with other folks—like me—throwing our weight in along with you?"

She simply shook her head. "I thought you wanted a tour."

"We can tour and talk."

Sometimes she wasn't sure if she could walk and chew bubblegum around this man. She plastered on a smile. "Sure we can. And here's my office."

Eloisa swept the door open wide and gestured for him to follow her into the tiny space packed full of novels, papers and framed posters from literature festivals around the world. She placed the Dickens classic on a rolling cart to be shelved later.

The door clicked as it closed. She turned to find the space suddenly seeming way smaller with Jonah taking up his fair share of the room that wasn't already occupied by her gunmetal-gray desk, shelves and an extra plastic chair for a guest.

Maybe her office just felt claustrophobic because there weren't windows or even a peephole in the door. Not because they were alone.

Totally alone.

He hadn't planned on getting her alone in the library.

Yet here they were. Just the two of them. In her tiny, isolated office.

Jonah pivoted away to find some distraction, something to talk about, and came nose to nose with a shelf of books. Art books and history books, all about Spain and Portugal. She wasn't as detached from her roots as she tried to make out.

Jonah thumbed the gold lettering along the spine of a collection of Spanish poetry. He recalled she spoke the language fluently. "Have you ever met your biological father in person?"

"Once." Her voice drifted over his shoulder, soft and a little husky. "I was about seven at the time."

"That's years after the last-known sighting of him." Jonah kept his back to her for the moment. Perhaps that would make it easier for her to share. So he continued to inventory her books.

"I don't know where we went. It felt like we took a long time, but all travel seems to take forever at that age."

He recalled well the family trips with his three brothers and his parents, everything from Disney to an Egyptian pharaoh's tomb. Their vacations would have been so different from that mother-daughter trip to see a man who barely acknowledged her existence. Sympathy kicked him in his gut. "Do you remember the mode of transportation?"

"Of course."

"Not that you're telling." He couldn't stop the grin at her spunk.

"I may not have a relationship with my father—" sounds rustled behind him, like the determined restoring of order as she moved things around on her desk "—but that doesn't mean I'm any less concerned about his safety, or the safety of my brothers."

"That's right. Medina has three sons." He clicked through what he knew about Medina from the research he'd been able to accomplish on his own—when he should have been working. But damn it all, this was important. "Did you meet them as well?"

"Two of them."

"That must have seemed strange to say the least."

"I have a half sister, remember? It's not like I don't understand being a part of a family unit." Her voice rose with every word, more than a little hurt leaking through. "I'm not some kind of freak."

He turned to face her again. Her desk was so damn neat and clean a surgeon could have performed an open-heart procedure right there. Germs wouldn't dare approach.

Jonah, however, had never been one to back down from a dare. "Your mother would have already been remarried by the time you were seven."

"And Audrey was a toddler." She clasped her hands in front of her defensively.

Her words sunk in and…holy hell. "Your mom went to see her old lover after she was married to another guy? Your stepfather must have been pissed."

"He never knew about the trip or any of the Medinas." She stood straight and tall, every bit of her royal heritage out there for him to see. She ruled. It didn't matter if she was sitting in a palace or standing in a dark, cramped, little office. She mesmerized him.

And she called to his every protective instinct at the same time. What kind of life must she have led to build defenses this thick?

"Your stepfather didn't know about any of it?" Jonah approached her carefully, wary of spooking her when she was finally opening up, but unable to stay away from her when he sensed that she could have used someone to confide in all these years. "How did she explain about your father?"

She shrugged one shoulder. "She told him the same thing she told everyone else. That my father was a fellow student, with no family, and he died in a car accident before I was born. It's not like Harry talked about my dad to anyone else. The subject just never came up for us."

Jonah skimmed his fingers over the furrows along her forehead. "Let's not discuss your stepfather. Tell me about that visit when you were seven."

Her forehead smoothed and her face relaxed into a brief flicker of a smile. "It was amazing, or rather it seemed that way to me through my childish, idealistic eyes. We all walked along the beach and collected shells. He—" she paused, clearing her throat "—uhm, my father, told me this story about a little squirrel that could travel wherever she wanted by scampering along the telephone lines. He even carried me on his shoulders when my legs got tired from walking and sang songs in Spanish."

"Those are good memories."

She deserved to have had many more of them, but he kept that opinion to himself. Better to wait and just let her talk, rather than risk her clamming up out of defensiveness.

"I know it's silly, but I still have one of the shells." She nudged a stack of already perfectly straight note slips. "I used to listen to it and imagine I could hear his voice mixed in with the sound of the ocean."

"Where is the shell now?"

"I, uh, tucked it away in one of my bookcases at home."

A home she'd decorated completely in a seashore theme. It couldn't be coincidence. He gripped her shoulders lightly. "Why don't you go see him again? You have the right to do so."

"I don't know where he is."

"But surely you have a way to get in touch with him." The soft give of her arms under his hands enticed him to pull her closer. He should take his hands off her, but he didn't. Still he wouldn't back off from delving deeper into this issue. "What about the lawyer?"

She avoided his eyes. "Let's discuss something else."

"So the lawyer is your point of contact even if the old guy never bothers to get in touch with you."

"Stop it, okay?"

She looked back at him again hard and fast. Her eyes were dark and defensive and held so much hurt he realized he would do anything, anything to make that pain go away. "Eloisa—"

"My biological father has asked to see me." She talked right over him, protesting a bit too emphatically. "More than once. I'm the one who stays away. It's just too complicated. He wrecked my mother's life and broke her heart." Her hands slid up to grip his shirt. "That's not something I can just forget about long enough to sit down for some fancy dinner with him once every five years when his conscience kicks in."

He churned over her words, searching for what she meant underneath it all. "I miss my father."

His dad had died in a car wreck when Jonah was only entering his teenage years.

"I told you I don't want to see him."

Jonah cupped her face, his thumb stroking along her aristocratic cheekbone. "I'm talking about how you miss your mother. It's tough losing a parent no matter how old you are."

Empathy softened her eyes for the first time since they'd stepped into her office. "When did your father pass away?"

"When I was in my early teens. A car crash. I used to be so jealous of my brothers because they had more time with him. Talk about ridiculous sibling rivalry." He'd always been different from them, more of a rebel. Little did they know how much it hurt when people said he would have been more focused if only his father had lived. But he refused to let what others said come between him and his family.

Family was everything.

"We almost lost our mother a few years ago when she was on a goodwill tour across Europe." The near miss had scared the hell out of him. After that, he'd knuckled down and gotten his life in order. His skin went cold from just thinking of what had almost happened to his mother. "An assassin tried to make a statement by shooting up one of her events."

"Ohmigod, I remember that." Her fists unfurled in his shirt and her hands smoothed out the wrinkles in soothing circles. "It must have been horrible for you. I seem to recall that some of her family was there…. You saw it all happen?"

"I'm not asking for sympathy." He clasped her wrists and stilled her hands. She might mean her touch to be comforting, but it was rapidly becoming a serious turn-on. "I'm only trying to say I understand how you feel. But, Eloisa, once you're in the spotlight, there's no way to step back out."

"I completely get your point," she said emphatically. "That's why I've kept a low profile."

He brought her hands together, their hands clasped as he tried to make her understand. "You were born into this. There's no low profile. Only delaying the inevitable. Better to embrace it on your own terms."

"That's not your call to make," she snapped, pulling her hands away.

God, it was like banging his head against bricks getting this stubborn woman to consider anything other than a paradigm constructed a helluva long time ago. "Are you so sure about your father's reasons for choosing to close himself away?"

Her spine starched straight again, ire sparking flecks of black in her eyes. "What are you hoping to accomplish here?"

He'd been hoping to learn more about her in an effort to seduce her and had ended up pissing her off. But he couldn't back down. "You don't have to play this their way anymore, Eloisa. Decide what you want rather than letting them haul you along."

Her hands fisted. "Why does this need to get so complicated, and what the hell does it have to do with you?"

Anger stirred in his gut. "I'm the guy who's still married to you because it's so complicated. Damn it, Eloisa, Can you understand my need to do something, fix this somehow?"

"Maybe there's nothing to fix. And even if there is, do you know what I really want?"

"Okay. Mea culpa." He thumped his chest. "You've got me there. I haven't got a clue what you want from me."

"Well, prepare to find out." She clasped his face in her hands, only giving him a second's warning.

Eloisa planted her mouth on his.

He blinked in shock—for all of three seconds before he hauled her against him and kissed her right back.

As her arms slid around his neck, he decided the time had come to take this as far as she would go.

Seven

Eloisa couldn't decide if she'd just made the best or worst decision of her life. Regardless, she knew she'd made the inevitable choice in kissing Jonah. They'd been leading up to this from the second he'd stepped out of his limousine last night.

She pressed her body closer to his, fully, for the first time in a year, her mouth opening to welcome him. Last night's staged kiss outside the party had been too brief. She'd somehow forgotten how well they fit, the way she tucked just inside his embrace, his head angling down. He was taller than she was, but somehow it worked just right for her arms to rest on his shoulders while she burrowed her hands into his hair.

And ohmigod, his hair.

Eloisa touched and roved and savored his head, the slight waves curving around her fingers as if coaxing her to stay. No persuasion needed, she was on fire with want after a year without this kind of sensual contact.

She'd reached for him in frustration, her desire slipping past when her defenses were weakened by irritation. But now that he was touching her, stroking her, coaxing her body against his, she forced all that ire away, just put the whole argument right out of her mind.

Still, part of her feared he'd sparked something deeper inside just by caring enough to ask the hard questions others avoided. He confronted things she liked to keep tucked away.

Either way, she didn't want to argue. She wanted that connection she remembered from a year ago, and she didn't want to fight it another second.

"You taste like apples."

"My lip gloss," she gasped.

"Ah," he said, smiling against her mouth. "You're wearing lip gloss today." He traced her lips with his tongue, then dipped deeper, sharing the hint of flavor with her.

His kiss growing bolder, fuller, he backed her against the desk and she welcomed the bolstering because she wasn't sure how much longer her legs would hold. Jonah stroked her back, her sides, the tops of her thighs, nowhere overtly intimate but intensely arousing all the same. His hot breath caressed her neck a second before his mouth skimmed her oversensitive flesh. Her spot. *He remembered.* The fact that he still knew what she liked turned her inside out as much as the touch of his lips to her skin.

She bit back a moan, her head falling to rest on his shoulder. "We need to slow this down. I'm at work."

He pressed a finger to her lips, still paying detailed attention to her neck. "Shhh. We're in a library. Haven't you ever made out in the library?"

"Never," she answered, one word all she could manage.

"Or caught people making out in the stacks?" His hands slid up and down her sides, each time grazing farther and farther over her ribs, just below her breasts.

"A time or two." She'd sent them on their way like a good, responsible adult, but right now she was feeling anything but responsible.

Jonah nudged his leg between hers, the thick press of his muscled thigh sending sparks of pleasure radiating upward. And clearly she wasn't the only one feeling the effects of their clench. There was no mistaking the rigid press of his arousal against her stomach. He wanted her. Here. Now.

And heaven help her, she wanted him too and to hell with the emotional fallout later. Hadn't she thought just this morning about how wonderful it would be to indulge with Jonah, no marriage, no strings? And other than a piece of paper, they weren't really married. Their lives wouldn't be tangled up beyond these next couple of weeks.

"Let's continue this at my house." She took the leap. "Or at your place even."

"Trust me. I wouldn't risk getting you in trouble." He kissed her quiet again.

They had their clothes on. She was off the clock for lunch. He was only kissing her.

Kissing her senseless.

But still. Who could object? When she'd stumbled

upon other couples necking in the library before, while it had been mildly embarrassing for the people caught, all had just laughed good-naturedly. And she was locked in her office on her lunch break.

Why not?

"Okay then, I trust you," she vowed against his mouth, meaning the words for now, this moment.

"That's what I want to hear." A smile kicked up into his cheek as he lowered his head to hers.

She threaded her fingers through his hair again. Thick and luxurious, wild and sexy. Like the man.

Jonah angled her closer. His palms spanning low on her back, he urged her into a gentle rock against him. His leg pressed more firmly. Pleasure tightened more insistently. She ached for release but held back, nervous and excited by the notion of losing control. They were just making out, for heaven's sake.

Memories of a similar embrace in his rented home in Spain steamed through her mind, of him pressing her just this way against the kitchen counter when they'd made a 3:00 a.m. forage for food. Naked. Both of them had been exhausted and starving from their workout in bed. The images of then tangled with the present until the clothed kiss became so much more in her mind…. She could almost smell the sangria and fruit juices they'd licked from each other's bodies.

It had been so long, too long, a whole damn year without this feeling, a growing sense of frenzy no man other than Jonah had been able to engender. What if he were the only man who could stoke her passion to this level? What would it be like to go through life never feeling this level of want and pleasure and pure sensuality again?

The warm sweep of his tongue, the familiar taste of him, stoked her need higher, hotter, tighter. She wriggled to get closer. The tension gathered low, right where he so perfectly teased. He pressed his leg more insistently against, rocking it rhythmically against her until she realized…

Gasped…

Couldn't stop…

He caught her moan with his mouth. She arched her back, flinging full-out into her release. Every muscle inside her pulled taut as if to hold on to the sensation as long as possible, clenching up each sparkling aftershock.

Slowly, the warm flush along her skin began to cool. She shivered and he gathered her against his chest. Thank God he didn't speak. She would have been mortified, but she could barely think, much less talk.

Jonah brushed his mouth along the top of her hair. "Enjoy the rest of the lunch break and your sandwich. I'll pick you up for supper."

Then he was gone. The door to her office closed behind him with a gentle swoosh while she sagged into her chair. Eloisa smoothed a shaky hand over her hair, to her lips, against her still-racing heart.

She didn't regret her decision, but had to admit, she'd been so very wrong. Things with Jonah could never be uncomplicated. She'd just had the best orgasm of her life.

And he'd only kissed her.

He'd only kissed her.

Parked in her town house lot five hours later, Jonah shut off the engine on his rental car—top-of-the-line

Range Rover, the same sort he always picked and owned because it worked best for him on work sites.

He'd spent the afternoon settling into Pensacola a little deeper, renting wheels. He'd stopped by his penthouse suite to complete paperwork and calls, also lining up two of his employees to oversee the early work trickling in unexpectedly.

Basically, he'd spent the afternoon figuring out ways to make his schedule more open to Eloisa. Damn, how his brothers would laugh at him if they were here to see, but he refused to lose this chance to settle things with Eloisa.

With the scent of her still all around him, he knew he wasn't giving up. He had to have her.

Jonah draped his wrist over the steering wheel and stared at her door. Their encounter in the library had gone just as he'd planned…and yet it hadn't turned out at all the way he'd imagined.

No way in hell could he have imagined being this rocked by seeing her come undone in his arms. This was moving so fast and if he wasn't careful, she would bolt again.

Good thing he'd made reservations at a restaurant. He wasn't sure he could withstand another evening alone with her in her place.

He reached for the car door and his cell phone chimed, stopping him short. He unclipped it from his waistband. His mother's number from her airplane phone scrolled across the screen.

It still blew him away that diplomats and politicians around the world feared his mother's steely nature. Ginger Landis was tough, sure, but she was also fair with a soft heart.

He thumbed the Talk button and turned on the speaker phone. "Hey Mom, what's up?"

Jonah cranked up the Range Rover again so the A/C would keep the car cool on the muggy May afternoon.

"Just checking in on your schedule." Computer keys clicked in the background. Ginger was undoubtedly working while talking, the phone tucked to her ear, holding back her signature grey-blond bob that always stayed as in control as she did. His mom took multitasking to a whole new level: ambassador, wife, mom to four children and three stepchildren and known as a superwoman to boot. "I'm finishing up a summit in Washington. I'll be back in South America before you arrive in Peru for your next project. I'm looking forward to living near my youngest son, even if it's for a short time."

"Me, too." The Landises all spent so much time on the road with their careers, family visits were valued all the more. And while he had his ambassador mother's ear. "Hey, do you have any inside-track info on the deposed king of San Rinaldo?"

She hesitated for a beat before answering. "Why would you ask that?"

"Rumor has it, he's in Argentina." And his mom just happened to be ambassador to a small neighboring country.

"That's the word around town."

He knew his mother would never break security rules, but if she could just point him in the right direction…. "Officially or unofficially?"

"Honestly, I don't know the answer either way," Ginger said, her voice even tighter. He thought of it as her office voice. "Jonah, I can say that there is a compound in Argentina built like a fortress. There's a lot of activity going on inside and very little coming out. Either he's living there, or he's done a good job of creating a red herring."

"Medina has the money to accomplish that."

She laughed lightly. "That, I most definitely can confirm. The old king built a fortune beyond the royal inheritance. The estate continues to multiply itself. We know he has three sons—Carlos, Duarte and Antonio."

And he had a daughter, a daughter no one knew about. Eloisa, so unforgettable and deserving of so much better than she'd gotten from the people who were supposed to care about her.

And what about how *he* had treated her? Damn it all, Eloisa deserved to have someone a hundred percent on her side. "Thanks, Mom. I would appreciate it if you could ask around—quietly, please—about the Medinas."

"Certainly, I'll see what I can find." Curiosity slipped ever so subtly into her voice. "Would you like to tell me why?"

Eloisa's secrets weren't his to share. But the time would certainly come when his family would have to learn he'd married her. The fact that he'd hidden it for the past year was going to piss them off enough. "Is that a requisite to your help?"

"Of course not," she said, backing off smoothly. "I'll let you know if I discover anything soon. Otherwise, I'll see you in a couple of weeks."

"Looking forward to it. And hey, Mom? Love you."

"I love you, too, Jonah," she said softly before disconnecting.

Perhaps talking to his mom had heightened his conscience or maybe he'd just woken up. But regardless, he needed to shower Eloisa with romance as well as sensual enticement. He couldn't be sure how this was going to turn out. But he wasn't walking away or letting her walk away until he was damn sure everything was out in the open and resolved.

Jonah rang the doorbell and waited…and waited. No answer. Eloisa had told him she would be home around this time, but wasn't answering her phone or cell. His instincts burned. Something was off.

She'd given him a key and he intended to use it.

He opened the front door and pushed inside fast. "Eloisa? Are you home?"

His heart slugged his rib cage harder with each step as he searched her empty town house. Then he thought about her patio. The curtains were closed over the French doors. She must be outside relaxing.

He opened the doors to the patio and sure enough the chair was full. But the person most definitely wasn't Eloisa, or even a female.

Jonah scrubbed a hand over his jaw to mask his surprise and figure out what to do about this intruder who looked completely at home. As if he belonged in that chair, at Eloisa's place.

Jealousy cranked into high gear as he summed up his opponent.

A large male sat in the Adirondack chair—dark haired, about six foot three inches. The guy appeared toned, but Jonah had a few pounds on him. He just needed to decide what move to make next.

At first the guy's eyes seemed closed, but when Jonah

studied him further, he could see the man watching ever so carefully through narrow slits.

This guy was ready to pounce.

Jonah blocked the exit. "What the hell are you doing on Eloisa's patio?"

His eyes opened slowly, a haughty smile not far behind. "I've come to visit my sister."

Eight

Well, that took care of the jealousy.

Jonah stared at the guy in front of him claiming to be Eloisa's brother. How could he trust this dude was on the up and up? But then perhaps he was someone who'd just ended up on the wrong patio. After all, the stranger had simply said he was visiting his sister, no name given.

"Who did you say you're looking for?" Jonah asked.

The man smoothed the front of his dark suit jacket—no tie on his white shirt open at the collar. "Where is Eloisa? My sister. Our family lawyer informed us she has concerns. I came right away."

First, he needed to determine if this man could be trusted. Sure, he looked like he could be Eloisa's brother, same dark hair and brown eyes. The aristocratic air was there, too, but his skin was more olive toned.

Because both of his parents were from the Spanish region?

Still, he needed to go on the assumption that this guy knew nothing about Eloisa, that he could be some reporter searching for information...or worse.

Jonah shut the door to the town house and stepped closer to the looming guy in a dark suit. "And your name is?"

He thrust out his hand, lean and ringless, no jewelry other than a pricey watch peeking from his cuff. "I am Duarte. Hello, Jonah Landis."

Jonah jolted. How did the man know him? Sure his family name was easily recognized, but it wasn't like his face was familiar to the average Joe—or in this case, Duarte. "How did you get in here?"

"I jumped the fence."

This guy in a suit hopped fences? Odd, and not the sort of behavior he expected from a prince.

Still the fence apparently posed a security problem he would be addressing shortly. "Do you make a habit of that? Jumping fences? Breaking and entering?"

Duarte—or whoever the hell he was—arched a single brow slowly. "I would have come through the door but she is not here."

"Eloisa doesn't have any brothers. Just a sister named Audrey."

Duarte simply smiled. "Eloisa can clear this up soon enough. And as you noticed, I already know who you are, and I know how you are connected to my sister." He frowned slightly. "I guess that makes us brothers."

Jonah braced his feet, shocked that Eloisa would have

revealed their marriage to anyone, but she said she didn't talk to her family, only communicated through a lawyer. How had this guy found out? And was he even who he claimed to be?

This joker wasn't getting past him. "How about you leave a calling card?"

"Good, good." He nodded curtly. "I like it that she has you to protect her."

That threw him off-balance for a second. The last thing he'd expected was acceptance, encouragement even.

Except he knew better than to be swayed by calculated words. "What did you say you're doing here?"

"I've come to see Eloisa for our father. And you're wise not to trust me. That's best for her."

While they may have found a point of agreement, that didn't mean Jonah intended to back off pushing for whatever he could get out of Duarte. "Where does your father live?"

"Ah, you're tricky, not ever saying the last name either, never giving anything away. Your questions and answers are as nebulous as my own." He gestured toward the French doors. "Let's go inside. Less chance of being overheard."

"I don't think so. Until I hear from Eloisa that you're welcome, we can stay right here."

Duarte glanced around at the small fenced-in patio, vines growing up the wood, a small fountain in the corner with a cement conch shell pouring water into a collection pool.

And only one chair.

Duarte nodded regally. "We will stand here, then, until she returns."

Jonah leaned on the doorframe with affected nonchalance, every muscle still on high alert as he watched the man for any signs of aggression or deception. "So step out on a limb and spill your guts for me."

The strange guy threw his head back and laughed. Finally, he shook his head and quieted. "I travel everywhere. But our father? He can no longer travel anywhere because of his health, and he wants to see his children. You don't have to confirm anything I say. I don't expect you to."

"Dude, I'm thinking it's time to call the cops and arrest you for trespassing."

"I could give you all sorts of identification, but you know that IDs can be purchased. Instead I will tell you a story about the last visit Eloisa made to see her biological family when she was seven—I was seventeen. We all went on a picnic, then walked down the beach. We collected shells. Then Eloisa rode on our father's shoulders while he told her a story about a princess squirrel who could travel anywhere she wanted, anytime."

Damn. This guy could really be...

"Then he sang her songs in Spanish. Does that answer your questions?"

"You've definitely captured my interest enough to delay calling the cops." He might not know everything about Eloisa, but he was certain she would blow a gasket if her family news was splashed all over a police blotter where any newspaper could snatch the scoop.

"I'm not worried."

"You're a cocky bastard."

"Thank you." He slid a finger along his shirt collar,

the first sign that he felt the heat or any tension. "I'm not only here because Eloisa called the lawyer. I am also here because our father is sick."

"Your dad, the guy who sings lullabies in Spanish? How sick is he?"

"I am not the kind to predict worst-case scenarios. Let's just say he's very ill. A visit is in order before the opportunity is lost forever."

How would Eloisa take hearing Enrique Medina could die…or was already dead and she'd missed seeing him? He'd encouraged her to make contact with the old king if for no other reason that to settle the past, and now the clock was ticking. If this man could help persuade her, all the better. And with Jonah by her side, nobody would stand a chance at hurting her ever again.

In fact, there should be some apologizing and amends for needing such a dire prod to make this offer.

"Even if I might think it's in her personal best interest to see him, why should Eloisa—or any woman—visit a family you say she hasn't seen since she was seven? If that's all true, perhaps they should have tried harder to contact Eloisa more often over the years." The silence stretched between them, birds chirping, cars roaring and honking in the distance, even the ocean echoed distantly. "What? No disagreement?"

"Why would I argue when you're absolutely right? That doesn't mean Eloisa could live with doing the wrong thing now."

Jonah checked his watch. Where the hell was Eloisa? She should have been home twenty minutes ago. "Your family is exempt from the rules but she's not? She's supposed to do the right thing regardless? That's bull."

"She is a part of our family."

"Says you. I'm still not sure what you're talking about."

"It's her choice to live this way rather than claim her birthright." He tipped his head to the side. "You didn't know that? She and her mother chose a long time ago not to accept anything from him. He slipped help how he could. Surprise prize winnings, bonuses at work, even a fellowship to travel to Europe."

Eloisa would spit nails if she found out the whole trip was a setup. But given her prickly ways about money, that would have been the only way to get her to accept anything. "Most women I know wouldn't like being manipulated that way."

"Then don't tell her."

"Why are you telling me?" That put him in a tough position, forcing him to keep secrets. He hated lies. Always had. His father had hammered that into his head from a young age. His dad had been in the military before he'd gone into politics. He'd prided himself on being a rarity—a guy who shot straight from the hip, no matter what.

He'd always said the measure of a man was how he acted when no one was looking.

"I am hoping you can hold some sway over her to see my father for what may very well be the last time. She needs persuading. She's a stubborn woman."

"Wait. Hold on for just a damn minute. You say you haven't seen her, but you know all about her personality?"

He shrugged. Did this dude ever relay any emotion? "I never said we haven't kept close watch over her."

She definitely wouldn't like that. Even if this guy

was on the up and up, another possibility still existed. He might be a stalker. Family could stalk. And dealing with that possibility took precedence. "It's time for you and me to leave."

"You and I?"

"I'm not letting you walk away until I am one hundred percent sure who you are. I have connections of my own."

"Fair enough. Just one question first." Duarte's dark eyes narrowed as if zeroing in for the kill. "Who did you think I was when you entered?"

The sound of a key rattling in the front door jarred the silence between them. Damn it all. He should have moved faster. The hinges creaked and Jonah put himself between this man and the path Eloisa would take.

Eloisa filled the open French doors, two grocery bags in her arms and her mouth open wide.

"Duarte?"

Shock nailed her feet to the floor.

Eloisa blinked fast twice, unable to believe her eyes. It couldn't possibly be one of the Medina brothers.... Did he even go by Medina?

But she'd seen a few pictures over the years and she would never forget the faces of her faraway brothers. That summer she'd visited, Duarte had told her of his dream to take a new last name, maybe his mother's maiden name, and move out of the compound, into the world. Duarte had been emphatic about making his own way in the world.

She'd understood that, even at seven, when he'd talked about his plans for "getting the hell off this island."

Island? Until just this moment she'd forgotten that part of talking with him.

From his slick suit, gold watch and some kind of signature cologne, it didn't seem he'd done too badly for himself. She was glad for him if he'd managed to fulfill those dreams of leading his own life.

Although he had managed to send all her evening plans up into smoke.

Eloisa juggled bags of groceries in her arms as her purse dangled from her elbow. She would have set them on the counter when she'd entered the apartment, but she'd heard two voices on the patio and rushed out there, food and all.

She'd traded a favor at work and clocked out early. She was always the one staying late for others who had surprise dates.

It was fun to be on the other side of that for a change. So much for fun.

Both men stepped forward to take a sack from her arms, the food she'd bought with such grand ideas for her evening. She'd taken great care in making her selections at the market. Deciding had been tougher than she expected because what could you serve a tycoon world traveler?

She'd opted for a simple regional classic that might actually have a chance at being heavy enough for a big guy like Jonah—shrimp and grits, with slaw and biscuits on the side. She'd splurged on a bottle of good wine. Well, what she considered good, which could very well be swill by his standards. Not that it mattered now since they had an extra guest.

Her hands shook with nerves and she nearly dropped

her purse. How silly to be this uptight about making dinner for a guy.

Dinner for her husband.

She felt the smile on her face before she ever realized she'd reacted. Seeing him made her happy. Wow. What an awesome—and scary—notion.

Especially with this huge distraction between them. Before she could do anything, she needed to find out why her brother had shown up here so unexpectedly.

The space between them might be short—the patio was microscopic, after all—but there might as well have been a mile between them. Hugging this distant man she'd only spoken to once seemed awkward, even if they shared the same DNA.

And now that she thought about, how strange for him to be here. A trickle of unease tickled inside her stomach. "Come into the town house, gentlemen. Let's get those groceries inside before the shrimp spoils in this heat."

Eloisa flashed a grateful smile to Jonah. She couldn't miss the tic in the corner of his eye, but wasn't sure what put it there.

"Duarte," she touched her brother's arm lightly, "welcome. You might as well stay for supper. Unless you've already made other plans?"

Once in the kitchenette, Jonah's somber gaze stopped her midramble. "Your brother said he needs to talk to you."

"Right, of course. We have a lot to catch up on, I'm sure." God, this felt so surreal, having her brother here after so many years.

She put away groceries on autopilot. Holding a wrapped and taped bag of shrimp in her hands, she pivoted toward the refrigerator and almost slammed smack into her brother. "Sorry, uhm, not much space."

"How did you recognize me?" Duarte asked simply, with no preamble.

She looked into dark eyes identical to her own, ones that had also stared back at her from her father's face during that memorable encounter years ago. "You look just like him."

"Our father?" Duarte blinked slowly, his eyes more enigmatic than their dad's. The old king's eyes had been mostly sad. "You were only seven years old."

"But Enrique was younger then." Although in her childish view he'd seem so very ancient. "And my mother kept a picture of him from when they, uh, knew each other. She let me hide it in my sock drawer sometimes. I mixed it in with fan clippings and posters so no one would ever guess. And it's obvious I'm right."

She couldn't bear this standoff positioning. Eloisa strode past to shove the bag of seafood into the refrigerator. She had to be in control of something, even if it was making sure the shrimp didn't spoil. "Why are you here? Now?" Eloisa froze as a horrible possibility avalanched over her, far more chilling than the blast from the fridge. She spun back around. "Is he dead?"

"He's alive," Duarte reassured her quickly, even though his somber face gave her pause. "I'm here because you contacted the lawyer. And we would have been in touch with you soon anyway. Our father is sick, most likely dying. He wants to see his children."

"How many of us are there?" Damn, where had that cruel response come from? From the deep recesses of her late-night childhood fears and tears, no doubt.

Jonah placed a comforting, steadying hand between

her shoulder blades, while nudging the refrigerator closed with his foot.

Duarte stuffed his hands in his pants pockets. "Just you, our two brothers and, of course, me."

"Pardon me if I'm not so sure." Eloisa breathed deeply to expand the tightness rapidly constricting her rib cage with tension. "I am sorry he's sick, but I don't think we have anything to say to one another. Not after so many years."

She expected an argument, smooth persuasive reasons why she was wrong. But Duarte simply shrugged.

"Okay then. I'll let him know the message was delivered and you declined. Since you don't have any questions, I've completed my task."

That was it? He was leaving?

Duarte slid a card onto the sofa end table, simple white vellum with a number printed in raised, black ink. He anchored it with a paperweight. "You can contact me when you decide to see him."

When?

Another decade or two?

Duarte had simply shown up, rocked her balance until she didn't know what she thought, and then he was gone again before she could gather her thoughts. He hadn't come to *see* her. He'd come to pass along information. God, she was such an idiot, still hiding hopes deep in her heart like those pictures of her biological family tucked under her socks.

She wanted to cry but her eyes were dry after all these years.

Jonah stepped around her, nearly nose to nose with her brother. "I'll walk you to the door."

"No need." Duarte nodded to Eloisa, starting toward

the front door. "I'll let our father know you will be visiting soon."

She stifled the urge to scream out her frustration. Who did these Medina men think they were to blast into a person's life once every decade or so and wreak total havoc? "You're assuming a lot."

He pivoted back toward her fluidly. "There are many times when my life has relied on my ability to read people."

Duarte Medina slipped out of the door as quietly and quickly as he'd arrived.

Jonah rubbed between her shoulder blades. "Are you all right?"

"I'm fine. Totally fine. Why wouldn't I be? It was just five minutes out of my life. No big deal. Now he's gone and everything's back to normal again." She pulled away and yanked open the refrigerator. "I'll start supper."

His hands landed on her shoulders, squeezing gently with a sympathy and comfort that swept away her defenses. She shattered inside from endless vows that she didn't care if her father never fought for her. And when her brothers struck out on their own, they never even bothered to contact her. Years of being everyone's support and nobody's princess crashed down on her until she hurt so bad inside she couldn't find any corner of her soul to hide and escape.

She had nowhere to go except straight into Jonah's arms.

Nine

Eloisa blocked out the ache in her heart left from her brother's shocking visit and focused on Jonah. Just Jonah, with her, both of them hopefully naked very, very soon.

She wrapped her arms around his neck and flattened herself to him. He stumbled back a step and nearly slammed into the kitchen counter.

"Whoa." He gripped her hips, steadying them both so they didn't knock off the remaining groceries or tumble to the tile floor. "Let's slow this down a minute and think things through. I know you're upset—"

"Damn straight, I'm upset. I'm angry and hurt and confused and want it all to go away. You can fix that for me, so let's get to it."

She plastered her lips to his, opened, demanded. The ever-ready attraction between them blazed to life on contact, thank goodness. She welcomed the blissful sensation expanding within her, pushing everything else to the far corners. Less pain.

Total pleasure.

Muscles in his chest and arms twitched and flexed under her searching fingers. "Eloisa, I hear you and I understand. And God knows, I'm more than glad to comply until you're not able to think or talk, but I also have to know you're not going to bolt out of here afterward before I even have time to pull on a pair of boxers."

Eloisa nuzzled along his ear, kissing, nipping, whispering soft gusts of air over his skin as she buried her face in his hair. "We're in my home. That makes leaving a lot tougher for me."

"But not impossible," he insisted even as his hand slid down to cup her bottom and lift her closer, more intimately against him until she could feel the fly on his jeans straining against the thickening length of him.

"We're here to resolve things," he said, "not make them more complicated between—" He clasped her hand already making fast work of his jeans snap. "Take a breather, for now, anyway."

She flipped her hands to link in his as she met his eyes square on. "Jonah, look around you. Think. What did I bring in when I got home from work? Dinner. Wine. I planned a romantic meal because after what we did—" she paused, suddenly breathless at just the mention, the memory "—after the way you made me feel, I've been thinking about finishing this every second since. I've been planning what I want to do to you, how to make you every bit as crazy as you make me."

"Eloisa," he groaned, loosening his hold on her hands

until she flattened her palm to his fly. "You already make me crazy just by walking through my mind, much less the room."

"Then it's time to do something about that."

She peeled his black polo shirt over his head. Was it only last night he pulled up at her sister's party? It seemed like a lifetime ago, as if the past year apart hadn't even happened.

But it had and oh God, she couldn't let herself think about that. Better to focus on now, with him. He was right. They did need time together to work through their feelings or she—he too?—would spend forever wondering, wanting.

Growling low, he tunneled his hands under her dress, bunching it up and away in a deft sweep that left her breathless and bare, other than her icy-blue lace bra and panties. "Do you have any idea how gorgeous you look right this second?" He reached behind her to pull the scarf from her ponytail, releasing her hair. "I've lost a lot of sleep this past year thinking about you like this."

"I hope you're going to lose even more tonight." Her hair teased along her skin until she was ready to scream for a more insistent touch.

Thank goodness he didn't need any further encouragement. He kissed her again, backing her as he moved forward, their legs tangling in the desperate dance toward the stairs, which stopped them short.

But not for long.

Jonah ducked his shoulder into her midsection and lifted her into a fireman carry. Eloisa squealed, but certainly wasn't about to tell him no because he was making fast tracks for her bedroom.

Once in her room, he flipped her over and onto the

antique bed with a smooth sweep, the wooden thrift store find she'd painstakingly whitewashed. She bounced once in the middle of the pouffy comforter. A pink tulip print hung over the headboard.

Her haven where no one entered.

Until Jonah.

He traced her collarbone. "When I watched you sleep before, I fantasized about what kind of jewels would look best nestled right here." He skimmed his mouth along after his fingers' path.

"And here." He nipped her ears.

"I didn't think I slept," she gasped as his mouth trekked lower, "for even a minute that night."

"I didn't need more than a minute to picture you in my world."

Her breath caught as his words sunk in. Her eyes met his, so deeply somber for a second, then he smiled and she lost the chance to decipher what she'd seen.

"Besides," he said, shuffling away the seriousness, "I have an active imagination." He traced her belly button with his tongue, flicking her simple silver ring between his teeth. "Most definitely a diamond here."

Jonah kissed her hip, his hand sliding down her leg and scattering thoughts as quickly as the rest of his clothes and their underwear. "And anklets. There are so many options for stones I would have specially set for you to wear right there for trips to the beach."

A ceiling fan clicked, gusting over her bare skin and ruffling airy sheers that hung from bamboo rods. She felt like those curtains, fluttering and writhing with every brush and breath of Jonah's along her body. She grasped at his back, his taut buttocks, his chest, touching and tasting frenetically in contrast to his smooth exploration.

How could she be this hungry for Jonah when by all rights, he had taken care of her needs just a few hours before in her office? That should have at least eased the edge, but instead seemed to have only made her ache for more. Then he slid up along her, over her, the solid weight of him anchoring her to the bed and the moment so perfectly.

She slid the arch of her foot along his leg, opening for him, wanting him, welcoming him inch by thick, delicious inch.

"Shhh…" he whispered in her ear although she couldn't for the life of her remember what she'd said or asked for. "Patience. We'll get there."

Unable to wait, she slid her hand between them and clasped him, caressed him, coaxed him until his hands shook, too. He reached to the floor, to his pants, his hand returning with a condom. He tore open the packet and sheathed himself before she had time to do more than be grateful one of them was thinking clearly enough to take care of birth control.

Finally, he was inside her again, the pressure of him familiar and new at the same time, but then Jonah had always been an unpredictable mass of contradictions that shuffled her perfectly ordered world.

Braced on his elbows, he stared down at her, holding her with his vivid blue eyes. His jaw, tight with restraint, told her he ached for this as much as she did. She'd been tipsy when they'd been together before, but this time she was stone-cold sober, aware of every moment and sensation. And it was even better. Her senses were heightened, sharp, *responsive*.

He moved over her while the bed rocked under her. He was so large and gentle, completely focused on her and…oh my, what a heady feeling that was after so long in shadows. She wanted to stay right here and bask in the sparks showering through her, but knew there was no way in hell this could last. Maybe next time… There had to be a next time.

Frantic to hold on to the feelings, to him, she clenched around him.

"Eloisa…" His eyes closed, his jaw clamping tighter as he said her name again and again, telling her exactly how often he'd thought of her, the other ways he dreamed of adorning her in jewels, erotic images and possibilities she'd never considered and now couldn't forget.

She tried to answer, but words… She had nothing except a moan of increasing need. Jonah's hands fisted in the pillow on either side of her head, his head dropping to rest on her brow.

His hair slid forward, covering most of his face. She cupped his cheeks, her fingers playing with the wavy strands and wondered if he'd ever considered letting it grow longer. Somehow it seemed more lord of manor, leader of the land, with its extra length. He was the epitome of fairy-tale fantasies she'd only barely dared acknowledge to herself.

More, she wanted more of him, of this, of the whole fantasy. She hooked her heels behind his back and arched upward, accepting him deeper. Her fingernails scored desperate furrows down his back as the intensity gripped her, begging for release. This couldn't last much longer. It was too intense. Too much of everything and already the ending built and tightened and tingled through her in ripples she couldn't hold back any longer….

She didn't bother trying to hold back the shout of pleasure. Jonah thrust faster. She gripped his back harder. Sparks glinted behind her eyes much like the jewels he'd detailed earlier. With one last prolonged thrust, he buried himself inside her…and stayed, his face in her hair, his groan against her ear until his arms gave way and he rolled to his back, taking her, replete, alongside him.

His hand slid over her stomach, his finger tracing a circle around her belly button, his breathing ragged. "We're definitely going shopping for a diamond soon."

Her heartbeat tumbled over itself at the mention of diamonds…until she realized he meant navel rings, not engagement. Technically, they were already married anyway. But for how long?

Jonah continued to draw lazy circles with the backs of his fingers. A murmur of unease echoed inside her as she thought of their baby that had rested there, tragically too briefly. She should tell him, and she would, but how could she just toss it into the mix right now? More importantly, how could she trust he would stay? He'd made it clear he'd been angry with her for leaving. She couldn't help but wonder if he'd come looking for revenge.

Could he be that calculated? She had no way of knowing because as she'd told him before, they didn't know each other well enough to be certain of anything. Her best bet? Wait—a couple of days, perhaps?—to let the dust settle. To let her mind clear while she got her bearings. Then she would tell him about the baby they'd lost.

As the fan dried the perspiration on her body, she

wondered how long she could selfishly take from him before the truth put this tenuous connection to the test.

Reclining in Eloisa's antique bed, Jonah tested a lock of her hair between his fingers, so long and soft. He'd wanted to have her and walk away. He'd expected to put an end to their unfinished business by being with her one last time, and instead? He couldn't imagine how the hell he would let her go.

If they weren't married, he would have asked her to travel with him. Why not ask her anyway? Certainly they couldn't solve anything continents apart.

He knew her secret now, after all. Sure, being with him brought an added level of attention, but her heritage could too easily come out no matter what in an unexpected instant. Better to be prepared.

He was the man who could keep her safe.

Now he had to persuade her to go with him to Peru after her sister's wedding. And wouldn't waking up beside Eloisa daily be a pleasure? Not that he expected her to agree right away. She was stubborn, and she had a blind loyalty to her sister and stepfather that made him grind his teeth in frustration.

He needed to show her the way their lives could blend, that she deserved better from people. He cared about her in a way her self-absorbed family never had.

Jonah took in the every curve draped in a cotton sheet, a light purple. She looked damn good in that color. Natural purple diamonds were among the rarest. Like her. But he intended to shower her with jewels *and* his undivided attention.

He released the strand over her breast where it curled

to rest around the creamy swell. "I've missed you so damn much this year."

"We barely knew each other then." She rasped a fingernail lightly down his chest. "And things are happening so fast again now. Can't we just enjoy this moment?"

"Think how much we've learned in just a day of really talking. Let's talk some more." He splayed his hand over her rib cage, then upward to toy with a pert nipple. "I've missed being with you, seeing you, feeling you move underneath as you whisper how much you need me, need more of what I can give you."

She laughed, covering his mouth with her hand. "Okay, okay. I get the picture."

He nipped her finger, then drew it in to soothe away the sting with his tongue. "You can't tell me you never thought about those days together."

"Of course I thought about it." The sheets rustled as she sat up, hugging her knees to her chest. "You have a way of making an impression on a person that isn't easy to forget. Staying away was my only option for keeping my sanity."

"I make you crazy? Good." He swept her hair forward over her shoulder and traced down her neck to her spine, one vertebrae at a time. "Let's see if I can do it again."

"You know you do, on so many levels." Sighing, she rested her cheek on her knees as he made his way down her back.

"Then let's *talk* some more."

"I'm still finding my footing. I'm not exactly the tumultuous type, you know. Let's deal with the most basic level for starters."

"You've got a one-track mind right now." And while he sure as hell wasn't going to complain about that, he also noticed the way she wouldn't meet his gaze. Not a good sign.

She smiled, still not looking at him, instead inching the sheet ever so slowly off him. "What's so wrong with a married couple having sex? Lots of sex. In every room and vehicle at our disposal. We can talk the whole time. In fact, I've already got a pretty good idea of some things I'd like to say to you, too."

He clasped her wrist, stopping her, holding her until finally she met his gaze. "I'm being serious here, Eloisa. We shared something special just now. We'd be fools to just toss that away again. But for it to work, I need you to be honest with me this time."

Eloisa clutched a pillow to her stomach, the shadows and pain so intense in her eyes he wanted to scrap the whole conversation and just hold her. What in the world could have hurt her so deeply? He started to ask, but she pressed her fingertips to his mouth.

"Jonah, I hear what you're saying, and while I joke about all that married sex, honestly, in my mind—" she tapped her temple "—we're divorced. We have been for a long while. It's going to take time before I can reconcile all these changes. So much is happening so fast…I want to trust it…trust you."

"Then do it."

"That's easy for you to say. You're adventurous by nature." She eased her wrist free then clasped his hand. "Just this—" she raised their linked fingers "—is risky for me."

"I don't believe that, not after the woman I met a year ago." He paused, realizing, holy hell, she really was scared. There was a side to her he hadn't met in Spain. He honestly didn't know the woman he'd married. And if he intended to stand a chance with her now, he needed to push harder than he had before.

He had to understand her in order to keep her. He searched for the best place to start. "Are you upset about your brother showing up tonight? Hearing your father is ill had to be upsetting. Are you going to see him? Is that what's wrong?"

She looked down at the bedspread for so long he wondered if she would answer. Would she decide to cut him off at the knees? He wouldn't be pushed aside again without seeing this through.

"Eloisa?" He tipped her chin up with a knuckle. "I asked about your father."

"My father...right...uh, I haven't decided." Her grip eased on the hugged pillow. "I don't even know what to think about Duarte showing up here. It was so unexpected, I'll have to give this more thought."

"But you believed him when he said your father is ill." He sat up beside her, stroking her hair back from her face.

She didn't flinch away.

"My lawyer does keep me informed to a certain degree. I know what my brothers look like. They were already teenagers when I saw them before. Even if I don't know where everyone lives." She laughed dryly. "Actually I don't want to know. Being responsible for their safety would be too scary."

He didn't like the way they left her out here, unprotected. Then it hit him that he couldn't let her go. *He* couldn't leave her out here unprotected. There weren't many who could protect her at the level she needed.

But he was a Landis.

And even though there had been times he'd bucked the Landis conventions, right now he welcomed every bit of power the Landis influence could bring if it kept Eloisa from being hurt in any way—physically or emotionally—by her Medina ties.

The Landis influence and money could also bring her peace in other ways, pampering that by rights should have been hers from the start. "You need a distraction."

"You've done a mighty fine job of that tonight." Looping an arm over his shoulders, she leaned against him, kissing him with unmistakable promise.

His pulse jackhammered in his chest, throbbing through his veins thicker, lower, urging him to act now. He steadied his breathing and his resolve.

Stick to the plan. More time with her. Show her how well she could fit in his world, how easily she could leave her old one behind. "I'll up the ante. You took the afternoon off. Any chance you can call in sick for a couple of days?"

Interest lit in her eyes, followed by wariness. "I have to help Audrey."

"When's her next shindig?"

"Joey's family is throwing a party—" a tentative hope replaced the wariness on her face "—but it isn't until the weekend."

"So that's not a problem for you as long as you come back. Can she handle her own plans for two days?"

"I could take care of things by phone." Her words

tumbled over each other faster. "The bridesmaids' fittings are already done."

"That just leaves your job at the library. Can you get time off?"

"There are people who owe me favors." Her slow seductive smile turned him inside out. "It depends on what you have to offer."

"Trust me," he urged her, determined to make that happen on every level. "You won't be disappointed."

Ten

"Open your eyes."

Late afternoon nipping her arms with prickly heat, Eloisa pulled Jonah's hands from her face and gasped in awe. She stood on top of a building overlooking a massive canyon sprawled out in a craggy display of orange, brown and bronze rock. Wind tore at her clothes with an ends-of-the-earth force. She inched to the edge, grasped the scrolled iron railing and found she stood on top of a mammoth hacienda-style retreat, built on the edge of a cliff corner.

When they'd left Pensacola earlier this afternoon, Jonah had kept the windows closed on the airplane and the limo windows had been shaded. By their fourth hour traveling she was nearing the edge of her trust factor, but wow, had her patience ever paid off.

The property was deserted. Scaffolding remained

visible on one side of the expansive resort building, though no workers filled the platform levels of it today, their work apparently complete for the week. The historic hacienda appeared to have had a recent makeover, the scent of fresh paint mingling with the light fragrance of a potted crepe myrtle nearby.

She leaned farther over the rail. Terra-cotta pots were strategically placed around the patio with a variety of cacti—prickly pear, blooming hedgehog, spiking organ pipe, saguaro, even a towering Joshua tree. Below, in a stomach-lurching drop, away from the sculpted rooftop garden, cacti dotted the landscape in sparse and erratic abandon, no less beautiful. "This is magnificent. Where exactly are we?"

An eagle banked into a dive—*down, down, down*—so far it seemed impossible to continue, then it swooped upward again into the purple blue sky. Warm sun counteracted the dry breeze pinning her cotton halter dress to her skin.

"Does it matter where we are?" He dismissed the luxurious digs around them and pointed outward. "Can't it be beautiful just because it is, rather than because it has a fancy pedigree attached?"

She snorted on a laugh. "Spoken like a savvy investor who can see the possibilities in previously unappreciated properties."

He clapped a palm over his chest. "I'm wounded you would think I'm so calculating."

"You're practical, and I admire that." In fact, the more she learned about him the more she realized how she'd stereotyped him from the start. "You're not at all the reckless playboy I mistook you for last year."

"Don't go romanticizing me. I simply found a

job that suits my wandering feet and desire to create luxurious digs."

She started to laugh, then stopped to look beyond his casual dismissal of her compliment. "I think it's more than that for you."

"Maybe. I'm a guy. I don't analyze like you women. I just know that I like transforming things others have overlooked." He smiled distractedly before his eyes cleared again. "We're in West Texas, by the way. I figured that was about as far as I could go without you freaking out over the secrecy or worrying about getting back for your sister's party."

"You guessed right." She accepted his conversational shift for now since he actually had shared more than she expected. "I'm glad I took the leap of faith and joined you."

Thank goodness Audrey hadn't been upset by the prospect of her leaving for a few days. In fact, Eloisa had been surprised at how readily her sister had encouraged her to go away. Only a week ago, Audrey had been hyperventilating over punch flavors, insisting she needed Eloisa and the caterer's input on everything. Brides were notoriously edgy. She could understand and be patient.

Yet suddenly Audrey seemed calm. Go figure.

Regardless, that seemed a universe away now. She'd packed so carefully for this trip, choosing her most silky underwear, remembering to pack cologne, and her favorite apple lip gloss he'd so intensely—deliciously— noted in the library. Just this morning she'd even spied him sniffing the tube at her dressing table.

Yes, she'd taken care in choosing what to bring along, cautiously pinning high hopes on this outing.

She wanted reassurance they had a chance at a future before she could open herself up to him totally. This compressed time together, away from distractions offered that opportunity.

She trailed her fingers along the curved railing. "So this place is your work? I'm very impressed."

She couldn't miss his artistry as she looked down at the structure built in such a way she couldn't distinguish the old from the new.

"The resort is set to open in another month once the decorators have finished their gig inside. Working this place landed me a contract in Peru to pull off something similar with a nineteenth-century structure. It'll need expansion as well as renovation." He shook his head. "Enough about work. We're here to relax, alone up here where no one can see us and no one will dare interrupt. Now it's time for the real reason I brought you."

Jonah turned her to the right along the corner for even more canyon panorama and, just to her side...

Rippling water slipped off the edge of the building, somehow disappearing. She pivoted to find a rooftop pool, but unlike any she'd ever seen before. It stretched off the end of the building and seemed to blend into the horizon.

"Jonah?"

"It's an infinity pool," he announced.

It was magnificent. "Infinity pool. That makes sense in theory—" given the way it blended into the canyon view "—but I don't understand how."

Her feet drew her closer to the clear waters swirling over the blue tiles, sunlight sparkling diamondlike dots along the surface. The romanticism reached to her heart already softened by a night spent in Jonah's arms.

Even now, she could feel her body reacting to just his presence, the knowledge that she could have him right now and indulge herself in everything he had to offer. And he did offer her so very much on so many levels.

Eloisa reached for his hand, listening to his explanation and letting herself dream. Maybe, just maybe her instincts had been right that all they needed was more time.

Jonah linked his fingers more firmly in hers. "The pool is architecturally designed with the edge smoothed out until it seems to extend forever, blending into the horizon. Some call it a negative edge. A side is built slightly lower with a catch basin that pumps water back into the pool."

"That sounds extremely complicated." She didn't have to be an architect to tell this required incredible talent and expertise. She imagined the least miscalculation during construction could crumble the cliff. Much like the delicate balance and attention to detail needed in building a relationship. "Tell me more."

"An infinity pool can be built on a rooftop or into the side of a mountain or right against a larger body of water." He stretched a hand toward the horizon. "The effect is the same. While you float and stare out, boundaries disappear."

"Possibilities are limitless." That sounded good in theory, but felt scary for a woman who found comfort and safety in the cool confines of her dimly lit library stacks. She would take it one deep breath at a time, because the thought of turning back scared her even more than standing here at the precipice.

His arm dropped to his side. "There's an infinity pool in Hong Kong on the roof of a hotel that's the most amazing thing I've ever seen." He squeezed her fingers. "Wanna go?"

"What? Now?" Startled by his abrupt offer, she backed away a step, instinctively craving the safety of even a few inches away from wide-open abandon. "We just got to Texas. I'm still soaking everything in."

"But you want to go."

Did she? Could she just drop everything at his whim and see the world?

"I think so, maybe," she said to the adventure. To him. This didn't seem the place for stark realities and secrets. It was the ultimate place to lose yourself. Here, she didn't have to worry about what it meant to be a Medina or a Landis. "For a short time perhaps, but—"

"Quit thinking about afterward. Enjoy the now, here at the edge of a canyon. Take a risk, librarian lady."

She bristled instinctively. "Who says there's anything wrong with being a librarian in Pensacola, Florida?"

He tugged her closer to him, his hand soothing along her waist. "I never said there was anything wrong with your profession. I'm just offering you the chance to *experience* the books. You can have it all."

Stark realities intruded all the same, memories of her mother, memories of her own, even glimpses of her father's pain-filled eyes. Consequences for stepping out of her safety zone could be huge. "They killed my father's wife, you know. They assassinated her while trying to get to him." She looked into his eyes for answers, for reassurance. "Doesn't your family worry about that kind of lurking threat? Your father may have died in a car wreck, but you had to be aware of danger at an early age."

God knows, she had worried for her mother. And in

the darkest, quietest times of night, she even worried for herself.

The wind lifted Jonah's hair and flapped the edges of his sports coat. "I hear you, and yes, my family has lived with the reality of possible kidnappings and bribes and threats because of political stands. It's not fair, but that's how things are even if we gave away the money and left the public scene tomorrow. No one would believe we didn't have something hidden somewhere. The influence remains and we have a responsibility to use it wisely." He cupped her face in his sun-warmed hands. "You can't live your life dictated by fears."

She pulled out of his arms. Leaning against, leaning *on* him would be too easy.

"Tell that to Enrique Medina." Her chest went tight. How much longer did her father have left? "He's spent nearly three decades hidden away from the world, living out his life."

"If I knew where he was, I would tell him face-to-face."

"I thought you would have learned that when you found me." Maybe she'd hoped he knew so she wouldn't have to make the choice to search. Jonah would know, blindfold her and take her there. And only now did she realize she'd hoped he would do just that today. Good Lord, she was a coward.

"Medina keeps his secrets well."

"I guess he does." As did his daughter. Guilt pinched over what she should explain to Jonah.

He drew her to his side again. "What do you think he wants to talk to you about?"

"I have absolutely no idea. Probably just to say goodbye, which I should probably go along with. It sounds simple enough. Except I have this sense that if I step into his world, I will have made an irrevocable change." She blinked back tears until they welled back up inside her soul. She tipped her head up to look at him. "Jonah, we should talk."

He thumbed under her eye, swiping away dampness that must have leaked anyway. "I think we've done enough talking for one day."

She wanted to agree, reminding herself of her resolve to wait until she was sure he would stay before risking the pain that would come from sharing all. Still, her conscience whispered. "Seriously, Jonah, I need to tell you—"

"Seriously, stop arguing. We can talk about whatever you want later." He slid his other arm around her and pulled her flush against him again, rekindling the desire that had been barely banked all afternoon. "Right now, I want to make love with you in this pool while we look out at infinity."

Infinity.

Forever.

They could have it all. She could have the time to tell him the things that needed explaining. The possibilities truly seemed as limitless of the edge of that pool reclaiming and holding everything in an endless cycle.

Jonah kissed her and she allowed herself to hope.

Jonah hauled Eloisa closer, sensing something shifting inside her, tension flowing from her in a tide as tangible as the infinity pool streaming away. He didn't know what exactly brought about the change, but he wasn't one to argue when it brought her warm and willing into his arms.

"Inside," she whispered, "to your suite."

"Here," he answered. "We're alone. No one can see us, of that I'm certain. I designed this patio with complete privacy in mind."

Over the past few months, he'd tortured himself with fantasies of bringing her up here and baring her body to the sun. "Do you trust me?"

"I can't think of anything more exciting than making love to you out here in the open." Her arms slid around his neck, her fingers in his hair. "I want to trust you."

He noticed wanting to trust wasn't the same as giving trust, but still a step in the right direction. And since he had her in his arms, ready to have sex outdoors? No way in hell did he intend to dwell on semantics.

Eloisa slid his sports coat from his shoulders, his shirt open at the collar, no tie to bother with removing. Backing him toward the double lounger beside the pool, she toyed with one button at a time, unveiling his chest until the shirt whipped behind him in the wind.

Smiling, Jonah shook his head no and danced her toward the pool instead. Her eyes widened momentarily before she grinned in return. Eloisa kicked off her sandals and trailed a toe in the water.

Her sigh of pleasure left him throbbing against his zipper damn near painfully. But soon…so soon…

He toyed with the tie behind her neck holding her halter dress in place. A simple tug set it free and falling away to reveal her breasts to the sun. He nudged the fabric down around and past her waist to pool at her feet. She kicked it away behind her, their clothes littering the stone tiles, lifting on the wind and catching on the furniture.

Eloisa glanced over her shoulder with a flicker of concern. He guided her face back toward him again. "To hell with the clothes. We brought suitcases. I'll buy you more."

"In that case…" She unbuckled his belt, slipped it free and flung it out into the canyon, with a *flick* and a *snap*.

Her uninhibited laughter rode the wind along with the rest of their clothes and his shoes until they stood bare in the open together. Her breasts brushed his chest as she took him in her hand and stroked until he worked to keep his feet steady under him.

He clasped her wrist and draped her arm back over his shoulder. Leaning, he scooped her up against his chest and started down the stone steps, the sun-warmed water churning around his legs, his hips, around his waist and higher until he slid her to her feet again. The light waves lapped around her shoulders and she leaned into him with buoyancy.

He slid his hand between her legs, the essence of her arousal mixing with the water, leaving her slick to his touch. He tucked two fingers into her warm silken grip, stroking inside, his thumb teasing outside. Sighing, she pressed closer to him just as she'd done in the library, so hot, so responsive. So damn perfect he almost came undone from just the feel of her on his hand.

She sprinkled frenetic kisses over his face, working her way to his ear. "I want you inside me, totally, I want it all here. Now," she demanded.

"More than willing to accommodate," he growled.

Jonah cupped her bottom and lifted. She wrapped her

slick wet legs around his waist, the core of her pressing closer to him, her damp heat against him. He throbbed from wanting to be inside her again. And again. How often would be enough?

She slid down on the length of him.

"Birth control," he groaned into her ear. Only now did he realize they'd forgotten and he wanted to kick himself off the damn cliff for being so reckless with her. He never, never forgot. He always protected.

Her arms clamped tighter around him. "I'm on the Pill."

"You didn't mention that when we were together before."

"My thoughts aren't always clear around you, especially when we're naked. Now can we stop with the talking and move on to the fun part? I want this—I want you. How convenient for us both that you happen to be my husband, after all."

But she hadn't known that for the past months when they'd both assumed their divorce had gone through. He didn't want to know why she'd used it in the year they were apart. He chose instead to focus on how glad to have that last concern taken away so he could...

Plunge inside her.

Her head flung back, her wet hair floating behind her. He dipped his head to take the pink pert tip of her breast in his mouth. He teased her with his tongue, gently with his teeth, using his mouth in all the ways he wanted to touch her but couldn't since he held her, guided her.

The cool jet of water from the side of the pool didn't so much as take an edge off the heat pumping through him. Water sluiced between them as they writhed against each other. Her hair floated behind her, long and dark. Beads of water clung to her face, her shoulders. He sipped from her skin, the taste of her overriding any chlorination.

He palmed her upright until her head rested on his shoulder. "I want you to see."

To look out at the endless view, the endless possibilities *he* could give her.

Eloisa gripped his arms, her nails furrowing into his skin. He welcomed the tender bite into his flesh, the tangible sign that she felt the same frenetic need.

Water lapped around them, encircling them in a vortex as he clasped her closer. He had to make this last. He refused to lose her. While they'd made progress today, still he sensed her reservations. Whatever was holding her back, he needed to reassure her she didn't have to be afraid, because he could take care of her.

He *would* take care of her, sensually, physically and any other way she needed.

The primal drive to make her his clawed through him, intensified by the open elements. He'd come here for her and found it tapped into something inside himself he hadn't anticipated. Something basic and undeniable. He thrust inside her as her hips rolled against him, her breath hitching against his neck, faster as her skin began to flush with…

Gasping, she flung her head back again, her back arching, her eyes closed tight. He watched and savored every moment of her sweet release across her face, echoed in the spasms of her moist clamp around him, drawn out until…hell, couldn't hold back.

He surged inside her. The sunset shot purple, pink and orange spiking through the horizon as sharp and deep as the pleasure blasting through him. She was his, damn it. No more barriers, boundaries, secrets.

He'd won her.

Eleven

Eloisa surrendered to the languid weightlessness of floating in the water and watching the stars overhead. How blessedly freeing to put the world and worries on hold for once. She wasn't a wife, a sister, a daughter.

Today, tonight, she was simply a woman and a lover.

After Jonah had brought her to such intense completion while she stared over the infinity pool edge, they'd held on to each other for…well…she didn't know how long. At some point she'd floated away and he'd begun swimming lazy laps. They were simply coexisting in the water without talking. Being together so perfectly, even in silence, surpassed anything she'd imagined gaining from this time away.

The near-silent sluice of his arms through the water announced his presence a second before he passed. She reached out, grazing him with her fingers. His head slid from the water and he stood beside her, not even panting.

He shook his head, swiping back his hair. "Are you ready to go in? There's a cold supper waiting in the refrigerator."

She looped an arm around his neck and let her feet sink. "It's getting late. I just don't want this day to end."

"We're not even close to finished."

Scooping an arm behind her legs, Jonah pulled her to his chest again, carrying her dripping wet into the shallow end, up the stone stairs just as he'd brought her in earlier. Rivulets of water slid along her skin, caressing, then cooling in the early evening air. Her breasts pulled tight and she couldn't miss the way his gaze lingered appreciatively.

This new ease with each other was as thrilling as his hands on her body, but also a little frightening. She pulled her focus in on the moment, on these stolen days she'd promised herself.

He cleared the last step and walked under the covered porch, elbowing open double doors to a penthouse suite. The hacienda décor reminded her of the Old World Spanish manor home Jonah had rented a year ago. Was this simply the style he was drawn to naturally, or had he somehow been as caught up in their time together as she had been?

Bold tapestries hung on the goldenrod-colored walls. She bypassed surveying all else for later. Right now, her focus stayed on the king-sized bed, definitely a reproduction of the carved walnut headboard from the room they'd shared in Madrid. Linen was draped from the boxed frame overhead, wafting in the wind from the open doors.

He set her on the thick layers of cream, tan and burnt sienna, piped in red. On her back, she inched up the bed, soaking up the amazing view of muscled, naked Jonah against the backdrop of the pool blending into the horizon. He ducked into the bathroom and came back with two fluffy towels. Jonah passed one to her and began toweling his wet hair with the other.

Eloisa knew her own sopping locks would take eons to dry out so she turbaned the soaked mass. He pitched aside his towel and gave his head a quick shaggy shake before settling beside her on the pile of feather pillows.

Tracing lazy circles on his bare chest, she stared out the open double doors, the fresh air swirling the scent of Jonah and a hint of chlorination she would forever find arousing. "I can't believe the awesome sense of privacy here."

"That's something I work to achieve with any of my projects—" his hand settled on her hip, curving to a perfect fit "—seclusion, even if there are multiple units in the resort."

"You learned the value of privacy growing up in the public eye."

"To a degree." He slid an arm behind his head, his eyes focused on the faraway. "My parents did their best to shield us, make sure we didn't feel wealthy or different."

"They sound wonderful. You're lucky to have had parents like that."

"I know." He shifted uncomfortably, then smiled as

if to lighten the mood. "And if I ever forget, my mother will most definitely remind me."

She nudged her toes against his foot. "You must have been an adventurous child, looking for new territories to explore."

"I may have given my folks a heart palpitation or two." He trapped her foot between his.

"Today, I most certainly benefited from your adventurous spirit. Thank you." She stretched upward to kiss him, not long or intense, just holding and enjoying the contact for the sake of simply kissing, even if it wouldn't go further. Yet. She tucked back against his chest. "I never even dreamed of making love on a beach, much less something like this. The fear that someone could stumble upon us, rob us, even worse…"

She shivered and wished she could have attributed it to the wind kicking in faster as night set.

Jonah unfolded a downy throw blanket draped along the end of the bed, pulling it up to their waists. "You have to know I would never put you at risk."

Eloisa snuggled closer. "Not intentionally, no."

"Not ever." He stroked her shoulders. "You're tensing up again. Stop it."

She stifled a laugh at the notion he thought he could fix anything, even the state of her muscles…and then she realized she had relaxed again after all.

"There you go." Jonah trailed his fingers down her spine. "That's more like it."

"It must be the sound of the water echoing in through the canyon, the closeness to nature at its most soothing and stark all at once. How could anyone stay tense?"

"So you like making love outdoors? I'm totally

on board with that. We could do this in any number of countries while I work restoration projects."

Her stomach backflipped. "Like showing me another infinity pool in Hong Kong?"

"Exactly. The possibilities are as limitless as the horizon."

It sounded exciting…and aimless for her. "I couldn't live my life that, just following you around the world." She pressed her fingers to his lips. "Don't even say it."

"Say what?"

"Something smug about—" she lowered her voice to mimic his "—having sex in different countries is a fabulous goal."

A tic started in the corner of his eye. "There you go again with negative assumptions about me. I can't help but wonder if you're using that excuse because you're nervous about what happened out there between us. You know damn well I have a job, a goal."

With an exasperated sigh, he plowed his fingers through his hair. "Every time I start falling for your down-to-earth strength and your passionate nature, you withdraw. Why?"

He was right, and it stung. Still she wondered, "You have a job, but how would I fit in with your plan? I need a purpose of my own."

That silenced him for the first time. She waited through at least a dozen clicks of the ceiling fan overhead and was almost ready to crack, to apologize so they could take a few steps back.

Her cell phone rang from inside her purse. He must have placed it in the room along with their refrigerated meal they'd never gotten around to eating. Not that it mattered in the least to her how it got there. She was just grateful for the distraction.

Eloisa tugged the cover with her as she stumbled from the bed for her bag resting on the trunk at the foot of the bed.

The display screen scrolled "UNKNOWN."

Averting her eyes from Jonah's obvious irritation, she thumbed the Talk button. "Hello?"

"Eloisa? This is your father."

Her stomach pitched at just the word "father" even though she recognized the voice—Harry Taylor, her step-dad. She was just too on edge since Duarte's surprise visit. "What do you need, Harry?"

She said his name in answer to Jonah's questioning look.

"It's about Audrey," Harry barked with unmistakable frustration.

Her stomach flipped faster. What could possibly be so wrong? Why had she let Jonah persuade her into running away? She should have known better than to leave when her sister was in such a fragile state. "Is she okay? Was she in an accident or something?"

Jonah sat up straighter, leaning closer and resting his hand on her back. His steady presence bolstered her as she gripped the phone and waited for her step-dad's reply.

"Audrey eloped with Joey."

Her sister had done what? Eloisa could barely wrap her brain around the very last thing she'd expected to hear.

"Oh...uh..." She struggled for words and could only come up with, "Oh."

"I can't believe she would act so impulsively, so

thoughtlessly after all I've done to make the perfect wedding for her, to give my daughter the social send off she always wanted."

Eloisa bit back the urge to note it was the send off *Harry* wanted. "I'm sorry about all the money you lost on down payments."

"You don't understand the worst of it," Harry rambled, the frustration in his voice rapidly turning to anger. "She says she and Joey are moving away, cutting ties to start fresh away from his family. She's going to throw away all the influence of his family name."

It sounded to her like her sister had wised up. Now that the shock was beginning to fade, she knew that Audrey was better off.

Jonah gave her a questioning look.

She held up a hand and spoke into the phone. "It's for the best Audrey gets her life in order now rather than risk a messy divorce later."

And didn't that hit a little close to home?

Harry's laugh hitched on a half sob. "Eloisa? Where are you? How soon can you get back, because I really need your help right now."

"Uh, I went out for a drive." And a flight. And a swim. Followed by a resounding realization that she and Jonah had very different expectations from life. While she'd more than enjoyed the peaceful aftermath of their lovemaking, she couldn't spend her entire life just floating alongside Jonah. "Don't worry, Harry. I'll be home as soon as I can."

She disconnected the phone.

Infinity had an end after all.

* * *

Jonah tugged on jeans and a button down, slicking his still-wet hair back.

God, things had gone south with Eloisa so fast.

Her family snapped their fingers and she was ready to run to their side. On the one hand, that could be an admirable trait. As a Landis, he would behave the same way in a crisis. When his brother's military plane had gone done in Afghanistan, the family had all pulled together to hold each other up until Kyle was found safely.

When Sebastian and his wife Marianna separated after their adopted daughter was reclaimed by her biological mother, the brothers had sat together through that first hellish night and poured drinks for Sebastian.

He could go on and on with the list.

Then why was he so damn irritated over this? Because no one was there for *her*. Yet they expected her to drop everything for manufactured crises that seemed a daily occurrence in Eloisa's household.

Jonah watched her yank on a fresh sundress and wished he could have enjoyed the moment more. But she was packing. Leaving. Determined to return home immediately to do heaven only knew what. Her sister had left and married some other guy. It was a done deal.

But still, Eloisa was tossing her clothes into her little bag a lot faster than she'd put them in there in the first place. What was really going on here?

Eloisa looked up sharply. "I thought you said we were alone?"

He stopped buttoning his shirt halfway up and looked around, listened. The elevator rumbled softly, then louder, closer. "Decorating staff is downstairs, but there's no reason for them to come up here, and they don't have an elevator key for the penthouse anyway."

A ding sounded just outside the suite.

His muscles tensed protectively. He checked to make sure she was dressed on his way out into the sitting area. "I said no one would bother us. Apparently I was wrong."

And he damn well wasn't happy about the interruption.

He opened the door into the hall just as a carefully coiffed woman stepped out of the private elevator. He would know those sweater sets and pearls paired with perfectly pressed jeans anywhere.

His mother, of all people, had arrived in the middle of nowhere just when he happened to be with Eloisa. His mother's arrival was too convenient. She must know something or at least sense something. He could swear his mom had some kind of special maternal radar.

Could this day go to crap any faster?

Closing the door to the penthouse quietly to seal off Eloisa from the catastrophe in the making, Jonah swore softly as he stepped toward the elevator. "Hi, Ma."

Ginger Landis Renshaw swatted his arm even as she hugged him. "Is that any way to welcome your mother? You may have gotten taller than me by the time you turned thirteen, but you will still watch the language, young man."

His mother was all protocol out in the political world, but with her family she still kept things real—even though she was now an ambassador to a small South American country.

He glanced over his shoulder at the closed door. He

could only keep Eloisa under wraps for so long. His best hope was to head off his mom long enough to go back into the suite and warn Eloisa. Prepare her for the meeting. Most women he dated either froze up around his family, or worse. They kissed up.

He was certain Eloisa wouldn't be the latter, but he worried about the former. And she sure as hell was more than a "date."

At least his brothers weren't here. "Mom, I have someone with me. This really isn't a convenient time."

"I know. Why do you think I'm here? I want to meet this Eloisa for myself rather than keep waiting for you to get around to it."

Nobody got jack by Ginger. The only question that remained? How much did she know? A lot, apparently, if she'd already learned Eloisa's name.

The door to the suite opened. His window to prepare anybody was over.

"Jonah," Eloisa called softly. "I'm packed and ready to leave, but if you're busy with work I can call a cab." She pulled up short at the sight of his famous mother. "Excuse me, ma'am."

"Eloisa, this is my mother," he said, although it seemed no introductions were needed, "Ginger Landis Renshaw."

His mother pushed past him, her eyes both sharp and welcoming. "Call me, Ginger, please. All those names are too much of a mouthful. It's nice to meet you, Eloisa."

"And you, too, ma'am," she said simply, taking his mother's hand lightly.

No shaking in her shoes.

Thus far she seemed to be silently holding her

ground and letting Ginger fill the silence with a running monologue about her trip out. Eloisa had a quiet elegance about her, a way of smoothing over even awkward situations. It was easy to see why she was the rock of her family, why both her fathers needed her by their sides right now.

God, she was mesmerizing.

"Jonah? Jonah!" his mother called.

"Huh?" Brilliant response. He peeled his eyes off Eloisa. "Uh, what did you say, Ma?"

Ginger smiled knowingly before answering. "I was just telling your delightful friend Eloisa how I had a stopover in the area to meet with a congressman friend of mine. Since I was in the States, I gave my other boys a call so we could all meet up here for a family overnight vacation."

What the— "My brothers? Are here?"

"Downstairs checking out your latest work. It's all quite lovely dear."

Apparently the evening *could* get worse.

Eloisa stepped back, as if dodging the brewing family conspiracy. "Jonah, it sounds like you and your mother have a lot to talk about. I'll just call to check in with my father while you meet with your family." She nodded toward Ginger. "It was lovely meeting you, ma'am."

She disappeared back into the suite before he could stop her. Although he appreciated the chance to find out what was up with his mother's surprise visit.

"Mom, what are you really doing here? No way in hell were you and Matthew and Sebastian *and* Kyle just in the neighborhood."

"Language." She swatted his arms again and tugged

him into the elevator. "Let's talk in here where it's more private."

"Did the General come along, too?" He could sense the family closing ranks. Something was up. And as much as he wanted to go comfort Eloisa, he needed to make sure she wasn't walking into some kind of ambush.

God, he'd thought Eloisa was quick to answer the call of her kin. The Landises could round up relatives faster than most people could put dinner on the table.

"Hank couldn't make it back from his meeting in Germany in time. He sends his best." The doors swooshed closed.

"Mom, this is nuts." And part of the reason he needed to travel. Frequently.

"This is being a mother. I can hear it in your voice when something's wrong. It's a mother's instinct, a gift I have for all of my children." She nailed the Stop button. "You asked about the Medinas and so I tapped into some resources. I found out quite a lot as a matter of fact, most of it about you and Eloisa."

Okay, she'd definitely captured his interest. For Eloisa's sake, he needed to find out every bit of information his mother had been able to unearth. "What did you learn?"

His mother pinned him with a stare she'd perfected on all four of her boys. "That you're married. And I decided that since you've been married for a year now, if I wanted to ever meet this new daughter-in-law of mine, I had better take matters into my own hands."

Twelve

Stunned, Jonah stared at his mother and processed her bombshell, along with all the repercussions it could have for Eloisa. How had his mom found out about his marriage…? "Sebastian."

Ginger nodded slowly. "I went to him with some questions when I started looking into the Medinas. He thought I already knew."

Their mother always had been good about pulling information out of them unawares. He couldn't even be mad at his brother.

Jonah pulled his thoughts back to the present. Things were still so unsure with Eloisa he needed to tread warily. "Mom, I understand your impatience, but I need for you to hold back just a little while longer." As much as he loved his family, Eloisa was his primary focus. What else had Ginger found out? "What were you able to uncover about the Medinas? Did you learn anything about the old king?"

She leaned back on the mirrored wall silently and chewed the tip of her glasses dangling on a chain around her neck.

"How much do you know about Eloisa?" he pressed again.

Ginger dropped her glasses back to rest on the chain. "I know who her real father is. A carefully kept secret for over twenty-five years, a secret that seems to be leaking out since your marriage, otherwise I never should have been able to uncover her identity."

He went stone-cold inside. He'd never for a second considered he'd put her at risk by marrying her. But of course he hadn't known her secret then. What a convoluted mess.

One he would fix. "No one will ever harm a hair on her head."

"You're that far gone, are you?" Her face creased with a deep and genuine smile. "Congratulations, Jonah."

Far gone? Hell yeah. "I'm married to her, aren't I?"

"There are problems, obviously, or you wouldn't have spent the year apart." She held up a manicured finger. "I'm not trying to pry. Only commenting on the obvious. Of course, I don't know her, but I would imagine she has reason to be wary."

"Eloisa freaks out about being in the spotlight." He glanced at the closed doors, thinking of her on the other side waiting with her suitcase. "When the time comes, this needs to be handled with a carefully worded press release."

"That's all well and good, but I meant she's wary

of being a part of a family. I obviously don't know her personally, but what I have learned makes me sad for her, and also gives me some thoughts on the subject of why you two haven't been enjoying marital bliss for the past year."

"We were doing okay a few hours ago until all the families started calling and showing up."

"Oh, really? Didn't look that way to me."

His gut churned over the fact Eloisa might have already phoned for a cab or made God only knew what arrangements while he was talking to his mom. He couldn't let her up and leave when he was distracted again, and how could he ever hope for a relationship with a woman he couldn't count on to stand still for more than a few hours at a time?

"Son, you've been blessed with family traditions so it seems simple to you. Not so much to others. Like Eloisa perhaps."

"I know that, Mom, and I don't take it for granted."

"I don't know that I agree with you there. Not that I'm condemning you and your brothers for it. Children should enjoy those traditions and be able to count on them over the years. That gives them roots to ground them when storms hit. Like when your father died. You carried a part of him with you in our traditions."

"What are you trying to say?" He was damn near turning backflips to figure Eloisa out and now his mom was going on about Thanksgiving turkeys and Christmas trees? "Mom, you're talking chick talk, and I'm a guy."

"If you want to keep her, you need to help her feel secure." Ginger released the Stop button and leaned to kiss her son on the cheek. "Now go take care of your wife. I look forward to talking with Eloisa more downstairs whenever the two of you are ready. Your brothers and I will be waiting."

A half hour later, Eloisa waited in the resort lounge with her luggage and Jonah's immense family. She was nervous, even lightly nauseated at this unexpected turn.

She and Jonah had barely had time to talk when he returned from the elevator. He'd simply apologized for his family's surprise intrusion and promised to get her to Audrey before her sister returned from Vegas. He would take care of everything, he'd assured her, giving her a quick but intense kiss before escorting her downstairs.

Fresh paint—mustard yellow—tinted the air and soured her stomach even more. Being with Jonah offered a world of excitement, but very few moments of peace, in spite of the panoramic setting.

Archways framed the two massive walls of windows showcasing the canyon. Stars twinkled in the night sky, the moon climbing. He'd promised they would still leave for Pensacola this evening. He vowed he understood her need to check on Audrey, even if his eyes seemed to say he thought she was overreacting.

Meanwhile, she was stuck in the middle of a very bizarre family reunion. She forced herself not to fidget in the mammoth tapestry wingback. He promised only his mother and lawyer brother knew the truth about their marriage and her family. Apparently the other brothers just thought she was a girlfriend. Having people learn the truth about her background scared Eloisa to the roots of her hair—but at least she didn't have to deal with everyone knowing.

Yet.

She stared at all four Landis men sprawled on red leather sofas, the only pieces of furniture, other than her chair, not wrapped in warehouse plastic. All four men shared the same blue eyes as their mother. Their hair was varying shades of brown. Jonah's was longer.

But there was no mistaking the strong family jaw. These were powerful men, most likely stubborn men. She suspected they got it from their mom.

Ginger Landis Renshaw paced on the lanai, taking a work call, her shoulder-length grey-blond hair perfectly styled. Eloisa recalled from news reports the woman was in her early fifties, but she carried the years well. Wearing a lilac lightweight sweater set with pearls—and blue jeans—Ginger Landis wasn't at all what Eloisa had expected. Thank goodness, because the woman she'd met appeared a little less intimidating.

She'd seen Ginger on the news often enough, reminding Eloisa that she'd followed press coverage of the Landis family all year with more than casual interest. From her attention to the news blogs and video snippets on television, Eloisa knew Ginger was poised and intelligent, sometimes steely determined. Today, a softer side showed as she glanced through the window at her son then over to Eloisa before she returned her attention to her business call.

The whole group was beyond handsome, their unity, happiness and deep sense of connectedness tangible even through the airwaves. And yes, she'd been searching for even a glimpse of Jonah in those photos and broadcasts all year long, too.

How had his mother managed to build such a cohesive family? She searched Ginger's every move through the glass as if somehow she could figure out the answer like a subject researched deeply enough in her library. Then one of his brothers stepped in front of the window, blocking her view. She searched her memory for which brother...

The oldest, Matthew Landis, was a South Carolina senator and the consummate charming politician. "Our baby brother, Jonah, here has always been good at playing things low-key, keeping a lookout in such a way nobody even knew you were watching, but even we didn't see this one coming." Matthew turned to Jonah. "Where have you been hiding this lovely woman?"

Jonah reached from the sofa to rest a hand on her arm. "We met in Spain last summer."

He kept it simple, uncomplicated. How surreal to sit here so casually in this serene retreat while her world exploded around her.

Audrey's life in upheaval.

Secrets with Jonah so close to exposure.

Nowhere to hide from the fact that she was falling hard for Jonah Landis.

She folded her shaking hands in her lap and kept up the pretense of calm conversation. If nothing else, she had a brief window with his brothers before they saw her differently. She could use this chance to learn more about Jonah—from someone else this time. "He kept the lookout how?"

Jonah interjected. "Let's not go there right now."

Kyle grinned. "Let's do. The odds are three to one in our favor, bro."

The world of brothers was fairly alien to her, other than a few brief days nearly twenty years ago.

Sebastian—the lawyer—stretched his arms along the

back of the sofa. "He kept Mom from discovering our tunnels."

"Tunnels?"

Kyle—the brother who'd served in the military—leaned forward, elbows on his knees. "When Sebastian, Jonah and I were kids, during summer vacation, we would pack up sandwiches and Kool-Aid and head out for the day."

"You played at the beach alone?" She glanced out at Ginger and couldn't imagine her tolerating that.

"Nope," Kyle continued, "we went into the more-wooded areas nearby. Sebastian and I dug underground tunnels. Jonah stood guard and warned us if any adults came near."

Sebastian's solemn expression lightened. "We would dig the trench, lay boards over the trough and cover the planks with dirt."

"What about your oldest brother?" She nodded toward Matthew.

Kyle elbowed the esteemed senator. "Too much of a rule follower. He wasn't invited. Although I guess our secret is out now."

"Secret?" Matthew extended his legs in front of him. "Did it ever occur to you to wonder why those tunnels never collapsed on top of you?"

Scowling, Kyle straightened indignantly. "We built damn good tunnels."

"Okay." Matthew spread his hands. "If that's what you want to believe."

"It's what happened." Kyle frowned. "Isn't it?"

The more contemplative Sebastian even shifted uncomfortably until Matthew shook his head, laughing.

"After you two went inside, Jonah would go back out and fix your tunnels. He had me stand guard."

The stunned looks on Sebastian and Kyle's faces were priceless.

Matthew continued, "He was an architect in the making, even then."

Brow furrowing suspiciously, Kyle scrubbed his jaw. "You're yanking our chain."

Sebastian said, "You two collaborated against us?"

"We collaborated *for* you. And if you hadn't excluded us from hanging out in your tunnels we probably would have showed you how to dig them right in the first place rather than laughing at you behind your back."

Kyle slugged his brother on the arm, which started a free-for-all of laughter and light payback punches between the siblings. Did her Medina brothers share moments and memories like this? Did she have the courage to find out? They had no real connection to her other than blood.

But her sister, Audrey? They may not have had the perfect family circle like the Landises, but she loved her sister and her sister loved her. She had to be there for her.

As Jonah had been there for his brothers all those years ago, protecting their secret while making sure they stayed safe. Even as a little kid, the youngest of the crew, he'd been a guardian, a protector, all things that made her fall even harder for him now.

Her throat clogged with emotion and tears, and God, she didn't know how much more enlightenment she could take in one day. Her emotions were already so raw.

And scary.

She turned to Jonah, caught his attention and lightly touched her watch. *We need to leave,* she said with her eyes.

For more reasons than just Audrey. She needed distance to think, because sitting here with the Landises, she wanted to be a part of Jonah's world so much it hurt. This wasn't a family who ran from responsibilities or commitments. *Jonah* was a man to depend on.

And right now, she wasn't so sure she was the kind of woman he deserved.

The next morning, Eloisa propped her elbows on her kitchen island, a mug of tea in her hands as she sat on a barstool next to her sister. Her *married* sister.

A thin silver band glinted on Audrey's finger.

Eloisa and Jonah had taken a red-eye flight back, arriving just at sunrise. She'd hoped they could talk on the plane but he'd received a call from the Peru developers who were working round the clock on plans for the project he would tackle after leaving here.

Leaving her.

After they'd landed, she'd been stunned to find her sister waiting at the town house. With Joey who now stood out on the patio with Jonah.

Eloisa covered her sister's hand. "I'm sorry I wasn't here for you when you needed me."

"I'm an adult, in spite of what our father thinks. I made this decision on my own." Her mouth pinched tight. "Joey wanted to elope and leave this town from the start. I never should have let Dad talk me into a big wedding."

"Don't be too hard on yourself. We want the people we love to be happy."

Audrey looked out the patio doors. "I really shouldn't be so tough on Dad. I was as guilty as him, being charmed by all the money. Dad was always so freaked out about having enough for Mom. I remember this one time he bought her a diamond-and-sapphire necklace. She loved it, but the whole time Dad kept apologizing that it wasn't bigger. He said he wanted her to feel like a queen."

A queen? Had her father known more than she realized? If so, this was rapidly turning into the worst-kept secret on the planet. "Mom loved him."

"I know. I want that for my own marriage." She clasped both her sister's hands, her whisper-pale hair falling to mix with Eloisa's jet black. "It just took me a while to realize it's not about the trappings. I know you probably think I'm crazy for running off."

She thought of her own elopement a year ago. It had seemed so right at the time, she could relate to how her sister felt. Guilt pinched at a corner of her heart. Maybe if she hadn't kept it secret all year long, Audrey might have been encouraged to make her decision earlier. "I may understand better than you think."

She looked out to the patio where Jonah and Joey chatted like old buds. How easily Jonah talked to people, how quick he was to put Joey at ease. Jonah might not embrace the public eye as much as his famous family, but he'd certainly inherited a winning way with people. He'd certainly won *her* over a year ago—and last night. He'd slid under her boundaries in a way no man ever had.

Audrey gazed out at Joey with a seriously love-sick look in her eyes. "I only wish I'd followed my instincts earlier. It would have saved you so much work and time."

Her sister appeared amazingly calm. It seemed all the drama had come from Harry.

Eloisa sipped her tea while her sister shared details about her hurried wedding in a Vegas chapel. "And Joey says we really can't build a life for ourselves here. His family would be involved in anything we try." She took a bracing breath. "So we're relocating. We don't know where yet. He says that's part of the adventure, figuring out where. Maybe we'll toss a dart at a map."

Audrey was embracing the same kind of future Eloisa could have with Jonah. Was that why her sister's words sent a bolt of envy through her? Not that she wasn't happy for Audrey, because this would be a wise move for her. But it would be difficult to see Audrey living the dreams Eloisa had walked away from.

Her eyes tracked back to Jonah again, his broad shoulders, his comfort in watching out for other people, whether it was his older brothers or her. She wanted this happiness for herself, too. She wanted to trust they could work out a way for her to fit her life with his.

She wanted to find the same surety she saw shining from Audrey. There was a vibrancy and strength of purpose in her sister that hadn't been there before. Audrey had gone from pale and ethereal to glittering like a diamond.

"You're really excited about the new adventure."

Ashley clutched Eloisa's hands. "Is that too selfish of me? You've always been here for me and now I'm leaving you."

A deeper truth, an understanding resonated inside her. "You're living your own life. You deserve that. We won't stop being sisters just because you're married, even if you live clear across country. I'll come see you. Pick somewhere interesting, okay?"

Audrey nodded, tears in her eyes as she opened her arms. Eloisa gathered her sister close, hope for her own future glinting ever so warily inside her.

Jonah pushed open the French doors to the patio, his shoulders, his unmistakable charisma filling the void, filling her. She looked into those clear blue eyes of his and knew in her heart. He wasn't out for revenge. He was here for her.

He'd stood by her today during a family crisis. Had intervened for her during her sister's awkward engagement party, had hidden their secret from most of his family. He was a great guy and she trusted him enough to take the next step. She didn't want him to leave for Peru. She wanted longer to test out what they had before it was too late. She deserved a future of her own with Jonah, and the time had come to claim it, obstacles and all.

Starting with telling him about their baby.

Thirteen

Eloisa closed the town house door after Audrey and Joey. Their laughter and playfulness out in the parking lot drifted through, teasing and tempting her with what a relationship could be.

Jonah walked up behind her, swept aside her hair and pressed his mouth to the sensitive curve of her neck. Her head fell back to give him better access. After the day they'd had, there was nothing she wanted more than to lose herself in the forgetfulness reliably found in his arms. Then she could curl up beside him and sleep like a regular married couple.

Except that would be hiding. That would be using sex to shield herself from making the tough step of opening herself totally to Jonah. Letting herself love him.

And even scarier, letting him love her.

She was actually pretty good at loving other people.

Not so good at letting them be there for her. And wasn't that a mind-blowing revelation she would have liked the time to mull over? Except she was out of time.

Deciding to do something and actually following through were two different matters. But she was determined to see this through before they landed in bed.

Eloisa stroked along the open collar of his simple button-down, wishing her nerves were as easily smoothed. "Thank you for being so understanding about coming back here for Audrey. I hated cutting short your visit with your family."

"They're the ones who showed up unannounced." He looped his hands low around her waist. "We can have more time with them soon if you want."

"I do."

His face kicked up in a one-sided smile. "Good, good."

Jonah tucked her against his side and strode deeper into the living area, out to the patio. He drew her down with him in the Adirondack chair, settling her in his lap with such an ease and rightness it took her breath away. How could such a big-boned, hard-bodied man make for such a comfortable resting spot?

Eloisa nestled her head on his shoulder and gazed outward. That would be easier than looking him in the face. The sky turned hazy shades of purple and grey as the sun surrendered and night muscled upward.

Jonah thumbed along the back of her neck, massaging tiny kinks. "I'm sorry for not taking into account your job, and your need for security. I can understand why following me from job to job may not sound like the best of lives for you. We'll work together to figure out a solution."

God, he made it sound possible to find a compromise. She wanted to trust it could be that simple.

"Is that what we're talking about?" She swallowed hard against the hope. "A life together?"

"I think we're most definitely moving in that direction." His chin rested on top of her head. "It would be a mistake to pretend otherwise."

"Okay then—" she inhaled a shaky breath, not nearly bolstering enough "—if we're being totally honest here, there's something I need to tell you, something that will be difficult to say and difficult to hear."

His arms stiffened around her, but he kept his chin resting in her hair. "Are you walking out again?"

"No, not unless you tell me to." Which could very well happen. A trickle of fear iced up her spine. What if she'd put this off until too late? Would he understand her reasons for waiting?

"That'll never happen."

"You sound so sure." She wanted to be as certain. But hadn't being with Jonah helped her see she couldn't plan for everything? "You're always full of absolutes, total confidence."

"I have a vision for our future and it's perfect." He tipped her face up to his. "You're perfect. We're going to be perfect together."

"You can't really believe I'm perfect. And if you think that even on some level, what are you going to do when my many flaws show?" Of course she was afraid of rejection after a lifetime of being shuffled aside through no fault of her own. A child didn't deserve that. Except now, she was an adult and had no one to blame but herself. "What if I don't fit into the beautiful world of no boundaries that you've engineered for yourself?"

"We'll work at it. Think about your graduate studies in Spain. You enjoyed your research contribution. Maybe that's a path to blending our worlds again. Or we split time, both making compromises."

He was offering her so much that she wasn't prepared to think about yet. Not until she'd taken care of this old hurt. "That's not what I'm talking about. It's something different, something bigger, a mistake I made."

He stroked her forehead. "You're such a serious person, and while I admire the way you care about the feelings of everyone around you, I'm a big boy. Now just cut to the chase and say it."

"I haven't been completely honest with you—" her heart pounded so hard her ribs hurt "—about more than just my father."

"Do you have a boyfriend on the side?"

"Good Lord, Jonah—" her hands fisted in his shirt "—I've spent the whole year aching for you. There's no room for anyone else."

"Then no worries." He winked.

Winked, damn it.

"Jonah, please don't joke. Not now. This is difficult enough as it is." She pushed the words up and out as fast as she could. "After we split up, after I left you, I found out I was pregnant with your child."

His hold on her loosened, his face swiped free of any expression. "You had a baby," he said slowly, his voice flat, neutral. "Our baby."

She nodded, her heart hammering all the harder through pools of tears bottled inside. The grief, the loneliness and regret splashed through her again with each thud of her pulse. She should have called him then. But she hadn't and now it was time to face the consequences for that decision. "I had a miscarriage."

"When?"

"Does it even matter?" She hated the way her voice hitched.

"I deserve to know when…how long."

She flinched with guilt. He was right. He deserved that and so much more. "I miscarried at four and a half months. Nobody knew except my doctor and my priest."

She wanted him to know that while she hadn't told him, she'd nurtured and honored that life even if he hadn't been there to witness it. Even if he was going to walk out, he deserved to know that.

The first shadows of emotion chased across his face incredulity. "You didn't even tell your sister?"

"Audrey had just gotten engaged to Joey," she rushed to explain, and it sounded so lame now but had made such sense then. "I didn't want to spoil her special time."

"No," he said simply, his body shifting, tensing, no longer the welcoming place to land. Something had unmistakably changed between them. "I'm not buying the excuses."

She agreed, but still she'd hoped for some… understanding? Sympathy? Comfort after the fact? "What? I tell you my most heartbreaking secret and you just say 'no.' What's the matter with you?"

She couldn't bear to sit in his arms that had become so stone-cold. She rolled to her feet and backed away.

He stood slowly, his hands in his pockets. No warm reception for her revelation. "I think you didn't tell your sister because then you'd have to let someone get close to you, be a part of your life. Don't you think she would be hurt to know you didn't feel like you could turn to her?"

She hadn't thought of it that way before and she didn't know what to make of the notion now. Her confessions had churned up the loss for her, the retelling of it bringing to mind those dark hours when the blood loss started, then being in the hospital alone. The grief when the doctor told her the baby's heartbeat had stopped. The teeth-chattering cold after her D and C.

Would having her sister there have made the pain go away? Right now, with the memories fresh in her mind, she couldn't think of anything that would ease the loss for her.

And oh God, why hadn't she given more thought to how this would hurt Jonah? She forced herself to look in his eyes and confront the pain—and yes, the anger—she found there. "I should have told you then."

"Damn straight, you should have," he snapped, the anger seeping into his voice as well. "But you didn't. Because that would involve me being a part of your life and your family when it's easier to hide in your library with your books."

She gasped at the stab of his words. "You're being cruel."

"I'm being realistic for the first time, Eloisa." He paced the small stone patio restlessly, the frustration in his tone building with every step. "You talk about wanting a future together but you've been keeping this from me the whole time, even when we made love."

"I'm telling you the truth now. Just five minutes ago you said nothing could break us apart."

"Would you have told me if you weren't afraid I would find out anyway, now that all your secrets are coming out?" He pivoted back sharply to face her, the moonlight casting harsh shadows down his angry face. "When have you ever willingly let me into your life?"

She couldn't think of an answer. He'd led their relationship every step of the way.

He started toward her again. "All this time I've been wondering if you can trust me, and now I don't know if I can trust you. I don't know if I can be with you, always wondering when you're going to run again." He stopped pacing abruptly and plowed his hand through his hair. "This is too much. I can't wrap my brain around it. I need air."

He jammed his hands into his pockets again as if he couldn't even bear to touch her and left. The front door closed quietly but firmly behind him.

The first tear slipped free and pulled the plug out of the dam for the rest to come flooding down. Barely able to see, she walked back into her town house.

For the past year, she'd been immersed in her own pain and fears, never once thinking about how much she must have hurt Jonah when she'd left him. Now, standing alone with the echo of that lone door click in her ears, in her soul, she realized just how fully she'd screwed up in leaving him.

She was totally alone for the first time in her life. Harry was upset she hadn't persuaded Audrey to stay. Audrey was off enjoying marital bliss. And Jonah had left her. She had nowhere to turn.

Eloisa stood in the middle of her empty town house that had once felt like a haven and now seemed so very barren. She searched for something, any piece of comfort. Her fingers trailed over the glass paperweight, the one she'd made from shells and a dried flower, memorializing her baby's too-brief life. What would it have been like to share that grief with Jonah?

And now because of how she'd handled things, he was suffering the loss alone as well.

She gripped the cool paperweight in her hand—and revealed a plain white card with ten typed numbers, Duarte's number.

Perhaps there was at least one thing she could fix in her messed-up life after all. Perhaps she might as well make someone happy.

Jonah was going to get seriously trashed if his brothers didn't stop pouring drinks for him. But then that's why he'd come home to Hilton Head to be with his family.

Sitting on the balcony at the Landis beachside compound, he nudged away the latest shot glass on the iron outdoor table. He was still reeling from Eloisa's revelation about getting pregnant and losing their baby. Never once bothering to contact him about something so monumental.

Anger still chewed at his gut, along with grief for the child that could have been. And having a child with Eloisa? Even the possibility had his hands shaking so hard he couldn't have picked up the shot glass even if he'd wanted.

As much as he regretted not knowing about the life that had begun inside her a year ago, the knowledge of what happened made him realize the importance of getting things right with Eloisa this time. If birth control had failed a year ago, then it could fail again. He would not risk being on the other side of an ocean if Eloisa carried his child.

After their fight, he'd driven along the beach for about an hour until he'd calmed down enough to talk to her again. He hadn't known what he would say or how they could work through it. His ability to trust her had taken a serious blow. But he was willing to try.

Except once he returned to her town house, he found she'd already left. Her car was gone. Her suitcase was gone. Eloisa had run away again. Jonah had hopped the first plane to the only place he could think of to go. Home to hang out with his brothers.

Sebastian clanked down his crystal glass, the ocean wind kicking in off the waves. The surf crashed. Sailboat lines pinged against the double mast of the family yacht. "You have to figure out what speaks to her."

Frowning, Kyle leaned toward his brother with an almost imperceptible sway. "Marianna made you go to some kind of woo-woo, Zen-like couples retreat, didn't she?"

Sebastian reached for the bottle of vintage bourbon in the middle of the table. "What makes you say that?"

"'Figure out what speaks to her,'" Kyle mimicked in a spacey-sounding voice before laughing. "Really, dude, who are you and what have you done with my brother?"

Matthew clapped Kyle on the shoulder, the salty breeze filling their shirts, hinting at an incoming storm. "Don't knock it 'til you've tried it. There's something to be said for learning to speak their language on occasion. The benefits are amazing."

Sebastian smiled knowingly.

Jonah turned the glass around and around on the

table, a tic starting in the corner of his eye. He wondered for the first time how all his Neanderthal brothers had managed to find great women. What did they know that he didn't? What was he missing?

Hunger for making things work with Eloisa compelled him to flat-out ask. He sure as hell wasn't making headway alone. "You're going to have to 'speak' to me in regular-guy English if you expect me to understand."

Sebastian's face took on the lawyer look he assumed right before rolling out his best case. Of course the look was a little deflated by his cockeyed tie. "Okay, standard red roses and a heart-shaped box of chocolates are all well and good, and certainly better than not doing anything. But if you can think of something personal, something that says you know her...you'll be golden."

Kyle scratched the back of his head, his hair still worn short even after he'd finished his military commitment. "They really like to know we're thinking about them when they're not around."

Jonah eyed his brothers in disbelief. God, they were making his head hurt worse rather than helping. "Do you all get a group discount for the couples retreat?"

"Bro, make fun all you want," Matthew said. "You can have our advice or flounder around on your own."

"It's actually not that complicated," Sebastian explained. "Marianna adores our dogs." They both were nuts over their two mutts, Buddy and Holly. "One Valentine's Day, I bought Coach collars and leashes for the dogs, along with a donation to the local Humane Society."

Kyle jabbed a finger in his direction. "Remember when I got the laptop computer for Phoebe? Her squeal of excitement just about rattled every window."

Hearing how his brothers hit just the perfect note to make their wives happy offered up a special torture for him now that Eloisa had damn near ripped his heart out. "You had me tuck the wrapped computer where she would see it while you took her on a date."

Kyle smiled, his eyes taking on a distant air. "A late-night drive in a vintage Aston Martin convertible."

"Wow!" Matthew whistled low. "Nice move."

"Thanks." Kyle refilled his glass. "I'll give you the name of the guy who hooked me up. Now back to the computer." He turned toward Jonah, porch lights the only illumination, with the clouds covering the stars. "Phoebe was stretched too thin teaching her online classes and caring for the baby. I offered to take time off from work to watch Nina, even offered more nanny time, but she wasn't budging. The laptop gave her a way of working from anywhere."

His brother had done a damn fine job at blending two diverse lifestyles. Kyle and Phoebe might well have some good advice for Eloisa...if he hadn't walked out on her. If she hadn't followed up by walking out on him again as well.

It downright sucked being around these guys who practically oozed satisfaction and marital bliss.

Matthew snagged the bottle from his brother. "Extravagant is cool, too, you've just got to mix it up some with the practical."

Clinking the ice, Kyle lifted his glass for a refill. "What's Ashley's extravagance?"

Matthew's mouth twitched with a hint of a smile. "Don't think I can share that with you, my brother."

"Hey." Kyle raised his hands. "Fair enough."

The sound of a throat clearing reverberated behind them. They all four twisted in their seats.

Their mother's second husband—General Hank Renshaw—stood in the open French doors. His distinguished military bearing was still visible even after his retirement. His hair might be solid gray now, but he had a sharp brain that made him a major player in the national defense arena. "Hope you boys have saved at least one drink of my best alcohol for me."

"Yes, sir." Kyle snagged another glass from the tray they'd brought out with them and passed their stepfather—a lifetime family friend as well—a drink. "Maybe you can help Jonah here figure out how to get his wife back."

"Hmmm…" The General tipped back his glass with only a slight wince and dragged a chair over to the table. "Well, your mother likes it when I—"

"Whoa! Whoa! Hold on there a minute, General." The protests of all four brothers tumbled over each other.

Jonah agreed one hundred percent on that staying a secret. "That's our mom you're talking about. While I appreciate the offer to help, there are just some things a son doesn't need to know."

Matthew drained his glass. "The time we walked in on the two of you damn near gave me a heart attack."

"Okay, okay." The General chuckled lowly. "I get the picture." His laughter faded and he jabbed a thumb toward the door. "Now how about you three take the bottle and clear out so I can talk to Jonah?"

Chairs scraped back and his brothers abandoned ship. The slugging and laughs faded in the hall and up the stairs.

The General refilled both glasses. "Your dad was my best friend." He lifted his in toast. "He would be proud of you."

"Thank you. That means a lot to me." But not enough to clear away the frustration over failing when it counted most.

With Eloisa.

Why had she kept the news from him then? And now? He needed to understand that if they stood a chance at stopping this cycle of turning each other inside out, then running for opposite corners.

He didn't expect the General was going to be able to offer some magic bullet to fix everything any more than his brothers had. But still he appreciated the support. The General had been there for them after their dad died. He'd always vowed he was just helping out their mom the way she'd helped him after his wife died. But they'd all wondered how long it would take....

"It takes as long as it takes. But you don't quit."

How had the General known what he was thinking? "Have you added a mind reader medal to your already impressive collection?"

"Quit beating yourself up about the past and move forward," the General said with clipped, military efficiency. "Don't just curl up and admit defeat. You've got an opportunity now. Run with it."

"She's gone." Jonah reached into his pocket and pulled out the white card he'd found by her telephone, the same card he remembered Duarte Medina giving her. He flipped the number between his fingers. "She doesn't want to speak to me or see me again."

"And you're going to just quit? Give up on your marriage? Give up on her?"

His fingers slowed, the numbers on the vellum square coming into focus. His whole life coming into focus as well, because this time he wasn't letting Eloisa just walk away. There was a way to break this cycle after all. Show her how a real family came through for each other, everyone offering support rather than the one-sided deal she'd lived, always being the one giving. No wonder she hadn't reached out to him when she was hurting.

No one had ever given her reason to think her call for help would be answered.

This time he intended to show her that somebody loved her—*he* loved her—enough to follow and stay. "You have a point, General." He tapped the simple white card. "Lucky for me, I think I know exactly how to find her."

Fourteen

Eloisa sat on her father's garden patio overlooking the Atlantic, waiting. In minutes she would see Enrique Medina again. How surreal and confusing, and so not the joyful reunion she'd dreamed of as a child.

She turned to Duarte standing beside her somberly. "Thank you for arranging this meeting so quickly."

"Don't thank me," he answered with no warmth. "If it were up to me, we would all go about our lives separately. But this is how he wants it and, bottom line, it's his call to make."

His brusqueness made her edgier, as if she wasn't already about to jump out of her skin. She searched for something benign to diffuse the tension. "The rocky shoreline looks exactly like the one I remember from that single visit—magnificent. I often wondered if my memory was faulty."

"Apparently not."

And apparently Duarte would need more prodding to speak. "How strange to think our father has been so close all this time? In the same state even?"

Her biological father had taken up residence on a small private island off the coast of St. Augustine, Florida. One call to Duarte had set everything in motion. Her heart bruised beyond bearing, she'd been on a private jet, flying away from Jonah and the catastrophic mess she'd made of their second chance. Her throat clogged with more tears. She swallowed them and narrowed her attention to satisfying her curiosity about this place she'd thought of so often.

The towering white stucco house, rustling palm trees, massive archways and crashing waves... She could have been seven again, with her mother beside her, waiting for *him* to greet them.

Duarte touched her arm lightly, bringing her back to the moment. "Eloisa? He's here."

The lanai doors creaked opened. But no imposing king stepped out this time. An electric wheelchair hummed the only warning before Enrique came outside. Two large, lopey dogs followed in perfect sync. Confined to the chair, he was thin, gray and weary.

Duarte hadn't lied. Their father appeared near death. She stood but didn't reach out. A hug would have seemed strange, affected. The emotion forced. She didn't know what she felt for him. He'd needed her and beckoned. It was difficult not to resent all the times she'd needed him. Yes, he'd made contact through his lawyer over the years, but so infrequently and impersonally it seemed she was merely an afterthought. Her mind jetted back to that strange, but endearing, Landis family gathering at

Jonah's elegant Texas resort. This family reunion bore no resemblance to that one.

"Hello, sir. You'll have to pardon me if I'm not quite sure what to call you."

He waved dismissively, perspiration dotting his forehead. "Call me Enrique." His body might be weak, but his voice still commanded attention. The Spanish accent was almost as thick as she remembered. "I do not want formality or deserve any titles, king or father. Now sit down, please. I feel like a rude old man for not standing with a lovely lady present."

She took her seat again and he whirred the chair into position in front of her. The two brown dogs—Ridgebacks, perhaps?—settled on either side. He studied her silently, his hands folded in his lap, veins bruised from what appeared to be frequent IV needles.

Still, no matter the sallow pallor and thinner frame, Enrique Medina's face was that of royalty. His aristocratic nose and chiseled jaw spoke of his age-old warrior heritage. There was strength in that face, despite everything. And while his heavy blue robe with emerald-green silk lapels was not the garb of a king in his prime, the rich fabrics and sleek leather slippers reflected his wealth.

The old king gestured toward the doors. "Duarte, you can leave us now. I have some things to say to Eloisa alone."

Duarte nodded, turning away without a word, walking off with steps quieter than those of anyone she'd known. But he wasn't her reason for being here today. She'd come to see her father, to hopefully find some peace and resolution inside herself.

"I'm sorry you're ill."

"So am I."

He didn't speak further, and she wondered if perhaps he'd started to lose his mental faculties. She glanced up at the male nurse waiting patiently at the doorway. No answers there.

She looked back at Enrique. "You asked to see me? You sent Duarte."

"Of course I did. I'm not losing my mind yet anyway." He straightened his lapels. "Please forgive me for being rude. I was merely struck by how much you resemble my mother. She was quite lovely, too."

"Thank you." It would have been nice to have met her grandmother or even see pictures like other kids growing up. Maybe it wasn't too late. "Do you have photos of her?"

"They were all lost when my home was burned to the ground."

She blinked fast. Not the answer she'd expected. She'd read what little was reported on the coup in San Rinaldo twenty-seven years ago. She knew her father had barely escaped with his life—his wife had not. He and his sons had gone into hiding. And while she understood the danger, she'd never truly thought of all he'd lost.

Certainly losing a picture wasn't the same as losing a person, but to have lost even those bits of comfort and reminders… "Then we'll have to make sure you have a picture of me to remember her by."

"Thank you, but I imagine I will be seeing her soon enough." He spoke of his death so matter-of-factly it stunned her. "Which brings me to why I called for you, *pequeña princesa*."

Little princess? Small princess? Either way, she'd never dared think of herself with that title. More than anything, her heart stumbled on the endearment that Harry had always applied to his biological daughter and never to her. Not that she would let mere words sway her after all this time.

Enrique steadied his breathing. "There are some things you need to know and time is short. Whether I die or someone finally finds me, our secret will come out someday. Even I can only hold back that tide for just so long."

The thought of that kind of exposure sent her reaching for the lemonade beside her. What if the king's enemies sought him out again? Sought her out? "Where will you hide then?"

If he was still alive.

"I am a king." His chin tipped. "I do not hide. I stay here for the people I love."

"I'm not sure I follow what you mean."

"By staying here, it keeps up the illusion that I—and my children—are in Argentina. No one bothers to look for them. No one can hurt them the way they went after my Beatriz."

Beatriz, his wife who'd been gunned down during the escape. "That must have been awful for you."

And her brothers.

His chin tipped higher as he looked away for a moment unblinking. Seeing the Herculean strength of will in a man so weak...

He focused his intense dark eyes on her again. "It was difficult meeting your mother so soon after my Beatriz was murdered. I did love your mother, as much as I could at that time. She told me if she could not have my full heart, she wanted nothing."

She'd always thought her mother stayed away because

of safety reasons. She'd never considered her mom acted out of emotion. Harry Taylor may not be anyone's idea of Prince Charming, but he had adored her mother. Eloisa sat back in her chair and let Enrique talk. He seemed to need to unload burdens. For the first time, she realized how much she needed to listen.

"I am sorry I did not get to watch you grow up. Nothing I can do now will make up for the fact I was not the father you deserved."

The humble honesty of that simple statement meant more to her than any amount of money. She'd been waiting a lifetime to hear him admit he should have been a father to her.

And while that didn't erase the past, it was a first step toward a healing. She brushed her fingers over his bruised hand, words escaping her.

"I did decide to ask your mother to marry me."

"What happened?"

"I finally looked past my grief to see a new chance at love waiting."

"She didn't want to live here?"

"Oh no, she wouldn't have minded staying here. She told me so. I just waited too long to ask."

Oh my God. "She'd already married Harry."

"I fought for her six months too late," he said simply. "Don't wait too long to fight, *pequeña princesa*."

But her chance was gone now.

This time, Jonah had left her. She wanted to shout her hurt and pain over the way he'd left, even knowing she'd brought it on herself. He was the one who'd walked out, not her. Enrique didn't understand. How could he? He didn't know her. He couldn't, not from detective reports or however he'd kept watch over her life.

She started to tell him just that but something in his eyes stopped her, a deep wisdom that came from experiences she couldn't begin to comprehend. This man knew what it meant to fight.

And his blood ran through her veins.

Eloisa gripped the arms of her chair with a newfound strength. She was through hiding in her library and in her fears. She loved Jonah Landis and wanted a life with him, wherever that life took them. He was hurting and angry now, and she couldn't blame him. She hadn't put her heart on the line for him. Taking cautious to a new level. But she would remedy that now. She was in this for the long haul.

She would fight for him so damn hard he wouldn't know what hit him.

Pushing to her feet, she cupped Enrique's face in her hands. "You certainly are a devious old man, but I do believe I like you."

His laugh rumbled as he gave her a smile and a regal nod.

Eloisa backed away slowly until her hands fell to her sides. "I have to go, but I will come back. I just need to clear up some things with Jonah first."

Her father raised his hand and twirled a finger. "Turn around."

What? Frowning, she glanced over her shoulder. And her heart lodged squarely in her throat.

Jonah stood waiting in the archway, his hair slicked back and flowers in his hand.

Jonah barely had time to nod to Eloisa's father before the old king vacated the porch, leaving him alone with her. He owed Duarte and Enrique for making this reunion happen.

And he intended to repay them by keeping Eloisa safe and happy for the rest of her life.

He closed the last few steps between them, flowers extended. "I don't know what specific kind of gift you would want that 'speaks' to your soul, so I had to settle for flowers. But they're pink tulips, like the picture on your wall. I figured you must have chosen it because you like them."

"They're perfect! Thank you." Taking the flowers in one hand, she pressed her fingers to his lips with her other. The ocean wind molded her sundress to her body just the way it had when he'd seen her again outside her sister's engagement party. They'd covered a lot of ground in a few short days.

"Jonah, I so was wrong when I said we don't know each other." She brought the tulips up just under her nose and inhaled. "The flowers are lovely but you've already given me exactly what speaks to my soul. You give me infinity pools and walk with me through dusty castles full of history. You coax me out of my dark office and you even compliment my apple-flavored lip gloss. You know everything about me except—" she arched up on her toes, the flowers crushed lightly between them "—how very deeply I love you."

He swept her hair back and cradled her head, the subtle scent of tulips mixing with the tangy salt air and the essence of *her*. "I know now—" thank God "—and look forward to telling you and showing you just how much I love you in every country around the world. If you're up for the adventure?"

"I like the sound of those ideas you discussed earlier

for blending our lives together. I think I'm more than ready to bring my library research world out into the field again. As long as you're there with me."

She angled her head to meet his kiss, the taste of apples and the touch of her tongue familiar and far too exciting when they could be interrupted at any second.

"We should speak to your father."

"Soon," she said, her smile fading. "But first I need you to know how sorry I am for not telling you about the baby right when I found out, and then for not telling you once we got involved again. That was wrong of me to keep it from you. You deserved to know."

"Thank you for that. You didn't have to say it, but I appreciate hearing it." The knowledge of that loss still hurt, and he suspected it would for a long time. But he understood how difficult it was for her to trust. He expected he would still have some work to do in easing away barriers she'd spent a lifetime erecting.

But he was damn good at renovations, at making something magnificent from the foundation already in place. "I brought something else for you besides the flowers."

"You didn't have to bring me anything. You're being here means more than I can say."

"I should have followed you before. I should have been there for you."

She cupped his face. "We're moving forward, remember?" Eloisa kissed him again, and once more, holding for three intense heartbeats. "Now what did you want to show me?"

He reached into his pocket and pulled out two gold bands. Theirs. He'd kept them the whole year. Her eyes bright with her smile and unshed tears, she held up her hand. He slid Eloisa's wedding ring onto her finger, and she slid his in place again as well, clasping his hand tightly in hers. This time, he knew, those rings weren't coming off again.

Jonah tugged one of the tulips from the bouquet and tucked it behind her ear. "Are you ready to go inside now, Mrs. Landis?"

She hooked her arm in his, like a bride with her bouquet. "I'm ready to go absolutely anywhere...with *you*."

Epilogue

She had dreamed she was draped in jewels.

Languishing in twilight slumber, Eloisa Landis skimmed her fingers along the bare arm of the man sleeping next to her. She'd had the sweetest dream that her husband had showered her with emeralds and rubies and fat freshwater pearls while they'd made love. She stroked up Jonah's arms to face, his five-o'clock shadow rasping against her tender fingertips.

Eloisa flipped to her back and stretched, extending her arm so the sun refracted off her cushion-cut diamond ring to go alongside her wedding band. Early morning light streaked through the wrought-iron window grilles in the adobe manor home he'd rented for the summer. A gentle breeze rustled the linen draping over the bed.

What was it about this man that took her breath away?

His hand fell to her hip and she smiled.

Yeah, she knew exactly what drew her to him. Everything.

Growling low, he hauled her against his side. "The rubies, definitely the rubies," he said as he peeked through one eye, apparently not as asleep as she'd imagined. He flicked the dangling gems on her ears. "I've been dreaming of draping you in jewels for over a year."

"You certainly played out that fantasy last night." She reached underneath her to sweep free a sapphire bracelet that was poking into her back.

How delightfully ironic that he was the one giving her jewels and castles. Not that she needed any of it. She had peace and excitement, stability and adventure all at once with the man she loved. "You certainly brought along a king's ransom in jewels."

"Because you're a Landis, lady. That makes you American royalty." He rolled her underneath him, elbows propped.

Royalty. The word didn't make her wince anymore. She was coming to peace with that part of herself. She'd visited her father again. His health was still waning, his liver failing. She would have to face that, no more hiding for her. But thank goodness she had Jonah at her side to deal with the worst when it came around.

Jonah kissed her lightly, comforting, as if he read her thoughts, something he seemed to do more and more often these days.

Audrey and Joey were well on their way to opening a catering business in Maine, of all places. They said they planned to bring a little southern spice into lobster.

Harry planned to join them and manage the books, always looking out for his daughter's financial future.

Eloisa's family was expanding rapidly, with the Landises due in for a long weekend visit. Ginger had mandated they all needed to get to know their new relative better. Eloisa appreciated the overture. How silly to get so excited about being the belle of the ball.

But she couldn't help herself. The Landises had a way of making her feel special and welcome.

A part of their family.

Jonah toyed with the beaded pearls strung through her hair. "Have you given any thought to where you would like to live?"

"I figure when the right restoration project comes around for our home, we'll know it."

He gave her hair a light tug. "Can you narrow that down to a country for me?"

"Nope—" she threaded her fingers through his hair, drawing him down to her "—I'm through limiting my options out of preconceived notions." She nestled her leg more firmly between his, grazing him with the gold-flecked garter belt around her thigh. "Now, it's all about the possibilities."

* * * * *

"You are no more ready to walk away from me than I am from you," Geoff said.

"And if you want to lie and pretend that we don't you're welcome to try. But your body is telling me a different story."

"You're right," she said in a low husky voice.

"Then we're agreed."

"Agreed?"

"This isn't going to end until I'm in your bed."

"Geoff, I'm not sure that's a good idea."

He kissed her. He didn't ask permission or do it tentatively at all.

When he lifted his head, she was breathing heavily and her hands were on his shoulders and she tried to draw him back to her. She stared up at him with lust in her eyes and underlying vulnerability that made him wonder if this was a mistake. But then he remembered he was Geoff Devonshire and he never made mistakes.

Amelia Munroe was going to be his, and now they both knew it.

HIS ROYAL PRIZE

BY
KATHERINE GARBERA

All the characters in this book have no existence outside the imagination of
the author, and have no relation whatsoever to anyone bearing the same name
or names. They are not even distantly inspired by any individual known or
unknown to the author, and all the incidents are pure invention.

Published in Great Britain 2011
by Mills & Boon, an imprint of Harlequin (UK) Limited,
Eton House, 18-24 Paradise Road, Richmond, Surrey TW9 1SR

© Katherine Garbera 2010

ISBN: 978 0 263 88219 3

51-0511

Harlequin (UK) policy is to use papers that are natural, renewable and
recyclable products and made from wood grown in sustainable forests. The
logging and manufacturing processes conform to the legal environmental
regulations of the country of origin.

Printed and bound in Spain
by Blackprint CPI, Barcelona

To all of the ladies on the Jaunty Quills blog who let me know I wasn't alone when I felt like I was—thank you.

Katherine Garbera is a strong believer in happily-ever-after. She's written more than thirty-five books and has been nominated for career achievement awards in series fantasy and series adventure from *RT Book Reviews*. Her books have appeared on the Waldenbooks/Borders bestseller list for series romance and on the *USA Today* extended bestseller list. Visit Katherine on the web at www.katherinegarbera.com.

Dear Reader,

I'm both excited and sad that this is the last of *The Devonshire Heirs* books. Geoff is the oldest of the heirs and bound mostly by duty and familial responsibility. His heroine is Amelia Munroe—she's a tabloid darling, a millionaire heiress who's known mostly for her scandalous behavior.

Geoff and Amelia travel in the same circles most of their lives but have never had a chance to get to know each other until recently. So it's just Geoff's bad luck that a stipulation in his father's will is making seeing Amelia so difficult. She's always had a pack of paparazzi following her around and he is supposed to keep out of the papers.

But they both are fiercely attracted to each other and nothing is going to keep them apart.

I hope you have enjoyed meeting all of the heirs!!!

Happyreading,

Katherine

Prologue

Geoff Devonshire didn't have time for the biological father he'd never met. He had a jam-packed schedule and little time for much else today. But his curiosity was piqued, so he'd decided to attend this meeting at the Everest Group's corporate headquarters. His own office building was two doors down in a very posh section of London along the Thames next to the controversial cucumber-shaped city hall.

When he got off the elevator on the executive level, he was escorted to the boardroom at the end of the hall.

"Hello, sir. You are the first to arrive for the meeting. May I get you something to drink?"

The pretty, efficient secretary directed him to a seat at the table and when he declined a drink, she left.

Geoff walked over to the glass-lined wall and looked down at the river Thames. It was midmorning in March, and the sun was peaking through the heavy clouds that hung over the city.

The door opened behind him and he turned as he heard the secretary greeting another person. It was Henry Devonshire—one of his half brothers. The former rugby captain was now known for his celebrity reality shows.

They had never met before, and knew nothing of each other except what was in the press.

"Geoff Devonshire," Geoff said, offering his hand to Henry.

"Henry," he said, holding out his hand.

Geoff felt a bit strange meeting this man for the first time in his life. But the door opened again before he could say anything more and Steven Devonshire walked in.

All three of Malcolm Devonshire's illegitimate sons were now in the same room. Geoff realized that gossip magazines and celebrity Web sites would pay a fortune for a photo of the gathering.

Edmond, Malcolm's solicitor and all-around errand boy, stepped in and invited them to have a seat. Geoff sat back and watched the other men. Malcolm had admitted to fathering the three of them but had never really been a part of his life except to send a check once a month.

His mother, Princess Louisa of Strathearn, despite her lofty-sounding title, was a minor member of the current royal family. She had been a party girl and had relished her affair with Malcolm and the tongues it caused to wag. Until she'd realized she was only one of three women Malcolm was wooing. She retreated to her country estate and to Geoff's knowledge had rarely left in the years immediately after his birth.

Henry's mother was '70s pop singer Tiffany Malone. Henry was the middle son.

Steven, the youngest son, had been born to Lynn Grandings, a Nobel Prize-winning physicist. There had been a bit of a brouhaha when it seemed that both Geoff and Steven would attend Eton, but Geoff's mother had sent him to an exclusive boarding school in the States instead in a well-publicized exchange with a prominent senator's son.

Scandalously, they were all born in the same year with just several months between their birthdays.

"Why are we here?" Henry asked.

"Malcolm has a message for you," Edmond said.

"Why now?" Geoff asked. It seemed odd to him that their father would finally assemble the three of them in a room.

"Mr. Devonshire is dying," Edmond said. "He wants the legacy he worked so hard to create to live on in each of you."

Geoff almost got up and left. He wanted nothing from Malcolm Devonshire. He never had. Malcolm had devastated his mother. And as a man with two sisters, Gemma and Caroline, Geoff couldn't abide any man who would treat a woman so callously.

Edmond passed three file folders across the table to each of them. Geoff took his time opening the folder. He wasn't sure what he expected to see inside, but the handwritten note was a bit of a surprise.

Malcolm wanted him to run the airline unit of the

Everest Group and if his unit out-performed the other two, he'd inherit the chairmanship of Everest Group.

Geoff quickly assessed what running a business unit of a busy corporation would mean. Though flying was his passion, he'd never aspired to owning a commercial airline and his own business interests kept him very busy. But he wasn't about to just walk away from this. This was his chance to take what Malcolm had worked so hard to build and...what? A part of him was tempted to ruin it. Run it into the ground. He didn't need the money and his mum wouldn't take a cent from Malcolm. She had her own money.

While Henry and Steven talked to Edmond, Geoff leaned back in his chair. Edmond turned to him.

"Your thoughts?" Edmond asked.

"I don't need his money," Geoff said. He'd also inherited a title and a fortune from his maternal grandparents. He had never had to work a day in his life but he'd always pursued business with passion. His interests were varied and diverse but he liked to keep busy.

"May we have a moment to discuss this alone?" Steven asked.

Edmond nodded and left the room. As soon as the door closed behind him, Steven stood up. Geoff noted the way Steven moved, very carefully with controlled measure. He'd heard a little about him and the china company that he'd brought back from the brink of bankruptcy. Steven was a man with a lot of business acumen. Geoff suspected he'd be very hard to beat in this competition that Malcolm had set out for them.

"I think we should do it," Steven said.

"I'm not so sure," Geoff replied. "He shouldn't put any stipulations in his will. If he wants to leave us something, so be it."

"But this affects our mums," Henry said.

Everything that Malcolm had done since Geoff's birth had affected his mum. And Geoff wasn't sure what the outcome would be. His mum, Louisa, didn't want anything to do with Malcolm. But Geoff wanted something on her behalf. Something from Malcolm to make up for what he'd taken from her.

"It does affect them," Geoff said, thinking it over. "I see your point. If you two are in then I'll do it as well. But I don't need his approval or his money."

The men agreed. In the end the consensus was that they would accept the challenge laid down by the father none of them had ever met. Geoff left the building with Henry, who was quiet on the way down.

"Have you ever met him?"

"Malcolm?" Geoff asked.

"Yes."

"No. You?" Geoff had always assumed that Malcolm wasn't involved in any of their lives. He'd be surprised if he found out differently.

Henry shook his head. "It's interesting, this proposition of his."

"Indeed," Geoff said. "I have no experience running an airline."

Henry laughed in a genial way. "Nor I a record label."

"I have a feeling Steven has a leg up on us," Geoff said. "Look at what he did with Raleighvale China. I am used to running charitable foundations and businesses with a healthy cash flow."

"Me, too. That's the understatement of the year," Henry said.

After they parted ways, Geoff sat in his car in the garage, thinking about how he was going to add Everest Air to his already busy life. He'd find a way. He always did when it came to his responsibilities and duties.

Just once, though, he'd like to find something that was just for him. He did his family duty by attending royal functions and events that were important to his mother or sisters. Now he was going to try to turn a company that was owned by the man who had sired him into a profitable enterprise.

He wasn't doing it out of duty. He was doing it because he wanted to take his father's company and exceed all expectations, making it into a very profitable business. More profitable than his father had ever dreamed.

Geoff liked the challenge that was before him. Henry and Steven were both worthy adversaries, and meeting them under these circumstances seemed fitting. This was his chance to prove to himself that, as the eldest Devonshire bastard, he should enjoy the lion's share of the inheritance.

One

The event that same evening was long and boring—the kind of charity dinner that he'd rather not attend. But he was a Devonshire and a member of the British royal family and there were times when he simply couldn't decline. At least the William Kent Room at the Ritz was an exquisite venue.

His date for this evening was Mary Werner, the daughter of a billionaire office supplies executive. She was a suitable girl and would make him a proper wife, if that's what he was after. He knew that her family probably expected a proposal soon.

His half sisters—Gemma and Caroline, who were twenty-three and twenty-one respectively—called her his maiden bride. He pretended to growl at them for it but he knew they were right. Mary, as lovely as she was, was a bit too tame for him.

There was a spate of camera shutters clicking at the entrance to the ballroom. He glanced over his shoulder to see Amelia Munroe smiling for the photographers. She wore a bright red sheath, which hugged her generous curves, and held a small dog in one arm. The animal yipped whenever a flash went off.

There was a lull in every conversation in the room as all heads turned toward her. She said something in her distinctively brash American accent and then threw her head back and laughed. Suddenly he didn't mind being here quite as much.

"Oh, it's Amelia," Mary said quietly.

"Indeed. She does like to make an entrance."

"Yes, she does. Everyone is watching her. I wonder how she does it," Mary mused.

Geoff knew exactly how she did it. She drew attention because of the way she was built, the way she smiled, the way she laughed. She moved like a woman with loads of confidence. Her curly black hair was pulled up on her head and tendrils fell around her heart-shaped face. He couldn't see her eyes from here, but he knew they were a diamond bright blue. Men wanted her—hell, he did. And if Mary's reaction was any indication, women wanted to *be* her.

The atmosphere in the ballroom had changed. Though the paparazzi were kept at the door, the excitement spilled into the room as Amelia walked in.

"I guess the International Children's Fund must be one of her pet charities this year," Mary said.

"Must be," Geoff said. Hubert Grace, one of his stepfather's friends excused himself from the table and

Geoff shook his head as Hubert made his way across the ballroom to Amelia's side.

"What is Hubert doing?" Mary asked.

"I have no idea. I suggest we go back to our conversation, though," Geoff said.

He might be attracted to Amelia but he knew from past experience that the things he wanted most in the world were the ones that were dangerous to him and to his peace of mind. And with this new deal he'd agreed to with Malcolm, he had to be on his best behavior— something that had never failed to make him restless.

"Good idea. I wonder if she realizes how much of a distraction she is," Mary said.

"Does she bother you?" he asked.

Mary shrugged. "Not really."

Mary was a beautiful girl—a proper English rose with fair skin and thick, straight hair. Her eyes were a pretty blue that showed her keen intelligence. But she was tame. She allowed herself to follow the rules…much like he did on occasion. Their position oftentimes meant that they had to do what society dictated, especially in their circles.

He glanced back over at Amelia holding court across the room. He wanted to be over there but not one of the crowd. Given his rank and status in society he rarely settled for being one of the many, and this time was no different.

"Not really?" he asked Mary. "What is it about her that you envy?"

Mary took a sip of her wine and then turned to look at Amelia, who was still engaged in conversation with Hubert. "Everyone is watching her and talking about her—even me. I guess…I just wish I could walk into a room and make everyone else want to be me."

Geoff studied the American woman. She was gorgeous, from her kissable mouth to her curvy body. But more than that, it was her joie de vivre that drew his eye. She'd grown up rich and often turned up in *Hello!* magazine and YouTube video on her yacht in the Mediterranean. She'd had her share of scandals, but she never shrank from the public eye. He was intrigued by her.

"I think it's the fact that she doesn't follow the rules and doesn't care if anyone is bothered by that," Geoff said.

"I agree," his sister Caroline chimed in as she returned to the table. "You are talking about Amelia, right?"

"Yes," Mary said. "I envy her."

Caroline laughed. "I'm jealous of the way she commands the attention of everyone. I wish I did."

"You do, Caro, you just don't realize it."

"I think you might be the only one who thinks that," she said, smiling up at him. He adored both his little sisters, having practically raised them. His mum had bad episodes of depression and often took to her room for weeks at a time. And his stepfather had died when the girls were four and six years old.

"The right man will see that as well," he said.

"And when will he come along?" Caro asked.

"When you are thirty," he said with a mock growl.

"Until then, I'll just have to have fun with Mr. Wrong."

"Not if I have anything to say about it."

"You don't," she said with a giggle. "You are too busy running Everest Air."

He scowled. Malcolm's "gift" was a pain in the ass. With the spike in crude oil prices and the slowing economy, the air industry was feeling the pinch. Geoff was coming up with some creative ideas to keep the airline in the black, but it was taking up more time than he wanted to devote to his job.

He decided it was time to start working hard *and* playing hard.

"Too true, Caro," he said.

Mary was quiet during their conversation and he suspected it was because she was expecting an offer of marriage from him soon. As much as he liked Mary, when he tried to imagine spending the rest of his life with her, he couldn't do it.

She was simply too quiet. He had more fun talking to his sisters then he did talking to her, and in the end he guessed that made the decision he'd been mulling over about marrying her so much easier. It wasn't fair to Mary or himself. They both deserved more from their relationships.

He had a life of duty and obligation, and he wanted his marriage to be more than a merging of family names and titles. He wanted the real thing—unlike what he'd seen in his parents' lives.

He knew that he could never turn his back on his responsibilities but he also knew that he'd always had in the back of his mind the fact that he was going to have a good marriage.

His mum's affair with Malcolm Devonshire had changed her. She'd said as much more than once when she was having her dark spells. And her marriage to Caro and Gemma's father had been made purely to restore the reputation she'd destroyed with her affair.

So he'd seen the obligation side of marriage and it had left him feeling empty. When he'd been younger, he'd seen his sunny mother wither whenever she read an article about Malcolm until she spent more time in her home then she did at the social obligations she used to enjoy.

And he knew he wanted more than that. He wanted someone different—a woman who could stir his passions. He heard the husky sound of feminine laughter and glanced across the room to where Amelia held court with several eager young suitors. He wanted her.

She spent a lot of time in the spotlight, something that he'd learned to avoid as a young man. But that didn't seem to bother him at the moment.

Geoff was used to going after what he wanted and used to getting it, and Amelia Munroe would be no different. He was going to have her.

He took a sip of his martini and leaned back in his seat as the emcee talked on and on. He thought back to the time he'd spent with Amelia on a philanthropic trip to Botswana. He remembered how compassionate and sincere she had seemed there. Not the spoiled heiress whose every move was catalogued by the press, but a woman who'd sat in the dirt and comforted a child who was crying. A woman who'd spoken the local language to the people who were collecting the water and medical supplies that their group had brought with them. She'd casually mentioned she'd learned the language on a trip years earlier to the same region.

Seeing that side of Amelia had intrigued him. But seeing her tonight in full form had reminded him that she was a complex, confusing, beautiful woman. One that he was suddenly hell-bent on getting to know better.

Amelia Munroe smiled at Cecelia, Lady Abercrombie, and nodded as the older woman talked about the fiasco at her dinner party a week earlier. Amelia wished she were indeed the careless person she was portrayed as in the tabloid media because then she could just walk away from Cecelia. But she couldn't. Lady Abercrombie was one of her mother's closest friends and when she wasn't rambling on endlessly, Amelia genuinely liked her.

"Well, to make a long story short," Cecelia said, "be glad you didn't come."

"I'm not glad I missed your party. It sounds like it was very interesting."

"If you'd been there, it would have been more than interesting," Cecelia said. "How was Milan?"

"Wonderful. Mother has designed a new line that is going to be simply spectacular. I can't wait for the world to see it."

"I'm going next week for a sneak peek," Cecelia said. Though in her early fifties, Cecelia looked at least fifteen years younger, with a trim, athletic build and perfectly coiffed blond hair. But what really made her look young was her smooth skin—something that Amelia's mother, Mia Domenici, attributed to the spa treatments Cecelia had twice a year in Switzerland. Something Amelia's father never approved of.

"I'm sure you'll have a lovely trip," Amelia said.

"I can't wait. Oh, I see Edmond, Malcolm Devonshire's man of affairs. I want to find out how Malcolm's health is, dear, do you mind?"

"Not at all," Amelia said and watched the other woman walk away. Cecelia was a gossip and always knew every detail of the personal lives of their set. She turned to survey the room and saw a man walking toward her.

She knew him in an instant. Geoff Devonshire. They attended many of the same functions and served on the board of the International Children's Fund together.

There was something about the man, with his dark, thick curly hair and piercing blue eyes, that she couldn't resist. She thought back to a photo she'd seen of him once, standing next to his Learjet in a pair of slim-fitting jeans—and no shirt.

Yummy. The man had chest muscles like the Italian models that her mother hired for her fall shows.

But unlike most men, Geoff had never paid her much attention. It was maddening, actually.

"Good evening, Geoff," she said, as he stopped in front of her. She stood up to give him the customary kiss on each cheek, but he startled her by putting his hands on her waist and brushing his lips against hers. Her mouth tingled from the contact and she tilted her head to the side to study him, trying to hide the fact that he'd caught her so off guard.

She was the outrageous one!

"That was a bit friendly," she said.

"I can be a cheeky bastard," he replied with a half smile.

"As can Hubert," she said.

Geoff laughed as she gave the older man a wave.

"Scandalous," he joked.

It was an apt choice of words, Amelia thought. Scandal might as well be her middle name. Though she had been born to a world of wealth and privilege, she'd also been born into scandal. Her mother had been the mistress of Augustus Munroe, a married New York hotel mogul who had changed the way that people traveled. He'd revolutionized the hotel industry with his signature luxury-themed hotels.

"But I don't want to talk about Hubert," Geoff said, staring her down with his impossibly blue eyes.

She took a sip of her champagne. "You don't? What *do* you want to discuss?"

"Dinner. Tomorrow night."

"Why, Captain Devonshire, are you asking or ordering me out?" she asked, using one of Geoff's many titles. She was playing coy but was surprised. After ignoring her for so long, why was he suddenly interested in her? He'd been a decorated war hero in the first Gulf war with the Royal Air Force.

Geoff smiled. "I'm asking, of course."

"But aren't you serious about Mary Werner?"

"We have been dating casually. Is that a problem?" he asked. "I didn't think that exclusivity was something you usually bothered with."

Heat rushed to her face. Geoff thought he knew her, based on what? Stories he'd seen splashed in the papers? She had always been careful not to repeat her mother's mistake of dating and falling for a committed man.

"Maybe you don't know as much as you think you do," she said.

"There's no maybe about it," he replied. "I'm sorry.

That was rude and I have no excuse for it. Please accept my apology."

"Accepted," she said. "You should know as well as anyone that just because a story is on a Web site or in the tabloids doesn't make it true."

"Give me a chance to make it up to you with dinner," he said.

"Why? Are you just after the girl you've read about?"

"No, I'm not," he replied. "There is something about the girl behind the headlines that intrigues me."

Amelia was afraid to believe him. Geoff was different from every other man she'd met but that didn't mean she could trust him. She had learned little about Geoff from the rumor mill—just that he was a man who took his work and his life very seriously, putting duty first. She had thought they had little in common—she courted the media and he shied away from it.

"If you have dinner with me, there will be photos and stories about us," she said, wanting to make sure that he understood what her life was all about.

"I am aware of that."

She nodded. "Then I will see you tomorrow night."

"I will see to the details," he said. "I'll pick you up."

"See you then," she said. She turned and walked away. She was always the first to walk away. She'd started doing that when she turned twenty-one and realized that she didn't have to wait for someone to leave her again. Someone…she meant her father and all men.

Geoff was different, though, and that made it all the more important for her to walk away. She needed the power to be in her hands and not in his. He had knocked her for a loop by brazenly asking her out while sitting a few tables away with his date. What did this mean? Did Geoff even know, or was the attraction between them that he'd denied so long simply too strong for either of them to contain?

She busied herself with the crowd of B-list celebrities she was hosting at her table in an effort to get her mind off Geoff. She knew that most of them had accepted her invitation to this event in hopes that they'd get a photo with her that would end up in tomorrow morning's papers.

She danced with each of the men at her table, trying not to notice where Geoff was. When it was time for her to go up to the front to narrate the slide show that documented her recent trip to Botswana, she found herself distracted by images of Geoff on the trip.

She remembered seeing him talking with the local businessmen, and helping out when a citizen had a flat tire. He seemed to be more than just a handsome face, more than a man who was doing his duty because it was expected of him. Though she'd been surprised that he'd asked her out. It would be nice to spend some time with a man who was more than he appeared to be.

Geoff started to return to his table but was stopped when he felt a hand on his arm. He glanced over his shoulder to see Edmond standing there. Geoff had been at numerous functions with Malcolm's right-hand man, yet this was the first time that he'd been approached by him in public.

"Yes?"

"I need a word."

"Certainly," Geoff said, leading the way through the crown to a quiet alcove. "What's up?"

"I saw you speaking to Amelia Munroe…"

"So?"

"I wanted to remind you of the stipulations of your father's—"

"Of Malcolm's will? He's never wanted anything to do with me, Edmond. I'm not going to let him dictate my life now."

"Understood, sir. But please be careful. I don't want you to lose your share of the Devonshire fortune."

Geoff walked away from the older man without responding. He was more than frustrated with the entire situation. He thought about just walking away, but his mother deserved something for the happiness that Malcolm had stolen from her.

Geoff returned to his table in time to greet Mary as she left the dance floor with Jerry Montgomery. Jerry was a nice enough fellow—an American sports reporter who covered British sports for ESPN. He had a toothpaste-ad, American smile—super-straight white teeth and a confident grin.

For some reason Geoff had never really liked the fellow. He couldn't say why and didn't spend a lot of time thinking on it. But Mary liked him. In fact she was flushed from dancing. She gave Jerry an intimate smile as he walked away. Geoff realized that Mary liked him. He also realized that he wasn't jealous in the slightest. In fact, he was relieved.

"Nice dance?"

"Yes. I simply love that song," she said. The song

in question was "I've Got You Under My Skin," made famous by Frank Sinatra. The song was a standard that evoked memories of his mum teaching him how to dance.

"I'm glad he offered his services, then."

"Me, too," she said somewhat shyly. "Where is Caroline?"

"Gone for the evening. She said this party was too tame."

"I guess it is, by her standards. By yours as well," she said. There was a question in her voice as her eyes cut across the room to Amelia.

"Ah, well, this is the kind of function that I have to attend."

She smiled then, the closest thing to a genuine expression of joy that he'd seen all evening. "Duty calls."

"Indeed it does. But I've had enough for tonight. Shall we?"

Geoff saw Mary home but didn't feel like heading back to his luxury townhome in the leafy-green area near Greenwich. He was restless and not sure what he needed, but he knew that sitting at home wasn't it.

Actually, he did know what he needed, but he couldn't have it until tomorrow night.

Normally, when he felt this way, he got in his plane—his favorite classic 1983 Lear—and took off for a few days. When he was in the sky he wasn't Geoff Devonshire, bastard son of Malcolm and Princess Louisa of Strathearn. Instead, he was simply Geoff and there were no rules, no obligations and no one who wanted anything from him.

Instead, he found himself at a club just off Leicester Square where a friend of his deejayed. He entered through the back to avoid the paparazzi who covered the red-velvet rope area and found a small booth in the rear of the darkened club.

The electronic beat of the music pulsed loudly and he felt everything inside him stir as his thoughts again turned to Amelia. He wanted to make sure she had no ill feelings regarding his comment about her tabloid life. He called his butler, Jasper, and asked him to send Amelia a little gift, something he thought she'd appreciate. And something that would show her that he saw her as more than just the scandal girl the world thought they knew. He'd picked up a carving in Africa he'd seen her admiring—maybe he'd known all along he was going to ask her out. He jotted a note on his personal stationery that he had Jasper bring him and sent the man on his way.

His mobile phone rang and he glanced at the caller ID before answering it. It was his vice president at Everest Air. Given the time of night, it probably wasn't good news.

"Devonshire here."

"It's Grant. We have a major problem. My contacts with the baggage handlers union said they are getting ready to strike."

"We don't employ them, the airport does. Right?" Geoff said.

Running the airline was taking some time to adjust to. As a former RAF pilot, he knew planes and understood what it took to fly them. And as a businessman he knew how to make money, but there were intricacies to the airline business that he was still learning.

"That is correct."

"So let's talk to their boss and see what we can do to sweeten the deal. Who is in charge?"

Geoff heard the rustle of papers on the other end of the line. "Max Preston."

"Let's have him to the office tomorrow. Pull out all the stops and make sure he knows that we want to listen to him. Listening is key in these situations."

A lot of his team at Everest Air was waiting for him to prove himself, to show them that he had the right stuff to run the company. And Geoff wouldn't have it any other way. He'd spent a lifetime making sure that everyone knew he didn't coast through on his father's coattails.

"I've had to deal with all kinds of hostile people, including rebels in Uganda who didn't think that my foundations had any business there. But I sat down with them, I listened and the rebel leader talked," Geoff said, remembering that long night when he'd sat across a fire from a man with an AK-47 cradled in his arms as he expressed the same desires that most men had. A desire to be heard and treated fairly. These were things that Geoff couldn't provide but he had been able to promise he would talk to his friends in government and was able to successfully gain some concessions for the rebels.

"I had no idea. I thought you just travelled around partying with your other rich friends."

"Grant, are you jealous?"

"Hell, yes, mate. Who wouldn't want that jet-set life?"

"It's not as glamorous as you might think."

"Nothing ever is. What time are you thinking for this meeting tomorrow?"

"Early. We want Max to have time to go and talk to his people once we've talked to him."

"Will do. I'll let you know when it's arranged," Grant said.

Geoff smiled to himself. "That's perfect. We want to make sure that no one's travel is disrupted because of this baggage handler situation. I think your suggestion is spot on."

Grant laughed. "Thank my wife for that one. She made the suggestion over tea."

Geoff smiled to himself. Women were able to sometimes get to the heart of an issue. Something he'd learned from his sisters and his mother.

Grant was going to be a great asset to him at the airline. He had been working there for the last three years, and though the profits weren't surging under his leadership, they had been steady.

Geoff knew from his own business interests that constant vigilance would be the key to making sure that every quarter increased their profit margin. And he could do that with men like Grant on his team.

Winning the competition against his half brothers was important to him because this was a family thing. And he always succeeded when he put his mind to it.

He looked at his watch and realized he'd spent exactly two minutes not thinking about Amelia. Her grin flashed in his mind and the scent of her perfume lingered with each breath he took.

He couldn't wait to see her tomorrow night and get

to know the woman behind the glare of the paparazzi flashbulbs because he was having a hard time reconciling the two very different sides of her that he'd seen. She was a puzzle that he wanted—needed—to solve.

Two

Amelia loved London in the morning, despite how crowded the city was with workers heading to their offices and tourists rushing from palaces to Big Ben. To be fair, her morning started after rush hour and well into the congestion charges that were in effect in her neighborhood. It was a crisp, spring morning. She put on a pair of running shorts, a sports bra and a pair of sneakers and headed out the door.

But her cell phone rang before she'd hit the elevator. She glanced at the caller ID to see that it was her older brother, Auggie. She shook her head and thought about letting it go to voice mail, except the one time she'd done that he'd been reaching out for help.

"Morning, Auggie," she said.

"Sis, I need a favor."

She leaned against the wall in her foyer. Why was she

surprised? Her brother was the kind of man who always needed something. But she had almost lost him to drug use, and she'd made him a promise that if he got clean, she'd always be here to help him stay that way.

"What kind of favor?"

"I can't make the Munroe Hotels board meeting this afternoon. In fact, I need the entire week off. Do you think you can cover for me?"

"No, Auggie, I can't," she said. Auggie had a serious problem with responsibility. Though she was the one who somehow always made it into the papers, Auggie truly lived his life as if he didn't owe anyone anything. His therapist had told her to stop enabling him.

He was only eleven months older than she was, and given the circumstances of their birth and highly dysfunctional family, they'd had only each other to rely on while they'd been growing up.

Her parents were passionate lovers who couldn't keep their hands off each other, but they didn't know how to relate to each other outside the bedroom. They were both a little too self-absorbed to be good parents. In essence, she and Auggie had raised themselves.

"Lia, please?"

This was the hard part, she thought, because despite everything she loved Auggie and didn't want to have to tell him no. "I really can't. I have to be at the Munroe Foundation this afternoon. I'm presenting my report on Botswana."

"Can't you just reschedule it?" he asked.

She rubbed the back of her neck. If she did this for him, he'd start expecting her to run both arms of her family business again. Amelia had chosen the foundation because she liked the work. And Auggie had taken the public role of running the Munroe Hotels chain. She'd had to do a lot of behind-the-scenes "helping," since it appeared that Auggie hadn't inherited their father's business savvy.

"I can't."

"Lia, I'm not going to be there. If you aren't going to stand in for me, the board will probably decide to hold an emergency election for a new chairman and then there won't be a Munroe at the helm."

Her father would be very angry if they both missed the meeting. Amelia didn't want to do anything that would invite her father back into their lives.

"This isn't fair. You know I'm not supposed to run both organizations. I can't do it, Auggie."

"It's your decision, Lia. I think it might be better to let someone else take over."

"Do you want to make Dad crazy?" she asked. Her brother had a love-hate relationship with their parents. And while she tried her best to keep the peace from a distance, Auggie did his best to make sure that their parents were always a little bit uncomfortable.

Auggie chuckled. "That wouldn't bother me in the least."

Her dad was recovering from open-heart surgery and Amelia didn't want to upset his progress. "I'll do it. But you have to be back in the office in one week's time. If not, then I'm going to ask to have you removed. I'm not going to keep covering for you."

"You're the best, sis. Talk to you soon," he said, hanging up.

She ran every morning in Hyde Park and this morning

she really needed it. Auggie was frustrating beyond belief, but he was her brother. She passed tourists who were following the Princess Diana Memorial Walk and heading up toward Buckingham Palace for the changing of the guard later in the morning. She ran, trying to forget everything and enjoy the city under her feet as music blasted in her ears.

She should be thinking of her day or of this weekend's luncheon with her father but instead she was thinking of Geoff Devonshire.

He had the kind of brooding good looks that put her in mind of Mr. Darcy in Jane Austen's *Pride and Prejudice*. Objectively she thought that it was interesting that a man with aristocratic breeding would still fit a mold that was over one hundred years old. But then she had to laugh. Men hadn't changed in all that time. Women had been subject to their whims then and still were now.

The psychiatrist her mother had sent her to when she'd turned thirteen had said that Amelia had father issues. And that was still true.

She was always trying to prove herself to some man and Geoff would probably be no different. As much as she wanted to think that she didn't care, a part of her did. A part of her wanted to be at that quiet banquet table he'd occupied last night rather than at the center of attention.

His respectable girlfriend and his sisters had surrounded him. He had been born into scandal, as she had, but instead of being consumed in the paparazzi storm, he'd found a way to make a respectable life for himself.

In some way, she craved what he had. But then she

shook the thought aside. She was the media's favorite subject because she always did something outrageous. The very things that had gotten her on the cover of the weekly magazines had also gotten her father's attention.

Father issues, indeed.

At the entrance to her building she noticed Tommy, the photographer who always seemed to be following her, lounging against the wall. He had worn jeans, a baggy T-shirt and a khaki vest with lots of pockets crammed with lenses and backup batteries.

He snapped to attention as he saw her approach and took several photos as she entered her building. She suspected they'd show up on some Web site before the day was done. She'd probably replace whichever celeb they'd caught doing something unglamorous.

"Good morning, Ms. Munroe. There is a package for you."

"Thank you, Felix," she said to the doorman, taking the FedEx package that he held out to her.

Felix also handed her one of her own monogrammed towels and a bottle of water. She smiled at the Brazilian doorman. Felix did a good job of getting tips from her by always saying yes to all her little requests. He was very handsome and he'd come to the UK to find fortune as an actor, but he had found that his grasp of languages wasn't as good as he'd thought, so he'd started working here to improve his English.

She took the elevator up to her penthouse and entered the room. Lady Godiva was waiting for her. The miniature Dachshund was always happy to see her.

Amelia took a moment to pet her before walking over

to the floor-to-ceiling glass windows that lined the east side of her apartment. She sipped her water as she looked out over the city.

She wiped the sweat from her face, tossed the towel on the floor and looked at the package. The return address was from London. Someone had sent her a package last night.

Geoff Devonshire.

Lady Godiva danced around her feet with a tennis ball in her mouth. Amelia reached down and scratched her under the chin. Then she took the ball from the dog, tossing it across the room.

The dog scampered off after it and Amelia sat down on the arm of her black leather sofa and opened the package, intrigued.

What would he send her?

She pulled out a box wrapped in white paper with Geoff's monogram on the center of it.

For a moment, she couldn't make herself open it. She didn't want to think of Geoff as a real option. She just wanted him to be a sexy guy she was going to have fun with.

Not a man who would make her care.

"Stop being silly," she said to herself. She tore the wrapping and opened the box.

Her breath caught as she stared down at the exquisite African carving. She knew he'd gotten it in Botswana— she'd seen the carving when they'd been touring a village. Had he noticed her admiring it?

A piece of fine linen stationary was lying on top of the carving with a simple note.

I look forward to learning more about the woman behind the headlines.

Amelia told herself that he was simply trying to woo her, but her heart beat faster anyway. His actions had touched her. She took the carving into her bedroom and set it on her chest of drawers where she could admire it from anywhere in the room.

Steven called him at eleven and asked if they could meet for drinks later that evening. He wanted all three of them to have a chance to talk. Geoff knew it would be tight—he planned to take Amelia up in his plane and get away from the city. He knew that she liked the spotlight, but Geoff had learned from his mother that living under constant scrutiny made life difficult at best, and he thought she'd like the escape.

"Sure, I can do that. Why don't we meet at one of my clubs?" Geoff suggested.

"Just tell me where and I'll text Henry," Steven said.

Geoff made a few notes and took down Steven's mobile number. He'd never thought about having brothers before and at thirty-eight he worried he was a little old to start forming close relationships with Henry and Steven, but he was willing to try.

"Can I ask you a personal question?"

"Go ahead," Geoff said.

"Do you ever wish you'd gone to Eton? So we could have met earlier in life?" Steven asked.

Geoff had never thought about that. Growing up with sisters in his mother and stepfather's family, he'd often wondered about his father and the two half brothers he'd never met. But he'd known that meeting them would have devastated his mother, who wanted nothing to do with any of "Malcolm's mistresses' children."

"Sometimes. But I think we needed to live our independent lives," Geoff said.

"That we did. I'm looking forward to speaking to you later," Steven said before ending the call.

That was abrupt, he thought as he leaned back in his chair and spun toward the window that looked out in the direction of Heathrow Airport. This view from Everest Air was different from his office in the heart of London. His life had always been in flux and he'd always embraced change—he wondered if it was because of the way he'd grown up.

Why was he suddenly being so philosophical? He suspected it had to do with Malcolm's presence in his life after all this time.

He booked a table at one of his clubs and figured out exactly how much time he'd need to leave to pick up Amelia.

She was on his mind the rest of the afternoon. Only when Caro arrived to chat with him about a garden party their mum was throwing at the end of the month was he able to think of something else.

"I need your help, Geoff."

"You always do," he said with a smile.

She stuck her tongue out at him. "Mum wants to make sure that we have privacy. She doesn't want the party to be swarming with media."

"That's not a problem, Caro. They have never come to Hampshire and they won't now, especially not for this party. Henry is the one who is keeping them captive and with his very public persona, it should stay that way. I don't want this to weigh on anyone's mind."

She nodded. "I'll let Mum know."

"You do that," he said.

She smiled at him. "How's your maiden bride?"

"She's not mine." After last night's flirtation with Amelia, Geoff had barely given Mary a single thought. The vehemence of his response to his sister's question surprised them both.

"Really? I thought you two were getting serious."

He shook his head, but he wasn't about to discuss his love life with Caro. "Who are you dating now?"

"Paul Jeffries."

"The footballer?" he asked. Footballers were notoriously full of themselves and changed girlfriends with the passing of a season.

"The same."

"I don't like that. He's too…wild for you."

"Too bad," she said with a cheeky grin. "I'm twenty-one now. You can't tell me who to date anymore."

Geoff looked at her sternly. "If I see one photo of you in the weekly rags, that's it."

She glanced at her watch. "Oh, look at the time. I've got to run."

"Caro?" She stopped at his office door. "I'm just trying to protect you."

"I know. Love you."

"Love you, too."

After she left, he wondered if perhaps he should be taking his own advice. Amelia embodied everything that he warned his sisters to stay away from. Not a day went by that he didn't hear some juicy tidbit about her on the *One Show*.

But he was different than Caro or Gemma, and he knew how to handle Amelia. Besides, he was a man used to getting what he wanted, and he wasn't about to let anything stand in his way.

She intrigued him. He'd first started noticing her on their last trip to Botswana. Something about seeing the woman who'd had a salacious video on YouTube sitting in the dirt with hungry, sick children had piqued his curiosity. She was complex, he'd realized, and he wanted to expose all the layers of the woman to get down to her core.

Dating her was going to be hard with his busy schedule and hers. He needed a solid reason for the two of them to spend time together.

He stood and stretched. Glancing out the window of his office he saw the Munroe Hotel chain logo in the distance and he had an idea. If he could partner with Munroe Hotels and create unique travel packages for the Everest Air consumer he would be able to positively affect the bottom line of the airline. It was precisely the kind of idea he'd been searching for. Something that would help him win the competition with his half brothers and give him a reason to spend more time with Amelia.

But did party-girl Amelia spend any time in the offices of Munroe Hotels? He'd have to research it and find out. He made a few notes on his legal pad. He and Amelia both came from similar backgrounds, with parents who were more interested in themselves than in their kids.

He'd always understood that the Everest Group was Malcolm's life, and besting Malcolm on his own turf appealed to Geoff. He liked the feeling that thought evoked. And he smiled to himself as she finished making plans for his evening.

He made reservations at a little African restaurant that he hoped would remind Amelia that they had met in Botswana. He wished he'd had the time to get to know her better then.

When they'd been on the charity trip to Africa neither of them had obligations that took up their time. He could have spent all of his time focused solely on her. But that didn't bother him. He was more than ready for Amelia. He only hoped she was ready for him. The real man, not the staid one that she might expect from his reputation.

Amelia wasn't used to waiting around for some man, so it unnerved her a bit that Geoff was coming to pick her up. She'd spent the afternoon at the foundation office presenting her findings and persuading the board of directors to adopt her proposal for the course of action they needed to take.

"Why are you nervous?" Bebe asked as the sat in a pub near Waterloo Station.

"I'm not," she lied. It was ridiculous to have nerves like this before a date. It was nothing more than a date. He was just a guy—one she would go out with once or twice. She'd dazzle him with her smile and her winning personality and then…he'd move on. The way men always did.

"You are such a liar."

"Bebe—"

"Don't 'Bebe' me. Anyone else might believe that you are perfectly confident, but I know you better and you are nervous."

Bebe was her best friend and had been since they'd met at finishing school. The two had bonded when they were both ugly ducklings. Bebe had been overweight with frizzy hair, and Amelia had had braces and been gangly. They'd been an odd-looking twosome back then. None of their classmates would have predicted that they'd turn out to be incredibly successful and renowned for their glamorous lives.

"He's different. I know he's not going out with me so he can get his photo in the society pages."

"So you don't know how to treat him?" Bebe asked.

"I'm not sure that's it," Amelia said. The after-work rush hour had just started and people were hurrying past the window on their way home.

"Whatever it is, be careful. You don't want to do something outrageous."

She swallowed hard. Bebe was right. She couldn't afford to let her nerves get the best of her—she tended to act without thought or restraint when that happened, and that meant regrets.

"I'll be fine. One more glass of wine and I'm set."

Bebe smiled at her. "You look fab. I love turquoise on you."

"Thank you, darling. My mother recommended it."

"How was Milan?"

"Fab," Amelia said, winking at her friend. "In fact, I brought you back a little something."

She handed Bebe the shopping bag that she'd carried in with her.

Bebe took the bag from her but didn't open it. "What's going on with you? You're not yourself. Is it more than that yummy Devonshire heir?"

Amelia shook her head. Bebe was the one person in the world who knew about all of Auggie's troubles, and a part of her wanted to just unload on her friend. But she knew exactly what Bebe would say. *Don't enable.*

Hadn't she heard those exact words from everyone before? She knew that she was to blame. She should just step out of the equation, but letting the Munroe Hotel chain go wasn't something she was ready to do yet.

"Nothing."

"Is it Auggie?"

Amelia shook her head in disbelief.

"How do you do that?"

"I know you. And it isn't that hard to figure out. You just visited your mum and everything's okay there. Your dad is recovering nicely from his surgery, so that leaves Auggie. What'd he do this time?"

"He needed some time off from work."

"And you covered for him?" Bebe asked.

"Please, don't. I know I shouldn't have, but I'm not ready to walk away from the hotel chain yet."

Bebe reached across the table and squeezed her hand. "I don't want to make you feel worse when things are already mucked up. Tell me everything."

Amelia spent the next thirty minutes talking to Bebe about the board's ultimatum that she take over running the hotel chain if Auggie was going to continue skipping out on meetings.

"Are you going to do it?"

"I have no idea. I could run both the foundation and the hotel chain, but that would mean giving up my life. I mean, I'd have to work 24/7 to make it happen."

"You can't do that," Bebe said.

Amelia knew that. Sometimes she wished she simply were the scandalous heiress that the tabloids made her out to be because it would be so easy to walk away from it all if she were that shallow.

She needed balance and wanted her life to be more than just her charities and her family business. She wanted to come home to more than Lady Godiva and to have someone who cared about her. Someone who would take care of her the way she watched over Auggie.

"I have until the next board meeting to decide. So that's three months."

"You'll come up with a plan," Bebe said. "I'm here for you, whatever you decide. Just be sure that you're doing what's best for you."

Bebe gave her a hug as they stood up to leave. As they walked out, Amelia heard whispers about her as she passed. She put on her carefree smile and walked through the crowd. She wasn't sure she could keep that smile in place all night but she was going to try her damnedest.

Bebe was the only friend who knew there was more to her than her party-girl image and she intended to keep it that way. No matter how much time and money she donated, the media never covered that. Instead, they only printed stories about who she was seen with. She was afraid to let anyone see the real her, afraid that she'd lose a part of herself if she did, and she wouldn't be able to handle that.

Geoff seemed to be different than the other men she'd dated before but she was afraid to believe in that. Men had let her down and she had a hard time trusting her judgment as a result. For all she knew, he could be just like the rest of them.

Tonight she needed to be poised and sure of herself. She didn't want him to guess that she'd spent extra time thinking about her outfit or what she would say. She wanted him to see the woman the world thought she was. A hotel heiress with nothing on her mind but the next big party.

That would be harder than it sounded, she thought. Being that vapid took a lot of work. She smiled at the bellman as she walked into her apartment building and went up to her apartment.

Her sweet little dog was waiting for her and she scooped her up and held her close. For a minute she wished she didn't always have to be on when she walked out her front door. And she almost wished that she could let her guard down and share with Geoff how difficult it was to keep up the illusion of Amelia Munroe.

Three

Amelia laughed and all heads in the restaurant turned to look at her. Geoff was getting used to the fact that she commanded attention—and took his breath away as well. She was charming and funny, something he'd already known from the time they'd spent together in Africa. But tonight, despite the impression he'd had, she didn't even seem aware of the attention she garnered. Her focus was entirely on him.

"So there you were, caught by your superior in a compromising situation. What'd you do?"

"I told him I was doing my duty for queen and country."

She laughed again, and it was then that he realized her laughter never reached her eyes. She was laughing because the story was meant to be funny but there was something upsetting her.

"Are you all right?" he asked.

"Yes. Why do you ask?"

"Your eyes."

"My eyes?"

"Yes, I can tell that you aren't really engaged in what I'm saying. Don't get me wrong—you're a wonderful audience. But your heart isn't in it."

Those very eyes of hers widened. "How did you know?"

"I just do. What's on your mind?"

"It's not worth discussing. Especially when I'm having dinner with a sexy guy like you."

Geoff reached across the table and captured her hand. He stroked his thumb over her knuckles. "I'm more than just a guy."

"Sexy guy," she said.

He was tempted to let her distract him from the topic, but he knew this was a chance for a real conversation and he wasn't going to pass it up.

"That's not going to work. Later on, when I claim my goodnight kiss, we can talk about how sexy you think I am. But right now I want to know what's on your mind."

She turned her hand over in his and threaded their fingers together for a moment before pulling her hand back. "It's a bit heavy for a first date."

"You and I are beyond first-date stories. Tell me, Amelia."

"I have to—" She shook her head. "I can't do it. I know you mean well, but if I tell you about this, then we certainly won't be having the date you signed up for this evening."

He knew there was a lot more to this woman than met the eye. Now he was going to find out just how much more.

"Trust me. I'm very good at keeping confidences."

"Are you?"

"Yes. And no matter what else happens between us, I'd like to believe we are at least friends."

As a flash of surprise flickered in her eyes, he realized that she wanted to believe that, too.

She leaned forward. "I…how much do you know about my family?"

"We have a bit in common in our births, don't we?"

"Yes. Well, you have more in common with my brother. My parents married before I was born."

"But there was scandal around you both."

"Yes, there was," she said, then shook her head. "You really don't want to hear this. And to be honest, I don't think I want to tell you. Please, let's go back to enjoying our evening. Tell me more stories from your RAF days."

Geoff leaned back in his chair and took a sip of his wine. Letting this go would be so easy to do. It might be the gentlemanly thing to do. But he was more interested in being real than anything else. He wanted to know the girl behind the image. He wanted to be more to Amelia than every other man she'd gone out with. He wanted to know the real woman, and just now, he'd had a glimpse of her and he couldn't go back.

"I do want to know," he said quietly. "My family is complicated as well. I know that it's not always easy to balance our own lives and still take care of familial duties."

"You've just made it sound as if we have more in common than just our scandalous births?"

"We have a lot in common, love. We already know that from the time we spent in Botswana."

"I guess we do."

She cut a piece of her filet mignon and took a delicate bite. He waited, hoping that if he gave her some space and showed her he could be patient, she'd let him in, even if just a little.

After a few moments she put her fork down and leaned in close again. "I'm not sure I *can* talk about it. I don't like to."

"Just tell me what's troubling you," he said. "You can trust me." He needed to know what was on her mind. It hadn't taken him very long to figure out that Amelia was everything he'd hoped she'd be and more. She was smart and sassy and so damn sexy that he'd had a hard time keeping his mind on the conversation. Until now. She was in pain—he could see it. And he wanted to be the one to help her.

"I have to find a way to convince the board of directors at Munroe Hotels to keep my brother in his position as chairman. And I have no idea how to do it without throwing myself into running the company full time."

He was surprised. He'd expected her answer to be something else. Anything else, really, except this.

"Do you know anything about running the chain?" he asked.

"Plenty. I've done it before. But with my responsibilities at the Munroe Foundation, it's too much work to do both."

"And your brother?"

"He's not…well, simply put, he's not a man like you, Geoff."

What kind of man did she think he was?

"In what way?" he asked.

"He has never put family and his responsibilities before himself, and I have the feeling he never will," she said. "The thing I have to decide is if I'm going to keep covering for him, or let him sink and let my father's dream of keeping the hotel in our family die."

Amelia knew she was saying too much. But there was something in Geoff's beautiful, stormy blue eyes, something in the way he held himself and the way he leaned in when she talked, that invited intimacy and made her want to tell him all her secrets.

And that was dangerous.

She didn't mind sharing about Auggie and the Munroe Hotel chain, but there were other secrets that she knew she'd have to be careful to protect. Secrets that would be very damaging to her if Geoff didn't prove to be the man she was starting to believe him to be.

She doubted he had any idea that she held an MBA from Harvard, since she'd gotten her degree under her mother's maiden name to keep the paparazzi from following her there. Or that he had any clue that she'd been the one to run the chain in the late nineties since Auggie was the figurehead then. She'd kept her name off everything while her brother was in and out of rehab. Those were the type of tidbits she'd been careful to keep out of the public domain. She'd found that if anyone saw beyond the party-girl image she'd carefully cultivated they were confused, and often expected things from her she simply couldn't give.

"Why are you trying to save your brother's skin?" he asked. "Isn't he older?"

This was a mark of the man that Geoff was, she thought. That he saw her as a little sister and therefore someone who should be cherished and protected. She knew that much from watching him interact with Caroline and Gemma. Everyone knew that although the women were his half sisters, Geoff would do anything for them.

"Auggie and I are almost twins—only eleven months apart—so I don't really think of him as my older brother."

"He should," Geoff said.

She smiled at him. "I guess the rumors about you are true."

He arched one eyebrow at her. "Which rumors?"

"The ones about you putting your family first," she said. As much as she knew that many people would say she had a better family situation, Geoff had the real family, something that her parents had never managed to create.

Amelia had realized early on that having parents who were married but couldn't stand each other was hardly an advantage. And her parents' public fights had often managed to feed the fire of tabloid gossip about them.

What would it have been like to grow up with someone looking out for her?

And would that really have been any better. Because if her childhood had been different she wouldn't be the woman she was today.

And as Sandra Bullock said…"I complete me." Those words could definitely be applied to her. And she needed to remember that.

"What are you thinking?" he asked.

"I'm sorry. Let's stop talking about this. I don't need you to solve my problems."

"I don't recall offering anything more than a shoulder."

"Touché."

"I have an idea that will be beneficial to both of us," he said.

"What?" she asked.

"A venture between Munroe Hotels and Everest Air. It will give you something to take to your board of directors and it will give me a new line of revenue at Everest Air."

"Why do you need a new line of revenue?" she asked. She'd heard rumors there was a competition between the Devonshire heirs, but the details had been kept close to the brothers. Would Geoff trust her enough to tell her what was going on?

"I need an edge to make sure that my business unit outperforms Steven's and Henry's. We're competing with each other—did you know that?"

"I did. I don't know the details… You could use the paparazzi to help your cause…."

"I can't. That's not my way, but what do you think about my offer?"

"I'll think about it," she said.

There was a commotion at the front of the restaurant and she turned to see Tommy and some of his paparazzi friends scuffling with the maitre d'.

"I hope you don't mind seeing yourself in the papers," she said.

He tipped his head to the side and studied her carefully. "Why do you think they follow you around the way they do?"

"Probably because I invited their attention. When I was younger I didn't realize how my actions were goading them on. And now it's too late to get rid of them."

"Why did you court them?"

She didn't really want Geoff to know how shallow she had been. He couldn't understand that she went from being a gawky, awkward teen to a beautiful woman overnight. And the attention was heady. Once she realized that it also garnered her father's attention, she'd been unable to resist.

"I thought—that's a lie. I didn't think at all. I just lapped it up like anyone else who gets some fame after years of being overlooked. It was like a drug and I was addicted. But then things got out of control."

She thought about that YouTube video—she was topless on her yacht with several of her mother's male models. It practically looked like she was orchestrating an orgy.

After that incident, she'd known she was going to have to take control of the media. She'd learned how to use them. They wanted something salacious so they'd get paid, and she needed her name in the headlines so that when she wanted to shine a spotlight on a cause, she could get the attention she needed.

"It's very convenient to have my little media hounds with me. They follow me to Africa when I go, and I get some pictures of the real plight over there back in the papers here. It's a trade-off and right now it's worth it."

"That's a very wise strategy," he said.

"I'm not known for being wise."

"That might be because most people are fooled by the smoke and mirrors. It takes a lot of smarts to keep the world believing you are nothing more than an empty-headed heiress, doesn't it?"

She shrugged. "Don't make me out to be a saint. I do love a good party and a good time. It's simply that at some point, we all have to grow up. And when I did, I looked around and realized that the only real assets I had were my family money and the media who follow me around."

He lifted his wineglass toward her. "You are definitely my kind of woman."

She lifted her glass and took a sip of her wine. She wasn't sure why but hearing him call her his kind of woman sent a little thrill through her entire body. She wanted to pretend that he didn't matter, that he was a guy just like all the others, but tonight had proven to be so much more than just a getting-to-know-you kind of date. Tonight had shown her that he thought of her as someone worth spending time with, someone he wanted to do business with, someone he felt he could trust. And it terrified her.

Geoff paid the bill and then escorted Amelia out of the restaurant. He knew that he'd gambled by going out with her tonight but despite his reputation for putting family and duty first, he was a man who seldom denied himself the finer things in life. Amelia Munroe was definitely one of the finer things in his life.

He put his hand on the small of her back as they walked out of the restaurant. Her hips swayed with each step she took and he couldn't help but admire her figure.

She glanced over her shoulder at him, her eyes smoldering with the same desire as his. Apparently she liked the feel of his hand on her. Almost as much as he liked touching her. No matter that she was still an enigma to him, that she wasn't what he had expected, that she hadn't exactly accepted his business proposal. He needed her. He needed her in his bed and he wanted to know all her secrets.

He wanted to be the man who made her forget her public persona, her family concerns, her work. And no matter what the cost, he was going to have her.

"Amelia, over here!"

"Who's the mystery man?"

"Devonshire, give her a kiss!"

The calls continued. Geoff ignored the paparazzi as he always did—he'd barely ever given them a chance to get a good photo of him. He signaled the valet to bring his car and when it arrived, he—not the valet—held open the door for Amelia.

"Come on, Amelia. Give us something we can use," one of the men said.

She smiled up at Geoff. In that instant, he realized how luscious her lips were. All evening he'd kept his mind on the conversation by looking straight in her eyes, but now he was failing miserably. All he wanted was to taste her, to know what it felt like to feel her lips against his. And he didn't give a damn who saw them. She stood up on tiptoe and wrapped her arms around his shoulders. He leaned down, intending to give her just a buss on the mouth, but he couldn't.

Their lips brushed and he felt an electric pulse down his body straight to his groin. He wanted to groan but controlled himself. Instead, he wrapped his hand in the hair at the back of her neck and tugged gently so he could take control of the kiss.

He plunged his tongue deep into her mouth. Her taste was addictive. He couldn't lift his head—not yet. He wanted more of her. Her lips were full and soft, and that expressive mouth that he'd watched all evening was finally his.

There were catcalls and whistles. Finally he came back to himself, remembering where they were. But he didn't give a damn about any of that. He wanted to be alone with Amelia so he could keep exploring her.

He lifted his head and looked down into her wide, dazed eyes. Her lips were shiny and swollen from his kisses. For a brief moment, he thought he had her, that he'd finally figured out how to master her. But she turned her head to the photographers and blew them a kiss before getting into the car. She was amazing, completely unpredictable. Dangerous.

He walked around the front of his car and seated himself, pulling away from the photographers calmly, though his gut instinct was to put the pedal to the floor.

Amelia made him forget the rules he always lived by, made him forget that he'd always tried to escape scandal by living above reproach. For once in his life, he didn't give a damn about that.

"You are a dangerous man, Geoff Devonshire," she said.

He spared a glance for her as he downshifted and saw that she held her fingers to her lips. She was staring pensively out the windshield and he wondered if she was playing a game that was getting out of control.

"If you play me like that again, you will regret it."

"I already do," she said. "You make it too easy to forget my own rules."

He almost laughed, and refrained from commenting on how similar they were.

"I'm surprised you'd admit that."

"Why wouldn't I? It's the truth. I don't think we should see each other again," she said.

"Like hell we shouldn't," he replied. "I'm not letting you go yet."

"I think I have some say in the matter," she said dryly.

He put his hand on her arm, feeling the shiver that went through her body.

"You are no more ready to walk away from me than I am from you. We have unfinished business," he said. "And if you want to lie and pretend that we don't, you are welcome to try, but your body is telling me a different story."

She reached over to his thigh and ran her fingers up the inside of his leg. He felt the lightest touch of her fingers against his erection and shuddered. He wanted her hands on his naked flesh. He wanted his mouth all over her naked body.

"You're right," she said in a low husky voice that made him even harder.

"Then we're agreed."

"Agreed?"

"That this isn't going to end until I'm buried hilt-deep in your sexy little body."

"Geoff, I'm not sure that's a good idea."

He pulled off the road, onto the lay-by, stopped the car and leaned across the gearshift. He took what he needed and gave what she wanted, kissing her until he felt as if he were going to explode if he couldn't explore more than her mouth.

When he lifted his head, she was breathing heavily and her hands were on his shoulders, trying to draw him back to her. She stared up at him with lust in her eyes and just a hint of panic that made him wonder if this was a mistake.

But it was too late now—there was no turning back. Amelia Munroe was going to be his and they both knew it.

Four

The kiss was beyond anything that Amelia had expected. Her body responded with ferocity and she had no say in the matter. Mr. Darcy had nothing on Geoff Devonshire when it came to sex appeal. He pulled the car back onto the highway and she realized she had no idea where they were going.

"Where are you taking me?" she asked. "I didn't even realize we'd left London proper."

"I'm taking an easier route. I was planning to take you home, unless you had something else in mind. I'd love to take you flying."

"Not tonight," she said. "What did you think I'd have in mind? I don't have an exotic love nest in the country, if that's what you're asking."

"Which wouldn't exactly be exotic," he said.

"I think I've just proved my point."

"Which is what, precisely?" he asked with a smile.

She shrugged. "I guess that I'm not what you might think."

"Love, I discovered that last night," he said. There was a kind and gentle note to his words that warmed her.

"Last night I thought you were a bit of a…"

"Prick?"

She laughed. Dammit, life would be a lot easier if Geoff were a jerk. "Maybe, but you did redeem yourself tonight."

"Did I?" he asked. "How? By kissing you?"

She didn't say anything for a few minutes. When she didn't like the way a conversation was going, she simply stopped it. It was avoidance, pure and simple, but she found that it was her only option. Her defenses disappeared around this man and it made her feel lost.

"Tell me."

"You're very bossy. I suspect it's because you're an older brother."

"Perhaps. But rumor has it I was bossy even before the girls came along."

"Truly? How interesting."

"Is your brother bossy?" he asked. He took the exit that led to her Hyde Park apartment.

"Auggie? No, he's demanding but that's not the same as bossy."

"No, it isn't. I have been called demanding as well," he said.

She could see that. Geoff was refined and very polite, but there was that underlying will in him that said he liked to have things his way. Like the way he'd kissed her. He had taken no prisoners and left her a mass of aching need. She wasn't used to that in the least, but she didn't mind it—in fact, his aggressive nature was becoming quite a turn-on. He wasn't the kind of man she could run circles around, like most of the others. Geoff would always want to be in charge and for once in her life, she was ready to loosen the reins a little.

"I'm a bit bossy at times myself," she confessed.

"More than a bit. The last meeting we had at your foundation, I heard you barking orders like the CEO of a major corporation."

"So if I tell you to drop and give me twenty…?"

"I'll drop and give you twenty of whatever you want, Amelia."

She felt her face flush and the ache in her body intensified. She couldn't think about anything but getting his lips on her again as they approached the high-rise apartment building she lived in.

"Want to come up?"

"I'd love to," he said.

"You can leave your car in the garage," she said.

He parked in one of the spots reserved for guests and then came around to open her door. When he reached down to offer her his hand, she had butterflies in her stomach. Geoff was different—something about him practically made her feel like a nervous schoolgirl. Granted, she wasn't used to such gentlemanly behavior. She knew she wasn't going to have to worry about him wanting her to do something kinky so he could brag about it to his friends. Guys like that she could handle because she knew exactly what to expect from them— they were a dime a dozen. But not Geoff.

Her imagination began to run away with her. She was hoping that in the morning he'd still be in her bed. And they'd wake up together and have breakfast.

No, she thought. *I'd better get a hold of myself before this gets way out of hand and I show him too much.*

She used her key card to activate the elevator in the main building. Geoff kept his hand on the small of her back as they waited. His fingers were fanned out and he made a small circle with his index finger that made her entire lower body start to pulse.

"You didn't have to invite me up," he said.

"I know."

A few years ago, after the video turned up on YouTube and she'd been hounded by men who assumed she was kinky, she'd established a new rule for herself—no sex on the first date. But she wasn't sure she was going to be able to stick to that rule tonight.

A part of her believed that if she didn't do it now, she might never be brave enough to let him this close again. She knew tomorrow she'd have regrets that stemmed from letting him see too much of the woman she was.

She'd have to find a way to put distance between them again, to convince him that she was just an heiress who liked a lot of attention. And the only way to do that was to take what she wanted tonight and walk away tomorrow.

But that was tomorrow. Tonight he was hers and she vowed to enjoy every second.

Amelia's penthouse was an eclectic mix of classical and modern styles. She had sleek Japanese tables and plush Italian leather sofas in her living area. The floor-to-ceiling wall of glass that overlooked London allowed the viewer to see all the way to Buckingham Palace.

On the wall was a large Monet from the artist's time in Argenteuil. On another wall was a painting of Amelia done in the Andy Warhol "Marilyn Monroe" style, with four of the same images in different colors.

Her small dog bounded out of the bedroom as soon as she'd walked in the door.

"How's my Lady Godiva?" Amelia asked, bending over to pet her dog.

The miniature Dachshund stood on her back legs with her tail wagging. Amelia scooped the little dog up and brought her over toward him.

"This is Lady Godiva. Godiva, this is Geoff," Amelia said.

He scratched the dog under her chin. Amelia set the dog down. "Go to bed," she commanded.

The little dog trotted off to a large pillow in the corner and circled around several times before lying down.

"Impressive," Geoff said.

Amelia smiled. "Would you like a drink?" she asked.

"Yes," he said.

She went to a wet bar in the corner and reached under the counter. "Cognac?"

"I'd enjoy one."

She gestured toward the sofa. "You can have a seat over there, or if you'd like, the stairs in the corner lead to my rooftop garden."

"I'll wait for you," he said.

She took out two large snifters and warmed them in her hands before pouring in a generous portion of the dark-colored liquor. She carried the drinks over to where he waited. He was watching her closely and she felt the butterflies fluttering again.

She handed him a drink and they toasted.

"To this evening."

"To us," she said. "I think the garden will be nice tonight, since it's not raining and not too cloudy. Want to give it a try?"

"I'd love to."

She led the way to her sanctuary, knowing full well that it was only a matter of time before her need would get the better of her.

He followed her up the wrought-iron staircase that was in the corner of the living room. She climbed up steadily in her high heels. He tried to do the gentlemanly thing and not stare up her skirt as she climbed but it was hard to resist looking. After all, he'd been thinking about what was under her skirt all night.

The cognac was good but it didn't taste as addictive as her mouth. He wanted to taste her again. But since they'd entered her apartment she'd been keeping her distance, and he was going to let her have all the space she needed. It was enough that he was here with her.

She opened the door to the rooftop garden and stepped out into the night. He followed her, breathing in the heavy air. It was crisp and cool, and smelled like spring. There was a hint of rain but also the scent of blooming flowers.

She hit a button on the wall and small lights lit up the area. A fountain started filling the night with the gentle sound of flowing water. He looked around the garden oasis that he was standing in—from here it was hard to tell he was in the middle of one of the busiest cities in the world.

"I like this."

"I'm glad. I needed a place to escape to when I couldn't get away so I created this area."

"You created it?"

"I did all the work except the heavy lifting. I figured if it was going to be my retreat I didn't want anyone else up here. If I had workers helping, they'd sell the story to some paper and then I wouldn't have any peace."

He stepped closer to her and rubbed the back of her neck. Her life did take a toll on her, clearly. And he didn't want to add to the stress.

"I'm honored that you are sharing it with me."

"Count yourself lucky. I don't let just anyone up here."

"Why me?"

"You're different," she said, closing her eyes for a moment as his fingers stroked her neck and shoulders. Then she pulled away and walked toward the bench nestled in the trees near the fountain.

He followed her slowly. Amelia was different here in her garden. She wouldn't look directly at him, and it struck him that she was vulnerable.

She'd invited him to the place where she let down her guard and he wondered if she had second thoughts now.

"This is the second secret you've shown me tonight."

"What was the first?" she asked, looking at him carefully.

"That you are more than the shallow socialite. This is the real Amelia Munroe, and I feel very privileged that you brought me here."

"Come sit with me."

"Are you sure?"

She nodded.

He did as she asked. The bench was a solid wrought-iron frame with a thick padded cushion. He sipped his cognac and wrapped an arm around her.

"Do you wish you hadn't invited me up here?"

She shook her head and the silky strands of her thick hair brushed against his neck as she turned her face toward him.

"I'm not sure what to do now. With anyone else I'd be a little drunk and I wouldn't be thinking so much."

He wondered how often she drank simply to endure her life or merely because it was expected of her. He suddenly felt the need to protect her, shield her from what the world expected her to be.

"Really?"

She shrugged. "In the old days. I haven't brought a guy home in a long time."

He arched an eyebrow at her. "You've been seen with men lately."

"You and I both know that being *seen* with someone has nothing to do with actually *being* with someone."

He took their glasses and put them on the ground by their feet. Then he took her beautiful face in his hands, rubbing his thumb over the blade of her cheek and down to the full curve of her bottom lip.

"That's very true," he said, leaning in for the kiss that he felt like he'd waited ages to claim.

It wasn't the dramatic, lust-filled kiss he'd given her in front of the restaurant. It was deep and steady, and made promises that he wasn't ready to vocalize but that he couldn't help making with his lips. This woman was special and he wanted her in his arms for a very long time.

Amelia knew that inviting Geoff to her place wasn't the wisest decision she had ever made, but she didn't regret it. She'd had learned fairly early on that if she was going to be able to live in her own skin she couldn't regret anything. She'd have to just learn from it and move on.

Being in Geoff's arms felt too good for her to think about regrets. His hands skimmed up and down her back and she shivered with awareness as his mouth moved over hers.

He was touching her with such skill and tenderness that her head was spinning. He was passionate. And commanding. Everything that he was in business she realized he was in life.

She'd made a mistake in judging him. The way he'd probably made a mistake in judging her.

What if he expected something exotic from her? Thanks to the media's interpretation of the video that ended up on YouTube, past lovers had expected some strange things from her.

She pulled back. "Did you see that video?"

He stared down at her, his brooding eyes unreadable, and she wondered if this would be the moment that he left. Was this going to be the one thing that would make him think poorly of her?

Why had she brought it up?

"I haven't. I'm not the kind of man who bothers with things like that."

"Oh, well, it was a long time ago. I mean I know that everyone thinks it just happened yesterday but I was a lot younger."

She was babbling. She couldn't help it. Every part of her was outraged that the video had been shared the way it had. She hated that everyone thought they knew intimate details about her because of one mistake.

"Amelia, love, you don't have to explain anything. I've done things in my past that I wouldn't want the world to watch online. What you and I share together has nothing to do with a video."

He kissed her so softly and tenderly then that she almost wept. She felt like he was truly kissing her, Amelia, not some idea or expectation of her.

He was healing a part of her she hadn't realized needed to be healed. She wrapped her arms around his shoulders and tunneled her fingers into the thick hair at the nape of his neck. She held him to her, realizing in that moment that she didn't want him to let her go.

She needed this more than she'd expected. When his mouth moved over hers and his hands explored her body she didn't care about the what-ifs—she didn't want to think about tomorrow or about consequences. She just wanted to feel.

She touched the buttons at the top of his shirt and undid them while he caressed her from shoulder blade to breast and back again. He found the zipper in the side of her dress and drew it down slowly. Every caress seemed to last longer than the first. And the feel of his hands on her body was an exquisite torture that she couldn't get enough of.

She reached for the neckline of her dress, wanting the fabric out of the way so that she could feel his hands on her flesh, but he stopped her.

"Not so fast. I wish to savor you."

She shivered at the note of lust in his voice. No one had ever wanted to make slow love to her before.

"I want your hands on me."

"They are," he said, running his hands down her back, spanning her waist and bringing them back to her front.

She realized that he wasn't going to be hurried. He would take his time until he drove her insane with pleasure. Two can play at this game, she thought, reaching for the buttons of his shirt again and undoing the rest of them.

She pushed the fabric open and finally had her hands on his chest. It was well muscled and lightly dusted with hair. She ran her fingers from his neck to his waistband, following the line of his sternum. She lightly scraped her nails down his chest and he shuddered as her touch moved over his abdomen.

"Do you like that?"

"Yes," he growled.

She smiled to herself as she reached lower, stroking his erection through the fabric of his pants. He grew harder and longer under her fingers as she found his zipper. But instead of lowering it, she simply stroked him harder through his pants. His hips shifted, following her touch, and she leaned forward to kiss his chest.

He smelled so good. She took a deep breath of

his unique scent—she'd never smelled anything so wonderful in her entire life.

His hands were back on her body, slipping inside the opening of her dress and finding the clasp of her bra between her shoulder blades. He kept one hand there, splayed across her back as he drew her forward. The other hand pulled the loosened dress away from her body.

"Take your arms out of this dress," he said, his voice shot through with desire.

She followed his commands. He pushed the bodice of her dress and her bra straps down until she was naked from the waist up. The night air caressed her bare skin as she studied his face.

He held her wrists loosely in both hands and stared down at her. She wondered if she was pleasing to him— every man liked something different in a woman's body. She hoped he got as much pleasure from looking at her as she did from seeing him.

He brought his free hand up to her mouth and touched her lips before drawing one finger down her body. He traced the line of her collarbone and then moved lower. His fingers fanned out to caress her chest and then the full globes of her breasts.

Her nipples tightened and she wanted to feel his fingers on them. She shifted her shoulders but again she was reminded that he wouldn't be hurried. When he could tell she liked what he was doing, he seemed to slow his pace even more, making her whole body ache with desire.

His hands spread down her back, bringing her forward until the tips of her nipples brushed against his chest.

She shivered as her blood began to run heavier. He held her firmly in his arms, making very sure that she stayed where he wanted her to. She tipped her head back and met his dark blue eyes.

"Are you sure this is what you want?" he asked her.

She couldn't really think—all she could do was feel and every atom of her being cried out for Geoff. She nodded.

"You have to say it. Before this goes any further, do you want me, Amelia?"

She reached up and cupped his strong jaw in both her hands. Then she leaned in and spoke her words against his lips.

"Yes, Geoff. I want you."

Five

Geoff had never held a woman like Amelia. She made him feel alive in a way that he had never experienced before. And now he was going to claim her for his own. A part of him felt that she was already his, that he wouldn't feel this strongly about a woman who wasn't meant to be in his arms.

He took control of the soft kiss she had initiated and brought his hands to her nipples at the same time. She moaned in the back of her throat, inflaming him even more.

He teased her with soft touches at first, running the pads of his fingers over her aureole. Then, when he felt her nipple bead under his finger, he scraped her lightly with his nail.

She tightened her hands on his shoulders and

pulled her mouth from his. Her head fell back and he hesitated.

"Do you like that?" he asked, wanting to be sure that he wasn't hurting her.

"Yessss."

He continued to caress her breasts and brought his mouth down the side of her jaw. He dropped nibbling kisses on her neck and when he reached the base of it, he suckled gently right over her pulse.

She came alive then. Her hands grasped him and her body moved over his until she straddled him. Her skirt pulled taut at her knees and she moaned in frustration.

He slid his hands under the skirt of her dress, pulling it up to her waist. She wore only a minute pair of bikini panties and he slipped his hands under them to cup her buttocks.

He moved one hand forward and felt the humid warmth at her center. He could no longer resist, rubbing one finger up and down her slit over her panties until she was moaning his name.

"What do you want?" he asked, whispering in her ear.

She shivered and shifted her body against his hand, trying to increase the strength of each stroke of her feminine center.

"You. Geoff, I want you."

"Not yet," he said, carefully moving her panties to the side so he could touch her bare flesh.

She made a soft sound when he touched her skin. He tugged harder on her panties and ripped the delicate fabric from her body.

"You owe me…"

"I'm going to give you an orgasm to make up for it," he said.

She gasped at his blunt words and a flush spread across her face.

He smiled to himself. He'd never had a woman whose passion matched his as perfectly as Amelia's did. She reached between them, grasped his zipper and freed his erection.

He felt the warmth of her center spilling over on him—it made him so hot and hard, he felt as if he would explode at any second.

But he wasn't ready to come yet.

He wanted her to have so much pleasure that she'd be addicted to him the way he was quickly becoming addicted to her.

"I have to tell you I'm unprepared," he confessed. He hadn't brought a condom with him since he hadn't anticipated this ending to the evening. "Are you protected?"

"Yes, I am," she said.

"Thank God."

She laughed. "Why, would you have been upset if we'd had to stop?"

He took both of her nipples in his hands and pinched lightly. She moaned and moved against him, her slit sliding over his erection.

"I don't think I could have handled that."

"Take me, Geoff. Make me yours."

He shifted his hips until the tip of his penis was at the entrance to her body, but he held still.

"Once you are mine there is no going back," he said.

"What do you mean?"

"This isn't a one-time thing. I'm not like the other men you've dated."

"This isn't the time for a conversation," she said, groaning, rubbing herself against him.

He put his hands on her hips and started to draw her forward as he thrust up into her body. She was tight, fitting around him like a velvet glove. She squeezed him so tightly that he had to stop and breathe to keep from spilling himself with just one stroke.

He held her hips as she tried to move and set about bringing her to the brink. He bent and caught the tip of her breast in his mouth. His tongue teased her nipple and he used the very edge of his teeth on her until she was clutching at his shoulders and frantically trying to move her hips in his hands.

He heard her long moan and then felt the minute tightening of her inner muscles as an orgasm ripped through her body. Only then did he let go of her hips and thrust up into her with all his strength. He took her mouth as he felt that telltale tingling at the bottom of his spine.

His orgasm was coming and he looked up into her eyes to find them half opened. He knew she was on the verge of coming again. He reached between their bodies and found the center of her pleasure, stroking her until he heard those sexy gasping sounds again that made him want to explode.

"Come for me," he said.

She did. He came a moment later, spilling himself inside her. He wrapped his arms around her back as she collapsed against his chest. He held her tight, resting his head on top of hers and realizing that he didn't know if he was ever going to be able to let her go.

Amelia couldn't catch her breath and didn't want to. Geoff's arms around her were solid and he held her close, as if she might disappear if he didn't. She loved it. She had wanted to find a man who would make her feel cherished for as long as she could remember, and it might be self-delusion, but right now, she felt cherished.

She felt Geoff sliding out of her body and the sweat on his chest was starting to dry, but he continued to hold her. She stayed where she was with her face resting against his neck and forgot that there was a world outside his arms.

The longer he held her, the more reluctant she was to actually get up. But she knew she couldn't stay in his arms forever. So she made herself do it.

She lifted her head, intent on disentangling herself from him. But he kissed her when she looked down at him. It was a soft, gentle kiss but she could still feel the passion that had flared between them.

"Where do you think you're going?" he said.

"I just need a second," she answered, suddenly feeling very exposed. This was much more than that fragile emotion she'd experienced when she'd brought him into her home for the first time. This was too intense. She had no idea what to do or say next.

She wanted him to stay—wanted to spend the night in his arms—but this was a first date. Dammit, this was another reason why sex on the first date was a mistake. If you truly cared about the person, things could get very complicated very quickly.

She used his shoulders for balance, climbed off his lap and stood next to the bench. Her dress started to fall to the ground but he caught it as he stood up and helped her with it. He wrapped one big arm around her shoulders and kissed her again. He kept her tucked under his arm.

"Shall we go back inside then?" he said.

She nodded. He reached down, tucking himself in his pants and fastening just the button. Then he lifted her into his arms.

"What are you doing?"

"Carrying you," he said.

"Why?"

"Because I'm not ready to let go of you yet."

He carried her down the stairs into her apartment. She gave him directions to the master en suite bathroom and he set her on her feet next to the sink. The bathroom was large and luxurious, something she'd insisted on when she'd had it designed.

"Would you care for a bath?" he asked.

"Geoff, you are going to spoil me."

"It's the least I can do. I did ruin your panties," he said.

She flushed, remembering how the sound of the ripping fabric had made her so wanton in his arms. "Yes, you did."

He adjusted the taps on the large tub and let the water run. She stepped out of her dress as Geoff quietly undressed next to her. She opened a jar of bath salts and poured a small scoop into the warm water.

She turned on the towel-warming rack and got an extra towel out for him. As silly as it sounded, she'd never bathed with another person before. Geoff seemed at home, though, and that put her at ease. He held her hand and helped her into the tub, then climbed in after her.

He settled himself back against the wall and drew her down so that her back was pressed to his chest. Then he took the loofah sponge she had on the tray next to the bathtub and poured some bath gel onto it. Her skin tingled in anticipation.

"Tell me more about growing up. How did you become a world-famous heiress?"

She tipped her head back against his shoulder and looked up at him, trying to see if he was teasing her, but his expression was sincere. "I think I'm more infamous."

"No, you aren't," he said. "Tell me."

"What do you know about me?" she asked. "I take it you don't want the story of my birth."

He laughed, a deep rumbling sound that echoed off the bathroom walls. "No, I don't. I know your father is Augustus Munroe and your mother is Mia Domenici, the legendary fashion designer."

"My father was married when he met my mother, but they have what she calls 'fiery passion,' and that, apparently, is something that can never be denied."

"It can't?" Geoff asked.

She shook her head, realizing that she understood now what her mother had meant. She'd never experienced passion like it until Geoff. Why him? What draws people to each other in such an extreme way? She was sure her own mother wondered why Gus Munroe had inspired that kind of passion in her.

"Have you experienced it?" he asked.

"Only once," she said. She didn't want to reveal that she was thinking of him, of what had just happened between them. She had no idea what this all meant to him. Perhaps she was just another woman to pass the time with until he found someone suitable to be his wife.

He stroked the sponge over her body. She knew she shouldn't want him again so soon but every time the sponge brushed over her breasts she felt an answering pulse between her legs.

"Have you experienced it?" she asked him.

"Define it for me," he said.

She shrugged. She didn't know how to put it into words without revealing that he was the man who'd inspired it in her. She really hoped that her affair with Geoff didn't turn out as disastrously as her parents' relationship had. Despite their marriage, they had never found the happily-ever-after that Amelia wanted for herself. She wondered if passion precluded happiness.

She hoped not.

"I don't really know how to put it into words. I only know that in my parents' case, it wasn't enough. They need each other desperately but can't live together."

"Sounds painful. Did you understand that as a child?"

She shook her head. "No I didn't. Auggie and I often felt as if we were on a sailboat in the rough sea, trying desperately to keep ourselves from capsizing."

Amelia had the sensation once again that she was revealing way too much. She decided to close her eyes—and her mouth—and revel in the feel of his touch, however long it lasted.

Geoff wanted to protect Amelia but she was a woman who had always scorned the protection of others, hadn't she? That had been his impression. Listening to her talk about her childhood, however, made him believe that she'd always had to make her own way and figure everything out on her own.

"I don't remember seeing much of you in the papers when you were a child," he said vaguely, fishing for information from her. He already knew that if he demanded it she'd simply clam up and tell him nothing.

"I spent most of my childhood in New York, but frankly, they weren't at all interested in me until I turned eighteen. I'm afraid to say I was a bit of an ugly duckling."

"There's no way I could believe that," he said.

She lifted one of her delicate shoulders. "Well, I was. I had braces and glasses. I was just about as awkward as a young girl can get, much to my father's great disappointment."

She was rambling a little and he realized she did that when she was nervous. "I'm sure you were lovely."

She shook her head. "You say that now but if you had met me back then, you wouldn't have even noticed me."

"That's where you're wrong," he said. "I have two sisters. If you were half as awkward as they were, I would have gone over to talk to you just to let you know you weren't alone."

She looked up at him, those wide weary eyes of hers trying to see if he was telling the truth. He hoped she could read the sincerity in his eyes. "So you became a sexy young woman and the paparazzi just swarmed around you?"

She laughed, a very sweet sound that made him want to hug her closer.

"Not exactly. I wore a very sexy dress that my mother had designed for me to my then-boyfriend's film premiere. And when they took photos of Andy and me, people started asking who I was. And Andy told them. We went to a few more functions together and then we broke up. But the paparazzi were still following me and at the time, I liked it. And so did my parents—it kept the family name in the public eye."

Andy was Andrew Hollings, one of the hottest directors in Hollywood. She lived in the world of celebrity and for a second, he wondered how a British peer measured up. But based on the way she'd responded to him, he didn't think he'd been found wanting.

He and Amelia were electric together. He had thought maybe there was fiery passion between them because of that addictive thing he felt for her. But he supposed it was just the newness of lust that made him feel that way.

He finished washing her, feeling himself harden as he touched her. He wanted her again. And he knew he'd take her another time tonight.

But not now. He wanted to know more about Amelia than how her body reacted to his touch. He wanted to know the secrets behind her eyes. He needed to find out every detail of her past and present.

Damn, he was obsessed.

How had that happened? It was sometime between the restaurant and here. Probably when she'd taken him out on her rooftop garden and shown him her own private hideaway—and let him into her luscious body. He struggled to focus.

"Is that when you decided to use the paparazzi?" he asked.

"This is going to make me sound like a spoiled brat, but please keep in mind that I was young and not very mature," she said.

"I will."

"Every time I had a photo in the papers or showed up on TV, my father would call me. I was speaking to him more than I had in my entire life. And though the conversations weren't meaningful, I finally had his attention."

"And you weren't about to give it up," Geoff concluded.

"That's right. I don't know what your relationship is with your parents, but I was largely forgotten. Auggie and Dad were close because they play polo together. But Mom was always in Milan and I was not very… fashionable, so I didn't fit in."

He suspected that having been left alone so much of the time was one of the reasons she was able to project such a strong sense of self—one of the many qualities that made her attractive to the public.

"Were you lonely?"

"A little, but not too much. I was at boarding school and then camps for most of the year. And my friend Bebe always invited me home with her for holidays."

"My childhood was similar," he said. "Except I was usually the one inviting mates home for the holidays."

"I don't know a lot about your upbringing. Caroline and Gemma are your half sisters?"

"Yes. My mother is Princess Louisa and my father is Malcolm Devonshire. They never married."

"I did know that. I heard that you and your half brothers were summoned to Malcolm's office by that attorney of his, Edmond. Is that an odd occurrence?"

"Do you know Edmond?" Geoff asked, surprised.

"I know of him," she replied. "He's one of my mother's friend's lawyers."

Geoff didn't want to talk about his brothers, but he couldn't continue to ignore her question. "It was the first time we'd met in person."

"That's odd. Why?"

"I'm not sure exactly. My mother is very sensitive to the subject of Malcolm's other sons, so I never brought up anything about them."

She turned in his arms to face him. "I'm sorry."

"Why?"

"Because that means you had no brothers to share with, to tell what was going on in your life. I don't imagine you had a close confidant as I did in Bebe."

"I had my half sisters eventually," he said. "I have a good life."

"I know. But you still missed out on that ideal childhood that everyone craves."

"Everyone?"

"Yes, we all pretend it doesn't matter that we didn't have our parents' attention but we all know it does. Our crazy childhoods shaped us into the adults we are."

She was wise, this sexy little heiress of his. He kissed her to get her mind out of the past and back in the present. He didn't want to admit that she might be right. He didn't want to give Malcolm any more control over his life than the man already had.

And when he had a naked Amelia in his arms he wanted to be focused on her and he wanted her attention on him. "I'm tired of talking."

"What do you want to do?" she asked, wrapping those long fingers around his head and pulling him down for a long, lingering kiss.

"I have a few ideas," he said in a growl.

"Do you?"

"Indeed," he said. "Why don't you show me your bedroom?"

He wrapped a warm towel around her and picked her up again, carrying her into the bedroom. He set her on the center of the bed and came down on top of her.

Six

Geoff woke to the sound of his mobile phone ringing. He reached for the device on his bedside table and hit a glass of water that spilled everywhere. He jerked upright in bed.

He was at Amelia's. She had propped herself up on one arm and was staring at him through a mass of tangled curly hair. Her lips were swollen and the sheet fell to her waist, baring her breasts. He forgot about the ringing phone and the water. Instead, he reached forward and touched her, running his finger down the centerline of her body and around her breasts.

"You're gorgeous."

She blushed and he saw that the color started just above her breasts and went up over her face. He leaned down to kiss her when his mobile phone started ringing again.

"Get that," she said in an amused tone.

He reached for his phone. "I spilled some water."

"I'll take care of it," she said.

He had managed not to knock the water over onto his phone. He glanced at the caller ID and saw that it was his mother.

"Hi, Mum."

"Geoff, we need to talk."

"Is it about the party? I already spoke to Caro. No one is going to follow me to Hampshire. The paparazzi are content to follow Henry around—he's the one who lives a life worthy of their headlines."

"Not anymore, darling. Have you seen *The Sun* today?"

"No," he said. "I don't normally read it." If his mother was asking about the paper, that could only mean one thing. "Is there a picture of Caro and that footballer she's dating?"

"No, Geoff, there isn't. There's a photo of you with Amelia Munroe. And I have to say you are giving them a lot to talk about."

"Mum—"

"Don't. Don't say anything. You can't justify your actions by saying that a girl like that is used to the attention."

"I wouldn't say that."

"Good. Because even socialites have feelings, Geoff. Every woman deserves to be treated with respect. Are you going to see her again?"

"Mum, I don't want to discuss this with you."

"Are you still at her place?" his mother asked.

"As I said, I don't want to discuss this."

"Make sure she understands where you stand. Don't lead her on, Geoff."

This was probably as close as he and his mother were ever going to get to discussing how she'd felt when it had been revealed that Malcolm had been dating two other women while he had been wooing her. "I would never do that. Amelia is different."

"Than who?"

"Everyone," he said.

Amelia had come back into the room. He did want to protect her from the scandal that the media attention could bring, but in this case, he guessed she might be better at dealing with it than he was. He would ignore it and the stories would go away. But for Amelia it was a way of life.

"I want to talk to you about this later. Why don't you bring her to dinner this weekend at your place in Bath?"

"I'll call you later. I love you, Mum."

"I love you, too, but we aren't finished with this."

He hung up and took Amelia's arm, drawing her down onto his side of the bed. He pulled her head down to his and kissed her. "Good morning."

"Is it good?" she asked.

"Indeed. It's very good," he said. He wrapped both arms around her, intent on making love to her before he went anywhere this morning. But his mobile phone rang again.

"You are one popular man. Why don't you answer that while I make us some coffee?" she asked. She walked naked across the room to the armoire and removed a pale blue dressing gown, which she wrapped around her body.

"How do you take your coffee?"

"Black," he said.

"I'll be right back."

"You don't have to leave," he said.

She raised a brow at him. "Yes, I do. They are all calling about me, right?"

"It's probably one of my sisters. The photo of our kiss is apparently in *The Sun* this morning."

She wrapped her arms around her waist in a defensive posture. Instantly, she seemed miles away from him. "That's nothing new for me. Are you okay?"

"Sure. There isn't anything to the story. It will fade away in a few days."

"It will?" she asked.

"Of course. I've found that if I don't give them anything to print, they grow bored with me and move on to something else."

She nodded. "I'll go get the coffee started."

She walked away and he could tell that something wasn't right. He had said something that had upset her.

He got out of bed, leaving his ringing mobile phone on the table, and padded naked to her kitchen. She was leaning against the counter staring at the granite surface as if it held a mystery she had to figure out. But when she sensed him, she busied herself with putting dog food in a bowl for Godiva and filling up her water dish. She set them both on a mat on the floor.

"Talk to me, Amelia. Tell me why you're upset," he said.

She looked at him, biting her lip for a moment. Then she shrugged. "I was hoping you and I would last longer than one night," she said. "But I guess we can't. We'd be all over the news constantly, and I know how much you'd hate that."

He pulled her into his arms and kissed her long and hard. He wasn't ready to walk away and he sure as hell wasn't going to let her walk away, either.

"When I said the story would fade in a few days, I meant *the press* would lose interest, Amelia, not that *I* would. I couldn't lose interest now if my life depended on it. We'll just have to keep a low profile."

Amelia wasn't too sure she wanted to keep a low profile. If she vanished from the public eye, would she still have any influence? She had always lived her life by her own rules. Now she realized that if she was going to be with Geoff, she'd have to adapt.

"I don't know if I can," she admitted honestly.

"Are you willing to try?"

She pushed the button on her coffeepot and put her Van Gogh mug underneath the spout. She reached above her head and took down a matching one for Geoff.

She handed him the black coffee when it was ready and took a sip of her mocha latte.

"You are asking me to change the way I normally operate," she said.

"Is that too much? I think it's justified," he said.

Of course he would. He didn't need the media to make his life manageable to keep the family business running smoothly, to garner free publicity for his causes—and to make his father happy.

"I'll try," she said at last.

"That's all I ask," he said, moving to her and taking her in his arms.

"You are still naked," she mentioned.

"Does that turn you on?" he asked.

There was something playful about him this morning. She wanted to smile but she couldn't. She'd overheard enough of his conversation to know that his mother had been concerned about that photo. And she was sure that wasn't a good thing.

"Let's go back to bed."

She shook her head. "I can't. I have to go to the Munroe offices this morning."

"To fix the problems left by your brother?"

"Yes," she said.

"Have you given my proposition any thought?" he asked.

"I haven't exactly had my mind on business, now have I?" she replied as he kissed her neck.

Geoff took her by the hand, leading the way back into her bedroom.

She watched his tush as he walked in front her. He was one fine-looking man naked. He wasn't hard-bodied like a weight lifter but he was in shape and everything was perfectly proportioned. She reached for him, wanting to touch him, when he turned around.

"What are you doing?"

"Admiring your backside," she admitted, reaching around and cupping his butt. "You have a very nice one."

He flushed, which made her smile. "Should we talk

a little business, or should we talk about my bum some more?"

"What's your proposition again? I'm a little distracted right now."

"I propose that we do a joint business venture, maybe some luxury vacation packages that would partner Everest Air with the Munroe Hotels. It would distract the board from Auggie's issues and we'd get to spend a lot of time together."

"So we'd work on this together?"

"Indeed we would. In fact, I think we should meet about it right now."

"In my bed?" she asked.

"Yes."

"I'm being serious, Geoff."

"Me, too. Let me make love to you and then I'll take you to breakfast and we can discuss the details."

Standing in her bedroom with light streaming in from the tinted windows, she had a hard time saying no to him. She wanted to be in his arms, but she had no idea if she should entangle herself further or escape.

This morning she was making business deals and promises and she wasn't sure why. Hell, that was a lie. She knew why. Geoff was too much a man for her to let him go this soon.

For the first time, she'd met a man she wanted to spend more than one night with. She'd met a man she wanted to get to know better. She wanted to see if their lives would blend, if she could change the way she lived so they could be together.

She'd met a man who had the potential to make her fall in love with him. It was as simple as that.

That should be the warning signal, she thought. That one reason should send her running away. Instead, she found herself slipping her dressing gown off her shoulders and letting it fall to the floor.

She pushed against Geoff's chest and he walked backward to the bed. He fell back and pulled her down with him.

She straddled his body and kissed him as his hands came up to rove all over her back and down to her butt. He murmured sexy words into her ear, which turned her on.

He positioned himself at the entrance of her body and she felt just the tip of his erection inside her. She rocked her hips and took him all the way inside. He felt so right inside her that she could scarcely breathe.

Last night she'd thought it had just been the magic of their first time making love, but he still felt right. He wrapped his arms around her and rolled over in one swift motion so she was underneath him. He took her face in his hands and kissed her long and deep as his hips kept driving into her until she realized she was going to come.

It happened quickly, taking her by surprise. He smiled down at her as she gasped, then he started pumping faster into her. A minute later, he came with a deep groan. She wrapped her arms and legs around him and held him with a strength that she hoped he didn't notice.

She was in deep trouble. She already cared for Geoff. She already wanted him to stay by her side and be the man she'd always secretly wanted to find.

And she knew that if he disappointed her, she wasn't going to recover from it easily.

* * *

Geoff left Amelia's to go home and get showered and changed. They were going to meet at his office midmorning to discuss the joint venture. As he entered his house, it felt strangely empty to him and he realized that he wanted to bring her here. He wanted to see her in his home.

This was getting out of control. He was as randy as he'd been at eighteen and no matter how many times he had Amelia, he still wanted her again, as if it were the first time.

She enchanted him. There was no other word for it. He was caught completely in her web. Everything about her just made him want her more.

He was aware that he had to walk a fine line here, and handle mixing his personal and professional life with care. He would keep Amelia and himself out of the spotlight from now on. He could do that if she agreed to it. It would be important for their new venture to project the right image.

He checked his mobile phone as he got out of the shower and saw that he had two missed calls. One was from Caro—no doubt some warning about staying out of papers like *The Sun*. The other was from Edmond.

He returned Edmond's call first.

"This is Geoff Devonshire," he said when Edmond answered.

"Thank you for returning my call."

"Not a problem. What can I do for you?"

"I'm not sure if you've seen the morning papers, but there is a photo of you and Ms. Munroe in it."

Geoff wasn't used to answering to anyone for his

actions and he didn't expect to start now. "I have seen it. I don't think it's a problem."

"In fact, there is. Your father is not exactly interested in having his company associated with the likes of Ms. Munroe."

Geoff took a deep breath. "Then it's a good thing he has handed over Everest Air to me, isn't it, since it's mine to run."

"This is a warning, Geoff. If you continue to see Amelia Munroe, you will forfeit your piece of the Everest Company."

"I think you would do well to remember that I am already a successful man and don't exactly need Everest Air."

"Again, this is just a warning," Edmond said. "I don't want you to do anything you might regret. And judging by what I saw at the benefit between the two of you, and in the paper this morning, you are headed for disaster. Stay away from her if you want to keep Everest Air."

If there was one thing Geoff knew he wouldn't regret, it was spending time with Amelia. Images of last night flashed through his mind and he closed his eyes.

"I want to speak to you about the articles that Steven proposed we take part in," Geoff said, changing the subject. "I'm not sure that my mother will do it. She's spent her entire life making sure she wasn't ever linked to the other Devonshire mistresses."

"I am aware of that, but I think the publicity would be good for the company, and would help put the scandal in the past as you and your brothers take your places in the company. Do you think you can try to convince her?"

"I'll ask but she's very sensitive on this subject. If she says no, then that will have to be the answer."

"I understand. Do you need to meet this week to talk about Everest Air?"

"Not at all. I have some new ideas we will be implementing, and we have the baggage handler situation under control."

"Sounds like you are taking to running the airline just as your father hoped."

"Please don't refer to him as my father, Edmond. You and I both know that Malcolm was little more than a sperm donor."

"Of course," Edmond said.

Geoff knew the older man wanted to say more—he could hear it in Edmond's voice. But to him, Malcolm wasn't a father. He had a mother and two great sisters. His family was complete without Malcolm.

"If that's all."

"For now," Edmond said and hung up the phone.

Geoff put on his Hugo Boss suit with a dark blue striped shirt and a yellow tie. His handmade Italian loafers fit perfectly and before he walked out the door, he glanced in the mirror, turning around to look at his backside.

He shook his head. Just because Amelia said she liked it.

He put his mobile phone in his pocket. His housekeeper was just coming out of the kitchen as he walked in.

"Good morning, Mr. Devonshire," Annie said.

"Good morning. I will not be home for dinner tonight," he said. "Will you alert the chef?" On the nights when he was home for dinner, Annie made sure he had a hot meal waiting for him.

"Very well, sir. And this weekend?"

"I will be going out of town," he said. He wanted to take Amelia away from the city. "I need the house in Bath prepared."

"I will see to it. Do you need meals there?" she asked.

"Just make sure the kitchen is stocked and I will take care of it."

"You will?"

He arched one eyebrow at her.

"I'm just remembering the smoky mess the last time you 'took care of it,'" she said.

Annie was cheeky, which was why he liked her. She was his mother's age but still had a sparkle in her eyes and enjoyed life. "I was planning to grill."

"Good idea."

"I'm planning a house party so make sure we have enough food for at least ten," he said.

He left his home with the feeling that everything was right in his world, despite the warning from Edmond. He knew that at the end of the day no matter how much Edmond and Malcolm wanted him to avoid scandal, the bottom line would determine the winner of the Devonshire will. And he wasn't going to let anyone give him an ultimatum involving Amelia Munroe. He wanted her, and he sure as hell wasn't giving her up.

Seven

Amelia dressed in the classic Chanel black suit that put Coco on the map and walked out of her apartment building. She'd straightened her black hair into a classic Audrey Hepburn updo and put on a pair of large, round sunglasses.

She'd thought about this outfit long and hard before leaving her apartment, trying to come up with the perfect elegant, low-key ensemble. She breezed past Tommy at the entrance, feeling like a kid who was sneaking out unnoticed when he didn't even glance twice at her.

At the corner, she hailed a cab to the Everest Air offices. Her iPhone buzzed, letting her know she had a text message.

She loved the iPhone function that made the text messages into a conversation. This message was from Bebe and was typical of her friend.

Bebe: How was last night?

Amelia: Nice. Will tell you later when we have drinks.

Bebe: No way. I want the story behind that kiss. It looked like it was more than nice.

Amelia realized that she had no idea how to describe what was happening between her and Geoff. She really didn't want to, either. Everything was new and fresh between them and she wanted to keep it to herself for a while.

But the published photo had made that impossible. It was something that she'd never considered before. Living her life in front of the camera had made sense for the young woman she had been, but the woman she was becoming might appreciate some privacy.

Amelia: Can't chat now. Let's talk later.

Bebe: Is he with you?

Amelia: Not now. I'm on my way to meet him.

Bebe: TTYL

Amelia resisted typing in text language because she loved words and it made her crazy to see things like *gr8*. She just couldn't make herself use those abbreviations.

The cabbie pulled up in front of the office and she stepped out of the car. As the cab pulled away, she caught a glimpse of herself in the plate-glass doors of Everest Air offices. She thought she looked very nice today, if she did say so herself. She hoped Geoff would think so, too.

She slung her Coach bag over her shoulder and walked

toward the building. The door opened as she approached and a tall, blond man walked out.

"Hello."

She smiled at him. "Hi."

"Can I help you?" he asked.

"I'm here to see Geoff Devonshire."

"Just my luck. I'm Grant, Geoff's second-in-command," he said, holding his hand out to her.

"Amelia Munroe," she said, taking off her glasses and taking his hand.

"You are even prettier in person than you are in your pictures."

"I won't keep you," she said graciously. He had that look in his eyes—the one that made her suspect he'd seen her YouTube video.

"I'll show you up to Geoff's office," Grant offered.

She couldn't think of a polite way to decline so she went into the building. The security guard, however, came to her aid.

"I'll need some ID, please, and to confirm your appointment with Mr. Devonshire."

"She's with me, Will," Grant said to the security guard. "This is Ms. Amelia Munroe."

"There are no exceptions, Grant. You know that."

Grant looked at his watch and then smiled at Amelia. "I'll leave you in Will's hands. It was very nice to meet you."

Grant left and Amelia was relieved to see him go. Being the woman that she was, Grant's reaction was one she was used to. But now that she was trying to keep a low profile for Geoff's sake, it had made her feel a bit odd to have a man staring at her like that.

"I'm not sure if I'm on his calendar yet. We spoke this morning," she said to the guard.

"You are in fact expected. But I need to see your ID and verify that he is in before I send you up."

She nodded and handed him her photo ID, thinking about the conversation she and Geoff were about to have. She had sent a message to Auggie this morning telling him that she was going to explain his absence by saying he was on a research trip to check out some of the newer Munroe Hotels. He had yet to get back to her, but she knew her brother would be more than happy to travel to the latest hotel opening and report back on its success.

She thought that moving him out of the executive offices and into a public role would be the best solution to Auggie's boredom and the board's impatience with him.

Now she just had to figure out how to convince them both that the solution she'd come up with would work. But she was confident she could do it, especially if she and Geoff could work out a partnership deal. The board would be ecstatic at the thought of a joint venture with an Everest company. It was a win-win situation.

"Here you go, Ms. Munroe," Will said, handing back her ID. She tucked it into her wallet while he called Geoff's office. And it was then that she realized she didn't know his numbers—any of them. He knew her address, but that was it.

She'd spent the night with him and she had no idea where he lived or how to get in touch with him. And that was a very weird feeling.

How was she going to ask for his number without appearing clingy?

This was uncharted territory for her and she had absolutely no idea how to react. What was it she was supposed to do?

"You are cleared to go up, Ms. Munroe," Will said. He pushed a button under his desk and the glass door leading into the elevator area buzzed. She walked over to it and opened it.

She went to the elevator, reminding herself that Geoff had suggested this. He wanted to see her. She knew he'd be thrilled that she wanted to pursue the partnership. She just had to relax and enjoy being with him. But in the back of her mind was that fear—that it wouldn't last.

Geoff looked up as Amelia entered his office, stunned by the sight of her in classic clothes. She took his breath away. Maybe it was the fact that he now knew the body underneath the suit. Or maybe it was just that he now knew her better than he had before.

God, he was starting to sound like a sap. What was his problem? She was still just a woman. One who could set him on fire just by entering a room, but still, she was just a woman. A woman who was here to conduct business.

He stood up to greet her. When his secretary left, he was tempted to pull Amelia into his arms and kiss her. But he resisted. He had to start controlling his impulses around her.

"You look lovely," he said. "This isn't your normal type of outfit, is it?"

"No, it isn't. I decided to try this out because we are doing business together and…the paparazzi aren't used to seeing me this way. I walked right past one of them who is always hanging out at my front door. He didn't even recognize me."

"That *is* good," he said, unable to keep his eyes from roaming over her body. "Please, have a seat. Can I get you a coffee or some water?"

"Water would be great," she said.

He pulled bottles of Evian from the refrigerator in his credenza and poured them both into highball glasses. Then he leaned back against his desk, not wanting to be too far away from her.

"Have you made a decision?" he asked her.

"I have. I'd like to proceed," she said, sounding strangely formal and slightly nervous.

"Wonderful. I've had a chance to talk to one of my managers about packaging our brands and he thinks it's a great idea. He'll be working with us on the project."

"Who is it?"

"Carson Miller. Why?"

"I met Grant downstairs and he seemed very familiar with me, did you mention the deal to him?" she asked.

Geoff caught a flash of something in her eyes and he wondered if Grant had tried to flirt with her.

"Did he make you uncomfortable?" he asked her.

She shrugged and tipped her head to the side. "Not really, but he was a little too friendly. And I'd rather not work with him."

"I'll speak with him," Geoff said.

She shook her head. "Don't do that. It was just me being silly."

"Silly in what way?" he asked.

She put her water glass down and stood up, walking over to his window with a view of Heathrow Airport.

"You made me realize last night that I am more than videos and publicity stunts, and he reminded me that to the rest of the world, I'm not."

Geoff didn't know how to respond to that. To him Amelia was always more than a girl in a video. And to most people she met she would always be. Because of the charity work she'd done and just her personality, she projected more than someone in a scandalous video would. But to a certain kind of man she'd never be more than her public persona.

"Amelia, if I talk to him—"

She turned around. "No, you shouldn't. That would just make matters worse. Tell me about Carson, and what you will need from Munroe Hotels."

He walked around behind his desk and sat down. "Give me your e-mail address and I'll forward the information to you."

"It's amunroe@munroehotels.com," she said. "I realized earlier I don't have any of your numbers."

"Nor I yours," he said, pulling out his iPhone and smiling at her. "Why don't you give them to me now?"

A second later they'd exchanged information. "Are you available this weekend?"

"For?"

"A trip to Bath. I have a house there and I thought it'd be nice to spend the weekend away from the city together."

She chewed her lower lip as she mulled over his invitation. "I'd like that."

"Good. My mother wants to meet you so I thought I'd invite her to dinner on Saturday."

"Your mother? Geoff, I'm not sure about that," she said.

Geoff wasn't a man who was used to hearing the word *no*. And he certainly wasn't going to let Amelia decline. "I promise, it will not be painful at all. She's a nice lady and she asked about you specifically."

"Does she want to talk to me about the photo in *The Sun?*"

Geoff had the feeling he was going to be on trial more than Amelia. His mother had always been very sensitive to the women he dated, always making sure he treated them properly. As if he wouldn't. He was her son and he certainly understood that women could be badly hurt by a callous man.

"I think she wants to meet you because we are dating."

Her eyes widened. "Are we dating?"

"I told you I want to let things develop."

"So that means we are dating in your mind. You should have said something."

"I just did," he said, grinning at her.

She shook her head. "You are one bossy man."

"Is that a problem?" he asked enjoying sparring with her. He could tell she was enjoying herself, too, by the sparkle in her eyes.

"I haven't decided yet."

He stood and walked around his desk. "Let me know when you do."

He put his hands on her narrow waist and drew her closer to him. She tilted her head back, anticipating his kiss.

He toyed with her for a moment before bringing his

mouth down on hers with the pent-up passion of having been in her presence without touching her. He knew that this business deal was going to be complicated because keeping his mind off her and on the bottom line was more difficult than he'd expected.

Amelia felt confused as Geoff kissed her. He had been so cool and businesslike when she'd first entered his office but now he was the passionate man she'd spent the night with. A knock on his door had him pulling away and again, she wasn't sure how to act.

Then she realized that she was being ridiculous. She couldn't let one man shake her so much. She tossed her head as the door opened.

"I'm sorry to interrupt, but Carson is here with some numbers for you. He said he thought you needed them for this meeting," his secretary said.

"We do. Please send him in," Geoff said. "Do you have time for a quick rundown of the proposal Carson has put together?"

Amelia pulled out her cell phone and glanced at her schedule. The only way she'd make her luncheon was if she left immediately from here. And that wouldn't work because she'd wanted to go home and change back into her normal clothes. "I can spare maybe five minutes. I have a luncheon at one and I need time to go home and change."

His brow creased and as the door opened he turned to the man and said, "Give me a moment." Geoff closed the door and leaned back against it. "Why do you need to change?"

"If I go to the luncheon dressed like this, then

everyone will know that I've changed. This luncheon is for teenaged mothers...I am going to use every media connection I have to bring attention to their need. I can't risk our relationship—"

She stopped as she realized what she was saying. Her motivation was her desire to keep her relationship with Geoff quiet—because he had asked her to. For a second, she worried that he was ashamed of her, and that was why he wanted to keep things quiet.

"Thank you, Amelia. I didn't realize how complicated this was going to be."

She had. "It's not a big deal but I will be later than is acceptable if I don't head out soon. Why don't you just e-mail me the figures Carson came up with? Do you suppose your secretary will call a cab for me?"

"She will. When can you meet again to discuss the details of our joint venture?" he asked.

She glanced down at her schedule again. "I can do it on Thursday, or early next week. I'm going to talk to my marketing person at Munroe this afternoon and I'll forward to her the e-mail you send me from Carson. Will that work?"

"Yes. I think next week is a good time to meet," he said. "But of course I'll be seeing you before then."

"Will you pick me up on Friday night or do you want me to meet you in Bath?"

"We can talk about that tonight."

Tonight? Had she missed something? She had accepted a dinner invitation from Lady Abercrombie and she couldn't miss another of her mom's friend's dinner parties. "I have an engagement tonight."

"Break it."

"Geoff! I can't just—"

"I want to take you flying," he said. "I had planned on doing it last night, but desire got the better of me and we ended up in your garden instead." He stared at her with such intensity that her pulse raced.

Flying sounded infinitely more appealing than Cecelia's would ever be. But if she went with him... he'd begin to know that she wanted to be with him all the time.

"You are tempting me," she said.

"Good," he said.

He stood there, just waiting for her answer. And suddenly she had a moment's panic. Was he using her? Was he wining and dining her—and sleeping with her—just to gain access to her family's business? Was she being stupidly naive?

She chewed her lower lip, wanting some kind of sign from him that he wanted to spend more time with her because he had real feelings, not because he was trying to manipulate her into a deal.

"What are you thinking?" he asked.

She thought long and hard before she answered. Was she going to treat Geoff the way she treated all the men she dated, or should she be honest and bare her soul, letting him see all her imperfections and insecurities?

What if he didn't like her? she thought. She'd never been good enough for any man before. Not the woman she was in front of the flashbulbs and the media attention, and with Geoff she wanted to be.

"Amelia?"

"I'm scared," she admitted.

"Of me?" he asked.

She shook her head. "Of letting you see the real me and finding out that you don't like her at all."

Geoff reached for her hand. "I adore you, Amelia. How could I not like a single thing about you?"

"Plenty of people don't."

"I am not 'plenty of people.' I know you in a different way, in a real way," he said. "This is all new territory for me, too. I'm trying to figure out how to make this into a relationship, but I've never been involved with a woman like you before."

"Okay," she said, looking into his eyes. "I'll go flying with you tonight. Should I meet you at the airport?"

"Why don't you do that? I keep my plane at London City Airport."

He gave her further details and she started to leave. But something pulled her back and pushed her right into his arms.

She gave him a kiss designed to arouse him and then stepped away. "So that you won't forget me this afternoon."

"It isn't possible, love, believe me," he said, his voice husky.

She winked at him and walked out the door.

Eight

Geoff walked into the Athenaeum Club as though he owned it. No matter what Edmond thought, there was little he or Malcolm could do to make him change his mind about Amelia. Geoff's place in society had been cemented by years of clean living and duty. He was meeting his half brothers for drinks, something the other fellows wanted to make a ritual.

And since the novelty of actually talking to the other Devonshire bastards hadn't worn off, he didn't mind meeting them.

He took a seat in the back of the bar and waited for Henry and Steven to arrive. Steven's idea to have all of their mothers interviewed in *Fashion Quarterly* was proving to be a pain. He understood that they wanted to generate buzz around the new Everest Group but Geoff was highly private. Letting anyone in was anathema.

Though now that he was dating Amelia Munroe he might have to revise that.

"Hello, mate!" Henry said as he approached the table.

Geoff stood and shook his hand. "Good afternoon."

"Seen a bit of you in the papers," Henry said.

"Just a bit," Geoff replied, shaking his head. "It will die down."

"You better hope it does. Edmond is a stickler about that scandal clause in the will," Steven said as he joined them.

"There is nothing scandalous about my relationship with Amelia."

"What is your relationship?" Steven asked.

"None of your business," Geoff responded.

Henry leaned forward. "I get that, mate, but if you are going to be in the papers…"

Geoff didn't like having to explain himself to anyone, especially these two. He was the oldest of them and he should be the one they deferred to. "Not that it matters, but we are talking about a business deal between the airline and Munroe Hotels."

Steven nodded. "Great idea. I think that's enough to keep Edmond off your back."

"How do you know about Edmond?" Geoff asked.

"He's calling all of us…trying to make sure we're not following in dear old Dad's footsteps, I'm sure," Henry said.

Steven laughed and Geoff shook his head. "We don't even know the man, how could we be anything like him?"

"Beats me. I'm just glad to know that I'm not the only one getting calls," Steven said.

"Me, too," Geoff added.

The men settled back to drink their drinks and discuss the business of the Everest Group, and for the first time since Edmond had called this afternoon, Geoff felt a sense of peace about the entire deal with Amelia. He knew how to manage his personal life and how to make sure that she knew where she stood in it.

Amelia dressed carefully for her evening with Geoff, putting on a pair of slim-fitting jeans and a designer top. She wrapped a scarf around her neck and then donned a leather bomber-style jacket. She put her hair up in a high ponytail as she checked her look in the mirror one more time.

Her afternoon had been full and busy, but she'd discovered that having Geoff's contact information was interesting. She kept wondering what he was doing and had been tempted to call him at least six times, but she'd resisted.

Everything about him made her feel unsure and excited at the same time. She wanted to know where he was and if he was thinking about her, but at the same time was so afraid to ask him and she hated the fear.

She'd always known exactly who she was and what she wanted from life. And now Geoff Devonshire was making her question all of it. Because now she wished to be the kind of woman that he wanted her to be.

She had tried to be one man's ideal before and it hadn't worked out for her. In fact, she was often trying to fill a need in a man, she thought. With her father, it had been dutiful daughter. With her brother, it was responsible sister. With other men, it had been exotic, sexy girlfriend. And all those roles had left her wanting.

She was all of those things and so much more and she was just beginning to understand that she needed to let herself be who she really was.

Her cell phone rang and she was tempted to let it go to voice mail but she needed a distraction from her own thoughts.

"This is Amelia," she said.

"It's Auggie. I got your message," he said. She heard music playing in the background and knew he was either in his car or at his place.

"What do you think? The board is adamant. They want to see something new from you or you're out," she said.

"And you're in? Is that what your agenda is?" Auggie asked.

He sounded paranoid, which probably meant one thing—he was using drugs. She closed her eyes, not ready to deal with her brother the addict again. "You know I'm not trying to take over your position. I'm trying to help you."

"Are you, Lia? I'm not sure anymore. Vickers told me that you argued with the board for a change in roles for me," he said.

"I did make that point but only because you hate being in the office. I've been thinking that you should be the new face of Munroe Hotels."

"You think so?"

"Yes. People want to stay with someone they know. I'm also working on a joint promotion with Everest Air that I think will bring in extra revenue. What do you think? You know the board better than I do, but I want to give them more profit to think about, instead of your absences from the executive offices."

"I like it, Lia. I'm sorry I thought you were out to get me," he said, sounding like his old self.

"No problem," she replied. She was never going to tell him about the fear that gripped her whenever she thought about him using again. Auggie hadn't handled the lifestyle as well as some of his peers. While she'd turned to scandalous behavior to deal with the pressure, Auggie had turned to drugs and it had almost ruined his life.

"Love you, sis."

"Love you, too," she said, hanging up. As much of a pain in the neck as he was, she needed her brother. She needed to know that he was going to be calling her and asking her to take care of things for him. He was a man that she knew how to deal with, she thought.

Maybe she hadn't always disappointed the men in her life. And with Auggie, she was her true self. She didn't have to pretend to be someone other than who she was. He had known her since birth.

Interesting, she thought. Maybe there was more to being herself than she'd realized. Maybe this was the key to the balance she craved.

She put on a final dash of lip gloss and headed out the door. She'd planned on driving herself, but the rain had changed her mind. She'd never really liked to drive in inclement weather.

If she took her car, Tommy and the other paparazzi would know where she was going and who she was meeting. She sat down on the edge of her bed. This was harder than it should be.

She'd changed clothes more times than she normally would today. She'd been sneaking in and out of her own apartment building and now she was going to have to... what?

Bebe. She'd call her friend. Surely Bebe could help her out.

She dialed Bebe's number.

"Hello, darling," Bebe said.

"I need a favor."

"Okay, what do you need?"

"I have a date with Geoff tonight and I don't want anyone to follow me. How would you feel about coming over here and providing some distraction?"

"I'd love to, but your boys aren't going to follow me," Bebe said.

"I know. I was thinking we could go together to a club and then I could sneak out the back."

"Why don't you just drive?"

"It's very wet tonight and my car is so recognizable," Amelia said. She had a vividly painted Jaguar that was very memorable, which was why she'd bought it. She liked people knowing she was behind the wheel, but not tonight.

Bebe laughed. "Come to my place. My dad's here and he can drive you wherever you're going."

"Your dad?"

"He has the Rolls and you know that you'd never be seen in a stodgy car like that unless you were going to visit your own father. They aren't likely to follow you in that car."

Bebe had a point. Amelia hung up and was on her way to Bebe's house a few minutes later in a cab. And though she knew she should be annoyed at all the subterfuge she was going through, she wasn't. She was simply excited at the prospect of seeing Geoff again.

Geoff was running behind schedule—something that rarely happened to him. He was driving his Bugatti Veyron toward London City Airport when his mobile phone rang.

"Devonshire."

"Hi, Geoff. It's Mary. Mary Werner."

"Hello, Mary. Can I give you a ring tomorrow? I can't really talk right now."

"That's fine. I just…well, I saw your photo in *The Sun* today and I wondered if you were still going to the breast cancer dinner with me next week."

He hadn't even thought to call Mary when the photo had appeared, which was not his classiest move. He realized that he needed to end things with her officially, even though she clearly already knew what the story was. "I think I can still manage that if you'd like me to."

"I would, Geoff. It would mean a lot to me, even though you are…uh…" She trailed off, unable to finish her sentence.

"I'm sorry, Mary. I should have called you. I know that we'd been dating a lot but—"

"Say no more, Geoff. I wasn't expecting an offer for my hand. We are really more friends than lovers, aren't we?"

"Yes, I think we are." Geoff couldn't tell if she was

upset or relieved. But she was a lot like him and he knew that duty came first to her. "I'm sorry things weren't different between us."

"Me, too. I like you but I think we would have bored each other to tears," she said.

He laughed. "We are similar."

"And you certainly never kissed me like you kissed Amelia."

"I think you'll find a man who will kiss you like that," he said.

"I'm going to. When I saw that photo this morning I was hurt, of course, but more than that I was envious. I want a man to kiss me that way and not care that the entire world is watching."

"I hope you find him," Geoff said. He wanted her to be happy.

"I'll see you next Wednesday?"

"Yes. I'll pick you up."

"Good night, Geoff."

Geoff felt relief that things had ended between him and Mary. They would have made a fine couple because they were both people who honored their commitments, but life would have been a quiet, slow death, he thought.

Having been with Amelia now, he knew he couldn't marry for his family's sake anymore. He needed a woman who stirred his passion. He needed a woman who painted his world with color, not bland responsibility. He needed Amelia.

His mobile phone rang again and he answered it.

"It's Henry."

"What can I do for you, Henry?" Geoff asked. Despite

the drinks they'd had at his club the other night he hardly knew his half brother.

"I wanted to invite you to a London-Irish game. My stepfather is the coach."

"I'd like that. When is it?" Geoff asked. He got the details from Henry. As Henry spoke, he decided to ask him for a word of advice.

"You have the media following you around a lot. How do you deal with it?" Geoff finally asked.

"I pretend that they aren't there. They are going to follow me anyway, and I can't deal with them so I ignore them. Why? Does this have anything to do with Amelia Munroe?"

Geoff wondered if he should have kept his mouth shut, but he wanted someone else's opinion and Henry was the only man he knew in this kind of situation.

"Yes, it does."

"I don't get the kind of coverage that she does. They follow her everywhere. But I find that just living your life is best. If you start trying to avoid them it can be a headache, and they always find you no matter what you do."

"That's not what I was hoping to hear."

"What did you want—a way to get rid of them completely?"

"Maybe."

Henry laughed, a jovial sound that made Geoff smile. "That's not going to happen, mate. *Ever.* Even if you weren't dating Amelia, they would still follow you because of Malcolm."

"They usually leave me be on that account," he said. Probably because of his mum. When the rumors circulated that she'd been put in the hospital for psychiatric evaluation and his stepfather had moved them out to the country for several years, the press actually took a step back.

"Have you talked to that Ainsley Patterson at British *Fashion Quarterly* about the interviews she wants to do? My mum is over the moon. She'd love to have her face in a magazine."

"She has a very lovely face," Geoff said. "My mum's not so keen on being in the article."

"I figured as much. I'm not sure that talking about the past is the right way to go. My family is used to the spotlight, though."

"That is true. What did Steven's mum say?"

"I heard he was going to Berne to talk to her in person. Steven believes this kind of article will help investors feel that the Everest Group is secure and that they won't need to worry about the future once Malcolm kicks it."

"Kicks it?"

"You know what I mean," Henry said.

"Steven has a lot of ideas about the company and they are usually solid. Edmond is very meddlesome when it comes to running our businesses," Geoff said.

"He is, and he's not afraid to butt into your personal business, either," Henry said.

"Indeed."

"I saw the photo of you and Amelia in *The Sun*. I don't think there is anything to worry about, but Edmond is of a different generation. He saw Malcolm almost lose the entire Everest Group when the situation with our mums went public. He'll do whatever he has to make sure that the company stays solvent."

"I don't answer to him," Geoff said.

"I hear you," Henry replied. "Your life is your own. Just watch your back—Edmond's not going to let you, Steven or me mess up the Everest Group."

"Thanks. How's the record label?"

"Good. I never thought I'd like it as much as I do," Henry said.

They chatted a few more minutes before he arrived at the hangar where his plane was kept and he hung up with Henry. He thought about what his half brother had said about Edmond, and Geoff knew he'd have to work the older man carefully because he wasn't about to give up Amelia.

Bebe's parents were at her house for their weekly dinner. Amelia had always envied her friend's close relationship with her family. Carlotta and Davis were both in their late fifties, and were a very attractive, romantic couple. They still held hands when they were in the same room, and she and Bebe had on more than one occasion walked in on them smooching.

"Do you have time for a drink?" Bebe asked.

"I'd love one," she said.

"Good. Dad's just mixed a pitcher of martinis. And they are pure perfection."

Bebe poured her a cocktail and then sat down next to her on the love seat in the sitting room. The walls were decorated in a soft blue with creamy white accents.

"Tell me about your date last night. And then I want

to know what he has planned for tonight," Bebe said. "This is exciting."

"Exciting?"

"Because you've never dated a man like Geoff Devonshire before."

"Geoff Devonshire," Carlotta said. "Is that who you're going out with? He's not your usual sort of man, is he?"

"Mom, not now. I want to get the details first."

"I know his mom, Amelia," Carlotta said.

Suddenly Amelia had a chance to learn everything she wanted to know about Geoff and his family. An unexpected feeling of relief washed over her. "I think I might meet her this weekend."

"Then it must be serious," Carlotta said. "He isn't the kind of man to bring home the women he dates."

"We've only been out once," she said, not wanting them to read anything into a relationship that she wasn't sure would last.

"And they are going out again tonight," Bebe said.

"And he already wants you to meet Louisa? That's encouraging. When Davis was courting me, I wanted to spend every second with him. When we were apart, I missed him desperately."

"That was, like, thirty years ago, Mom," Bebe said.

"But love doesn't change," Carlotta said.

"I don't know that this is love. We've only had one date."

Carlotta nodded. "But it feels different, right?"

"What feels different?" Amelia asked.

"Being with him. Don't you find that he's different from all the other men you've dated?"

"He's very different," she admitted. And that was part of why she was so enamored of him. But love? She wasn't ready to accept that. It was too soon. Everything was happening too fast.

She took another sip of her martini and realized that coming here and talking like this—about love—was making her nervous. What if Geoff couldn't love her?

Did that matter? Did she want him to fall in love with her? She had never dreamed of marriage because her own parents had made such a mess of it. But every once in a while, she'd thought that it would be nice to have a relationship like Bebe's parents had.

"I'm sure you two will make a good match. What time do you need to leave? Davis is ready to play chauffeur for you."

"Thank you, Carlotta. I'm ready to go now," Amelia said.

"Not so fast. I haven't heard any of the juicy details," Bebe said.

"I'll leave so she can tell you," Carlotta said. She patted Amelia on the shoulder as she went by, then stopped and looked back. "Being in love is the most wonderful feeling, Amelia, but it can also be very scary. It sometimes feels as if you're losing yourself."

Carlotta left and Bebe scooted closer to Amelia on the love seat, wrapping her arm around Amelia's shoulders. "Does it feel that way?"

"I don't know. I don't know what to do. A part of me wants him to love me and would do anything to make that happen. I mean, look at me, I'm sneaking around and changing cars like a spy in a James Bond movie."

"And the other part?" Bebe asked.

She shrugged. How could she put it into words? She felt just the way Carlotta had described—scared and euphoric at the same time.

"I just don't know. I've never felt this way about a man before."

"I think that's a good thing, darling. Let's decide that it is."

"And deciding will make it so?"

"Yes, it will. If things get serious I get to be your maid of honor," Bebe said.

Amelia shook her head. "Don't even talk about marriage. I'm not sure I can handle falling in love. What if I do but he doesn't? Or what if he wants me to change even more? He already has me trying to avoid photographers, which I've never done."

Bebe hugged her close. "You wouldn't do any of that unless you wanted to. This man isn't changing you, he's allowing you to be different. That's not a bad thing."

Amelia wasn't too sure about that. "I hope so."

"Darling, you know that you haven't been the scandalous heiress in years. The most daring thing you've done is jog around Hyde Park in a skimpy running outfit."

"True. I have changed. With Geoff, I'm going to have to give up the last part of that heiress I used to be."

"Used to be," Bebe said. "Don't be afraid to be the new you."

She'd never liked the old her and she wasn't sure who the "new" Amelia would be. But being with Geoff felt right, and as Davis dropped her off at the hangar, she didn't feel like this was a second date. She felt like this was the start of her new life.

Nine

Geoff had brought a picnic dinner and set it up in the hangar. When Amelia walked in, he felt a rush of emotion he couldn't identify and didn't even try. He had never met anyone who affected him as strongly as she did. She looked sexy and unsure as she paused in the doorway—it took every ounce of willpower he had not to go to her.

She glanced at the blanket he'd spread out on the floor. "We're having a picnic."

"I hope that's okay," he said.

"It's...perfect. Thank you," she said, her eyes lighting up as she took in the blanket, the food and the roses.

"How did you get here?" he asked, wondering if their picnic would be interrupted by paparazzi. He wanted privacy and the chance to enjoy himself with this beautiful woman he was coming to care deeply about.

But by the same token he didn't want her to have to jump through hoops to see him.

"Bebe's father drove me after the paparazzi left, figuring I was spending the night there. I was going to drive myself but everyone knows my car. And I don't like to drive in the rain."

"Why not?"

"I had an accident. I was fine but it shook me up. I hit another car when mine hydroplaned. It made me realize I couldn't control anything."

"How old were you?"

"Twenty-five. It's funny because, at the time, my life was kind of spiraling out of control. That was right about the time that the video hit YouTube and I was just acting out a lot. Wearing outrageous clothing and making sure that everything printed about me was titillating. And then the car accident happened," she said.

"But you were okay?"

"I was. I was taken to the hospital because of a scrape on my forehead. I had a concussion and the papers said I'd been drinking, of course."

"Had you been?" he asked.

"No. And I learned the hard way that the media just made up what they wanted to in order to sell more papers. I disappeared for a few weeks and came back with an agenda. Then I started really working for the Munroe Foundation. That accident changed my life," she said.

"I'm glad," he said. "And very happy you were okay."

He pulled her into his arms and hugged her close. Though she'd talked about the accident like it was no big deal, he realized that he might never have met her if things had seriously gone wrong. What would it be like if he didn't have Amelia? What if something took her away from him?

His thoughts turned to his phone call with Edmond. He had planned to tell her about it tonight, but he decided that business could wait. They could put out all the fires tomorrow. Tonight was about them.

She wrapped her arms around his waist and rested her head against his chest right over his heart. And though the self-protective part of him wanted to believe that this was just about lust and obsession, he knew deep inside that there was something more at work here.

He stepped back from her and led the way to the picnic he'd laid out.

"I hope you like chicken marsala."

"Love it. My mom's Italian, as you know."

"Can she cook?" he asked, pulling her down next to him on the blanket.

Amelia laughed. "Yes, but she doesn't. She has a chef. Though to be honest, she never did much cooking, even before she was 'Mia Domenici, famous fashion designer'."

"Wasn't she always famous?" Geoff asked.

"She was a model first. She started designing when my brother and I were toddlers. She attributes her success to being home with us."

"That's nice. She made you a part of her business then."

Amelia smiled. "I'd never thought of it that way before. I always thought she was bored with us."

"Or she didn't want to just be a stay-at-home mum.

Maybe she wanted you both to have something else to aspire to," Geoff said. He handed her a plate, sat down next to her and uncorked the wine.

"And look how that worked out. We both spend most of our time jet-setting around the world."

"And working for your father's company," he added. "I think you sell yourself short."

"It's easier to do that than to have someone else tell you that you don't measure up."

"You measure up very nicely, Amelia," he said.

He handed her a glass of wine and lifted his own for a toast.

"Salut!" she said.

"Salut."

They both took a sip. "What kind of car is that?" she asked, eyeing the sports car he'd parked in the hangar.

"A Veyron," he said. "They're very fast."

"They're also very hard to come by. You have to wait for them to be made, right?"

"Yes. But I put my name on the list a long time ago so when they started producing this model, I got one of the first ones."

"Why do you want a car like that?" she asked.

"I like to go fast. I've always had a thing for cars and planes."

"Let me guess. Probably because when you're at the controls of a plane or behind the wheel of a car, no one knows who you are," she said.

"Exactly," he said. "Driving is the closest I get on the ground to the feeling flying brings me."

"Truly?" she asked. "Just driving?"

"Well, until recently. I've found something else that makes me feel like I'm flying."

"What is that?" she asked.

"You," he said.

She looked up at him with those wide blue eyes of hers and he felt his heart skip a beat. "Me?"

He nodded.

She bit her lower lip and he reached across the blanket to stroke the side of her face. "What is it?"

"I just realized that I'm afraid to believe you."

"Don't be," he said.

"What if I fall?" she asked.

"I'll catch you," he said. And those words were more than reassurance, they were a promise that he knew he never wanted to break.

Amelia had never been in the cockpit of a plane before. She liked watching Geoff ready the small aircraft for takeoff. He showed her what he was doing as he did it, including her in every aspect of the preparations. She sat next to him as they taxied down the runway once they were given the all clear, and then they were in the air.

The cloud cover that had produced the rain earlier was gone and it was a clear night. They had headphones on so they could speak to each other, and Geoff gave her an aerial tour of the city, pointing out different neighborhoods and landmarks.

Some of it she could easily identify, but other parts were a mystery to her, as if she were seeing London for the first time. In the air, she heard the excitement in Geoff's voice. She could easily see why he'd had a successful career in the RAF. He was made to fly.

"I love this," she said. "I've never seen London like this."

"Up here you can see the entire city from a new perspective."

"It's beautiful at night. I've always liked the nighttime the best," she said.

"Why?"

She shrugged. "I think because at night, no one expects anything from you."

He laughed. "It's okay to mess up at night, is that what you're saying?"

"Yes, it is. Think about it. During the day, everyone has claims on you. But at night no one has any designs on what you should be doing. They might wish you were at home or perhaps doing something respectable, but no one expects you to be working."

"I think you're right to some extent. There are still obligations at night but you can beg off and the host won't think less of you," Geoff said.

Amelia knew that while she saw the evenings as a time to play and relax, Geoff and polite society saw things differently. For them, it was a time to shine.

"How did you get out of your dinner tonight?" he asked.

"By promising to have brunch with Cecelia in two weeks' time," she said. "She really is a dear friend of Mom's so I felt bad canceling. But she suspected that I might be canceling to spend time with you, so she was okay with that."

"She was? Why?"

Amelia got uncomfortable. Why had she brought this up? Everyone thought that Geoff was different from the usual men she dated. People like Cecelia and Carlotta thought that meant that she might settle down. But Amelia worried that she was Geoff's last wild fling before he found himself a respectable wife like Mary Werner—a woman who would never make waves and always say and do the right thing.

"She thinks you're a nice man."

"Nice?"

"Yes. That's a good thing, you know."

"It sounds boring. No man wants to be boring, especially when he's with you."

"I don't think you are boring," she said. "How could I?"

"Good. Now, do you want to take the controls?"

She shook her head. "No way. I like watching you do your thing."

"But I can't touch you if I'm flying," he said.

His words sent a pulse of desire straight through her body, making her moist at her center. She wanted his hands on her again. It felt like ages since last night.

"I definitely don't want to be in control of the airplane if you're going to touch me. I'd probably make us crash."

"Do I have the power to do that?"

"Yes, you do," she said. She took a deep breath. "You have more power over me than any other man ever has."

"And how does that make you feel?" he asked.

"Scared," she said. "Because I have no idea how you feel."

He banked the plane and started heading back toward the city. "You make me feel alive, Amelia. In a way that nothing has before—not even my fast cars and jet planes."

Amelia wrapped an arm around her waist and hugged herself. This was more than she'd expected him to admit. Was Geoff falling for her? She wanted to believe that.

Almost too much. Was she making Geoff into the hero that she'd always been afraid to hope would show up?

She reached over and put her hand on his leg as he continued piloting the plane. She loved the feel of his muscular thigh.

"I like it when you touch me," he said.

"I like touching you. I can't get enough of you."

"Really?"

"Can't you tell? Last night I told myself that I'd only have one night with you. But here I am again."

"What changed your mind?" he asked.

"You did," she admitted. "This morning, when you stood naked in my kitchen."

"Hmm…you can't resist a naked man?" he asked.

She looked over at Geoff and smiled. He knew that it was much more than not being able to resist a naked man—it was that she couldn't resist a naked Geoff. She could see that he knew he was the part that changed the equation. She wanted to build dreams around him—and that was dangerous.

Geoff landed the plane and pulled into the hangar but made no move to get out. He took his headphones off and helped Amelia with hers.

"Thank you for taking me flying," she said. "I've never done anything like that before. It was spectacular."

"I'm glad you liked it," he said. He'd really enjoyed having her with him in the plane. "I have a biplane with an open cockpit that I'll take you up in sometime. You'll really like that."

"Why?"

"Because you can feel the wind in your hair. I'll do a couple of barrel rolls so you can get the full effect."

"Full effect of what? Watching my life flash in front of my eyes?" she asked.

"You wouldn't be in any danger. It's exhilarating."

"You might think so, Mr. Daredevil, but I think I'll stick to a nice evening flight in a contained cockpit."

"As long as you're in my cockpit, I'm okay with that," he said.

She looked gorgeous, sitting in his plane. He'd been rock hard since she put her hand on his thigh, and now that they were back on the ground, he wanted her naked.

He reached over and slowly unwound the scarf from her neck, leaving the ends hanging down her body. "Take off your jacket."

She looked up at him and arched one eyebrow. "Am I finally going to feel your hands on me?"

"Oh, yes," he said.

"It's about time," she said with a cheeky grin.

"I want your breasts, Amelia. Take off your jacket and your blouse, but leave on that scarf."

A light flush covered her skin as she did what he asked. He watched as every inch of her torso was revealed to him. When she was naked from the waist up, he reached over to touch her left nipple. He'd noticed last night that her breasts were very sensitive and he wanted to play with them again, to get her as turned on as he was.

He rubbed his finger lightly over her nipple and then took the scarf and drew it over the tip. She shivered a little and bit her lower lip.

"Do you like that?"

"Very much."

He took the other side of the scarf and rubbed her right breast with it. Then he lightly pulled the scarf back and forth, teasing her breasts into taut peaks.

She squirmed in her seat and then leaned over and pulled his head to hers. His mouth met hers and she devoured him, her tongue thrusting deep into his mouth and her hands clutching at his shoulders. He moved the scarf back and forth faster and felt her fingers tighten on him.

"I want you, Geoff."

"Not yet," he said. "I want to see if you can come from this."

"No," she said. "I want to come with you inside me. Get naked."

He smiled at her sexual demands. She shifted her hips on the seat until she could push her skinny jeans and panties down her legs. And her crotch was offered up to him. He stopped thinking of anything but touching her and tasting her.

He reached over, tracing the thin line of hair on the center of her feminine mound. She was waxed smooth everywhere else. He leaned in closer and pressed his mouth to her, kissed her lightly and breathed in the feminine scent of her secrets.

"Geoff, what are you doing?" she gasped.

"Tasting you," he said.

He parted her with his fingers and ran his tongue down the center of her body, tickling the bud of pleasure revealed there. Her legs shifted to let him closer and he felt her hands in his hair.

He reached up and tweaked one nipple, and heard her gasp again. With his other hand he found the entrance of her body and thrust one finger up inside of her.

She arched her back and moaned loudly. He knew she was about to come and couldn't resist driving her over the edge. He used his mouth and hands to make her crazy until she was calling his name. He felt her core tightening around his fingers.

She leaned limply against the seat and reached down to unzip his pants. He quickly pushed them down over his hips along with his underwear and drew her over the console to straddle him.

She shifted on his lap, reaching down to position him at the center of her body. Then she impaled herself on him. She pulled his mouth to hers and he kissed her briefly, wanting to taste her breasts. He leaned down and took her nipple into his mouth, licking and sucking her.

He pulled strongly on her breasts with his mouth as she moved up and down on his erection. He loved the way she felt wrapped around him. He couldn't get enough of her.

She moaned his name and clutched at his shoulders.

He put his hands on her hips to hurry her movements as he felt his orgasm building.

He was about to spill himself into her but he wanted to make sure she came again. He bit down on her sensitive nipples to push her to the brink.

She tightened and called his name just as stars exploded behind his eyes. He groaned loudly and rocked up into her body three more times before he felt drained.

He rested his head against her breast and held her tightly to him as they both caught their breath.

Here in her arms he didn't think about the fact that they might be too different to make this work. He didn't think about the fact that obsessions could burn out and leave behind nothing. He didn't think about anything but the way she felt in his arms. And how each breath he took was filled with her.

He knew that he should address the attitude of Edmond and others who thought Amelia Munroe wasn't good enough to run a business or associate with him.

Ten

Geoff's sisters were waiting for him when he came home from work on Friday. He was exhausted. After two days of having the paparazzi follow him around, he was getting seriously tired of the spotlight that Amelia lived in—nothing was going to make him comfortable with it. He had to find some way to escape from the constant attention.

He'd been dodging calls from Edmond and his mother all day long. And now to find Gemma and Caroline here—he was tempted to get in the Veyron and drive away, away from the city and away from everything.

But he'd never been a running away kind of man and he wasn't about to start now.

"Hello, brats."

"Hello, hypocrite," Caro said.

"Is this about Amelia?" he asked.

"Yes. Why is it you can date someone and have your picture in the papers every day but I'm not welcome to bring Paul to your place on Sunday?"

He rubbed his hands through his hair and took a deep breath. "Bring him if you want to. I would enjoy talking to him."

"You have to be nice, Geoff, or I'm going to grill Amelia."

"Go ahead. She can handle herself. Can you say the same for Paul?"

She smiled at him. "Yes, I can. He is a professional."

"Enough, Caro. Geoff, I want to talk to you about Mum," Gemma said.

The older of his two sisters had always been the more serious of the girls. And she also had taken the role of mother hen at a fairly young age.

"Is she okay?"

"I'm not sure. She called me last night to discuss how you are with women," Gemma said. "I think the coverage of you and Amelia is reminding her a little of her relationship with your father."

Geoff didn't like that. The relationship of his mother and his biological father had set his mother on the path to seclusion from the world. It was only when she'd met and married the girls' father that she'd started to come out of her shell again.

"I think meeting Amelia this weekend will help ease her mind. I'm not Malcolm and I'm not toying with Amelia," he said.

"Good," Gemma said. "Now that that is settled. Who should I bring this weekend?"

"Who is on the list?" Caro said.

"You don't have to bring a date," Geoff said. He hadn't been planning on having a huge party—just his mother and sisters and Amelia.

"Well, if Caro is bringing Paul, I should have someone," Gemma said.

"Do you want me to invite someone for you?" he asked. He had already started going through the list of men he thought would be suitable for Gemma to date.

"No. I'll find someone. What time should we be at your place on Sunday?"

"Around noon," he said.

The girls left and Geoff went into his study. He had never thought of himself as Malcolm Devonshire's son, but he knew he resembled his father—more than the other two sons did. They all had Malcolm's eyes but Geoff had his features, too.

For the first time he thought about how that may have affected his mother. She'd always loved him, but seeing him as a grown man must be hard for her. And now, with the media glare on his relationship with Amelia, it seemed to be sending her into a panic.

It became doubly important to him to keep the hounds at bay. Not only so that he could have Amelia to himself but also so that his mother didn't have to relive what had been such a hard time in her life.

His phone rang and he answered it on the second ring.

"Devonshire," he said.

"Geoff, this is Edmond. We need to meet."

"I can probably squeeze you in on Monday, but you'll have to speak to my secretary."

"This can't wait."

"I can't see you this afternoon," Geoff said.

"I'm not going to be put off," Edmond said.

The last thing Geoff wanted was to meet with Edmond this weekend to discuss the older man's views on Amelia. They'd done their best to avoid the media and Everest Air was showing a profit.

"Does this have anything to do with the airline?"

"No, it's about Amelia Munroe. I have already warned you about continuing to see her."

"I'm a grown man, Edmond, you can't tell me what to do. Since the airline is performing better than expected, I don't see what you have to complain about."

Edmond let out a long breath. "Very well. I need to see you this weekend. I have some papers for you to sign."

"What papers?" Geoff asked.

"Your father—"

"Malcolm."

"Yes, well, he had heard about your relationship with Amelia Munroe—"

"The business one? That's the only one that concerns him," Geoff said.

"No. This one is with Auggie Munroe according to my sources. Anyway, Malcolm wants a sworn statement from you specifying that you will not be romantically involved with Amelia Munroe."

"I'm not signing that, so save yourself a trip." If he needed further proof that Malcolm Devonshire was an ass, he had it.

"You're backing yourself into a corner. If you don't sign it, you will lose all rights to your inheritance. That will nullify your half brothers' inheritance as well. Your father plans to ruin you if you ruin his plans, Geoff."

"Let him try. I'm my mother's son, Edmond, don't you ever forget that. My reputation is beyond reproach."

"Amelia's isn't," Edmond said.

He didn't like hearing Edmond threaten Amelia, and that was a threat, pure and simple. "Malcolm might be used to leaving women in his path like roadkill but I'm not. And I'm certainly not going to let you threaten her. I'm not signing any papers."

He hung up before Edmond could say anything else. He knew that his relationship with Amelia was going to have to either go to the next level or end, because the media and his biological father were doing their damnedest to tear them apart.

Amelia was surprised when she answered her door on Friday evening and found her brother standing there. He looked tired in his faded jeans and worn silk shirt. She stood there for a minute before stepping back to let him in.

"Do you have time for me?" Auggie asked.

That was the first time he'd ever asked her anything like that, and she wasn't sure what he wanted. She glanced at her watch. "I've got about forty minutes."

"Good. I talked to the board yesterday about your idea for making me the face of Munroe Hotels and they went for it. I am going to start by promoting the partnership agreement that you're working on with Everest Air."

"That's great, Auggie," she said. The board had of course already notified her but she didn't see any reason to tell him this.

"I'm here because I think that I should take over brokering the deal. I think that Devonshire will probably deal better with me man-to-man, and with you dating him, it doesn't seem appropriate for you to be doing business at the same time."

Amelia couldn't believe that this was coming from Auggie. "I'm not going to do anything to compromise the deal. And it's actually not official yet anyway."

"Fredrickson told me that unless you and I wanted to ruin the entire Munroe Hotels business, I need to step up and take control of this. Don't be upset," he said.

"I am. I've been running things behind the scenes for years and now because I'm dating Geoff, someone thinks I can't do it anymore? That's insulting."

"That's life," Auggie said.

"Men can be pigheaded."

Her brother laughed. "True, but until Fredrickson retires or gets booted off the board, there is little you or I can do about it."

Auggie sounded like he was ready to run the company for the first time in years. "You sound different."

"I am different now."

"Why? Does it have something to do with why you needed a week off?"

He shrugged. "I took time off because…well, let's just say I was dating someone but it didn't work out."

"A girl dumped you."

"Not a girl, Lia, *the* girl. And the only way I'm going to get her back is to straighten my life out."

"I'm glad to hear you say that. I hope you win her back," she said.

"I will. What about you and Geoff? Are you serious about him?"

"More serious than I've ever been before. But I have no idea if it's going to work out or not. I know that he doesn't like all the media attention and to be honest, I think I'm sick of it, too. But how do I make it go away?"

Auggie pulled her into a hug. "I have no idea. If you figure that one out, let me know."

"I will. Have you spoken to Father?" she asked. "About your new direction?"

"No. If I talk to him, he'll make me doubt myself. I think I need to do this on my own for once."

"I think so, too. If you need me, I'm here."

"I know you are. But I think I've leaned on you enough throughout our lives."

"I didn't mind it," she said. She liked knowing that she was the one who took care of Auggie. He was the one person in the world who'd always known what she really had to offer.

"My time's almost up. I think I'll go," he said. "Do you need anything from me?

"Two things, actually. Would you mind taking Lady Godiva for the weekend? I'm going out of town," she said. "I was going to have the dog-walking service take care of her, but I think she'd be happier with you."

"I don't mind at all. I could use the company," he said. "What else do you need?"

"One more week working on the deal with Everest Air. I'll finalize the terms we've been discussing, and then I'll turn it over to you."

"Okay," Auggie agreed. "But then you let me do my thing."

"Agreed."

A few minutes later he left with the dog in one arm. "Bye, sis."

"Bye, bro," she said as Auggie let himself out of her apartment.

She finished packing her bag for the weekend away with Geoff—she was meeting him in the parking garage in less than ten minutes. She was both looking forward to this weekend and dreading it.

She didn't know what his mother expected from her. This was the first time she'd met anyone's family. Normally the men she went out with were long gone from their families and lived in her world, the jet-set world where no one owed anyone any loyalty.

And that went double for her. But Geoff had a family and they wanted to meet her. She wondered if he was going to want to meet her family.

Doubt washed over her and she wondered what she was doing with Geoff. But she pushed it aside. When they were together, everything always felt right. She was with him because she liked the person she was in his eyes.

And he trusted her and believed in her. That's why they were doing business together. If he had any doubts, he never would have proposed the joint venture.

She liked the quiet moments that he found for them. And she loved the way he made her feel. He was in serious lust with her and she enjoyed every second of their lovemaking.

But that didn't mean that they belonged together or

that they'd last longer than it took for the passion to burn out between them, did it? What if she wasn't "the one" for him? She wanted to spend the rest of her days with Geoff and she was very afraid that no matter how things ended between them, she'd never be the same again.

She shook her head to clear out the thoughts—she was starting to drive herself crazy.

Amelia looked pensive when he picked her up. They didn't talk much as they drove out of the city. There were no cars following them, maybe because he was in a black Audi and not his flashy Veyron. Amelia was wearing a sexy outfit that was making it a little hard for him to focus. But he could tell something was wrong.

"What's on your mind?" he asked her once they were out of traffic and moving steadily along the highway.

"My brother stopped by tonight before you came to pick me up."

"And?"

"He talked to the board and he'll be taking over the partnership with Everest Air after we hammer out the details."

"Why?" Geoff asked carefully.

"The board didn't think it was appropriate for me to be dating you and doing business with you. I think they're afraid that if you dump me, the deal will fall through."

"That would never happen," he said.

"Dumping me or pulling out of the deal?" she asked.

He glanced over at her. She had large-framed black sunglasses on so he couldn't read her expression. But the tense way she held her body let him know that she was anxiously awaiting his answer.

"If our relationship ends, it's going to be because we both agreed that we'd taken it as far as we could."

She pushed her sunglasses up on her head and turned to face him. "Where do you see us heading?"

"I'm not sure. I just know that I don't like the thought of being without you."

"Me, too," she said. "When Auggie told me the board's concerns, I had to wonder if your own board wasn't saying the same thing to you."

Geoff shrugged, he knew if he told Amelia about Edmond's threats, she'd start to doubt herself and the business deal they'd carefully worked on. And Geoff knew he was more than capable of handling Edmond and Malcolm. Those two were mainly concerned about the bottom line, and as he'd told Edmond, he was his mother's son.

He'd ignore the media. With Amelia doing the same, they'd be okay. He didn't want to take a chance on doing something that would cause her to disappear. If Auggie took over the deal between their companies, it meant he wouldn't have a reason to see her all the time. And though the deal was being kept under wraps now, he wanted to let it out of the bag. He wanted to let the world see what kind of woman Amelia was and that she was his.

"I don't answer to anyone," he said.

"We all do."

"Everest Air is not the most important thing in the world to me."

"But it's your father's company."

"I never knew him. I still don't. He contacted me and the other heirs because he's dying."

"Oh, Geoff. I'm sorry. I didn't know he was sick. Does he want to make up for lost time?"

Geoff shook his head. "Hardly. He wants to make sure his company lives on long after he's gone."

She frowned at him. "God, that's cold. You deserve better than that from him."

"He's a stranger to me, so it doesn't bother me."

"Good. It's his loss. You're a fantastic man and I'm sure your brothers are as well. I can't believe he has never tried to get to know you all."

"His life was taking a different path," Geoff said. Hearing Amelia's perspective made him realize that he really had never needed Malcolm. He'd found his own way. The same way that Amelia had in her turbulent childhood.

"I'm glad our paths crossed," she said.

"You are? What made you say that?"

"I was thinking about how screwed up some parts of my life were before you. And I'm not saying this to add pressure to our relationship. But you have really given me some peace, and I enjoy it."

He reached over and took her hand in his, twining their fingers together as he continued to drive.

"You've brought excitement to mine," he said.

"Chaos you mean, right?"

Geoff brought her hand to his mouth and kissed the back of it before letting go. He didn't want to talk about how crazy her life was or how challenging he found it. He wanted to simply enjoy this weekend with her.

"I'm sorry," she said.

"Why?"

"You're trying to pretend that I haven't brought a headache into your life."

"I make my own decisions, Amelia," he said. "And I accept responsibility for them. Having you by my side is worth any of the problems that may have cropped up."

"Really? Sometimes I think it would be better for you if we just went back to our old lives. But I can't make myself do that."

"Good. I want you by my side," he said.

He knew that being with him and trying to avoid the paparazzi after a lifetime of engaging them must be taking a toll on her. He knew she was running around like a crazy woman to keep photographers from following her each time she met him. He appreciated the efforts she was making.

But at the same time he knew that they couldn't go on this way. He needed to find a way to permanently put an end to the media interference in their lives. He had no idea how to do it, but he could see the stress in Amelia and felt it himself each time they were confronted by a group of photographers.

He knew now how his cousins, the royal princes, felt. He'd often envied them, being the branch of the family to inherit the throne, but he couldn't live the way they did with their lives constantly under the scrutiny of everyone with nothing that was private.

As he entered the town of Bath, he had to slow down for traffic.

"I love Bath," Amelia said. "It's simply the prettiest place in England."

"I think some people would argue that, but I happen to agree."

He loved the lush green lawns, the flowing water of the Avon River that moved through the middle of town and the enchanting buildings. The influence of the Romans was still visible in the center of town near the legendary Roman baths. But the large medieval cathedral dominated the skyline of the city.

"How long have you had a house here?" she asked.

"Since my university days," he said. "I came here with one of my mates to visit his family and decided I wanted a home here as well. I wanted to come back often."

"And have you?"

"Yes, but this is the first time I've brought a woman here with me."

Amelia reached over to take his hand in hers and squeezed it tightly. "I'm flattered. And I'm sure I'm going to love it."

He was sure she would, too. And this weekend, he was determined to find a way to solidify his relationship with Amelia.

Eleven

Amelia had never expected to be so easily accepted into Geoff's family. His sisters were hilarious, treating him with love but also teasing the heck out of him. He was very much the patriarch of the family but he was indulgent as far as Gemma and Caroline were concerned.

Standing on the balcony overlooking the city of Bath on Sunday afternoon, she finally acknowledged that she had fallen in love with Geoff. It hadn't happened this weekend, she thought. No, it had started that very first night when he'd apologized for believing the worst of her. Then it had deepened when he'd kissed her in his car and made love to her on the rooftop, telling her that nothing mattered except what was between the two of them.

And everything that had happened since then had

just bound her more tightly to him, making her realize that he was everything she'd ever wanted in a man but had been afraid to reach out and take.

"So you like my brother?" Gemma said, appearing next to her.

"What makes you say that?" she asked.

"You are staring at him with stars in your eyes," Gemma said.

"That's embarrassing."

"Not really. I think he hung the moon, too. He's a bit arrogant but otherwise he's a great guy."

"He's bossy as hell," Amelia said.

Gemma sighed. "We've done our best but he simply won't listen to us. He still thinks he knows best."

"That's because I do," Geoff said, coming over to them and handing each of them a glass of Pimms.

"This is a girly conversation. Remember, you don't like those?" Gemma said.

"I'm interrupting it and changing it into a lovey-dovey conversation."

"See?" Gemma said looking at Amelia. "He's impossible."

"So are you, Gem."

His sister punched him playfully in the shoulder before walking away.

"I like your sisters," she said.

"They like you, too," he said. "My mum will be here in a short while. I should tell you something about her that I don't think I've mentioned. She's very afraid that I might treat you the way that Malcolm treated her. I think she'll want to speak to you."

"I'm not sure what to say. Why does she think that?" Amelia asked.

"I'm not entirely sure. But she said I should remember that even party girls have hearts that can be broken," Geoff said.

Amelia blinked. She knew she was going to like Geoff's mother. Any woman who would say that to her son had an inside knowledge of the world Amelia lived in.

"Everyone can be hurt," Amelia said, trying for a light tone. "Even business tycoons like yourself."

"Touché."

"Caro said that you warned her not to let her picture with Paul show up in *The Sun*."

"I did indeed. It's different with you and me," he said, clearly unashamed of the double standard he'd established for himself and his sisters.

"How?"

"We both know that I'm not just using you," he said.

"Maybe your sister knows the same thing about Paul."

He shrugged. "Until I'm certain of it, she's going to have to put up with my rules. I adore my sisters with their sassy attitudes. I don't want them to retreat from life because of men."

She understood exactly what he meant. "I'm glad they have you to look out for them. It'd be nice if everyone just dealt honestly with each other."

"Yes, it would," he said. "But that means trusting someone else not to hurt you, doesn't it?"

"Yes. That's the hard part," she admitted.

He hugged her with one arm. "I haven't betrayed your trust, have I?"

"No," she said.

"Amelia, there's something I need to discuss with you. It's about—"

"Geoff, darling, come and give your mother a hug."

Geoff pulled away without finishing, and Amelia could see he wanted to say more but now wasn't the time. He'd seemed concerned when he started to speak, but she had no clue what he'd wanted to say. Had she done something wrong? Was there some problem?

As she watched him with his mother, she realized that this was her secret dream. This family. A part of her felt that if she played her cards right, this could be her life. But another part felt insecure, like the other shoe was about to drop. Like she'd be lucky to make it through the weekend.

If he loved her, she thought, then everything would take care of itself. She just had to keep repeating that to herself.

Geoff wrapped his mum in a big bear hug and was surrounded by her slender arms and the scent of Chanel No. 5. It had long been her signature fragrance. Even though other designers had wanted to blend unique fragrances just for her, she preferred the one she'd worn as a young woman.

She wore a pair of wide-leg, camel-colored trousers and a fitted white blouse. Her auburn-colored hair was pulled back in a loose chignon and seeing her now, Geoff was struck by how pretty his mum was.

"Sorry to be late, darling," she said.

"Not a problem. I never mind waiting for you."

"That's good," she said with a smile.

"Mummy!" Caro said running over to them. "I can't wait for you to meet Paul. He's been eager for you to get here."

Paul joined them when Caro waved him over. He was an inch or two shorter than Geoff, and Geoff had used that to his advantage all afternoon, trying to intimidate the other man, but he'd stood his ground.

"Princess Louisa, it is a pleasure to meet you. Caro has told me so much about you," he said. He leaned in and gave her a kiss on the cheek.

"Please call me Louisa," his mother said.

"It would be my pleasure, Louisa."

Paul and his mum chatted as Geoff watched Amelia, waiting for the right moment to introduce her. She'd wandered over to Gemma and her date, Robert Tomlinson, the son of the current British prime minister.

As Geoff surveyed the balcony filled with his family, he realized that this was the life he wanted for all of them. He was tired of professional socializing and wanted to start having more time with his family and with Amelia.

He wanted the quiet domesticity that came with being a couple, and he wanted it soon. He was ready to be Amelia's. He just needed a signal from her that she wanted it, too.

For all he knew she would miss her wild lifestyle. He knew he kept her more than satisfied in bed, but there was more to life than that.

Realizing that her happiness was his chief concern sobered him up.

"She's a stunningly beautiful girl," his mum said as she came up to him.

"Yes, she is. You can't help but notice her when she's in a room."

"I can see that. What does she mean to you?" she asked.

"Mum, I've told you, I don't want to talk about my intentions with you. Not yet."

Louisa nodded. "I know you said that but I want to make sure you have more of me in you than Malcolm."

"There is no way to prove that to you," he said.

"I know, darling," she said, patting his arm. "I didn't mean that the way it sounded."

This had always been an issue between them. At times he wondered if Malcolm even knew what kind of wreckage he'd left behind when he'd abandoned Geoff's mother.

"Speaking of him, have you had a call from Ainsley Patterson or her assistant?"

Louisa took a deep breath. "I have. She wants to interview me and the other women."

"Are you going to do it?"

"Do you want me to?" she asked. "I really don't want to, but I also don't want to be the only one who doesn't participate."

"From what I understand, Steven's mother is reluctant to do it as well."

"The physicist, right?"

"Yes, Mum. I spoke to Ainsley and she assured me

that the piece is going to focus on all three of you from a fashion perspective."

She shook her head. "I'm still considering it. I know that it will mean publicity for the company but I really don't think we need any more money."

He smiled. Whoever had tried to use money as a reason for her to do the interview had made a huge mistake. His mother had more money than Midas and didn't think that was a justification for anything.

"If you don't want to do it, we can both walk away."

"You'd do that for me?"

"Of course I would, Mum."

"Thank you, Geoff," she said.

"Now where is Amelia?"

"I'm here," Amelia said, walking over to them.

He'd already started to figure out how much he loved Amelia, but seeing that shy smile on her face as she approached his mother simply confirmed it. He wanted to go to her and kiss her because he wasn't sure he could tell her how he felt, but he sure as hell could show her.

"Hello, Amelia," his mum said.

"Princess Louisa."

"Please call me Louisa."

"I have to tell you that you have raised three wonderful kids. The girls are very sweet and funny, and Geoff is simply the best date a girl could have."

He arched one eyebrow at Amelia's comment and she winked at him.

"Thank you, darling," Louisa said. "My kids *are* spectacular."

"They share your modesty," Amelia said with a laugh.

Louisa laughed along with her. "I like this girl, Geoff."

"Me, too, Mum."

"Now leave us alone for some girl talk," Louisa said.

"Very well," Geoff said. He reached around his mother and pulled Amelia into his arms and kissed her.

"You mean the world to me," he whispered before he left them to chat.

Louisa put her arm through Amelia's and led her off the balcony and out into the backyard where they could be alone.

"I hope you don't mind me pulling you away from the party," she said.

"Not at all. I wanted to talk to you as well. I'm so sorry about the photos that keep showing up of Geoff and me."

Louisa shook her head. "That's not your fault. Geoff's a big boy. He knows how to deal with the media."

"Ignore them?"

"Well, that has worked for us, but I think you have a different policy, don't you?"

"I do. I use them to keep my name in the public spotlight. It helps when I'm trying to promote the hotel chain or one of the charities I work with. But now…well, now that I'm involved with Geoff, they do seem to be in the way."

"I was like you once. Just living my life and enjoying every second of it. But everything has consequences."

"Of course. You should know that Geoff is a great guy. He's always treated me well."

Amelia knew that Louisa was trying to look out for her and it was important to Amelia that Geoff's mother realize what a wonderful man he was. He'd never tried to use her or treat her with anything other than respect.

"I know, he's a good boy. He always was. But the world we live in can change a man. Do you know that I was engaged to Malcolm?"

"No. I didn't know that. In fact, I know very little about your relationship."

"Well, when the news of it started circulating, that was when he started panicking. I think he was afraid I'd try to change him. To be fair, I probably would have, but who can really say."

Amelia understood. "My parents had a very tumultuous marriage."

"Are they divorced?"

Amelia laughed. "No. But they don't live together. Their passion is somewhat…all-consuming."

"Ah. So they can't give each other up but they can't live together either?"

"Exactly."

"Is that what you have with my son?"

Amelia tried to find the right words while they strolled through the beautifully landscaped backyard. "No. We have passion, but there is also peace. I don't know if this will make sense, Louisa, but my entire life has been very chaotic and being with Geoff just makes me happy."

Louisa squeezed her hand. "That makes perfect sense, darling. I think that is exactly as it should be."

"I'm so glad you think so," Amelia said, relieved.

Louisa stopped walking. "I need some advice and you might be the only woman I know who can understand this situation. I've been asked to do an interview with a fashion magazine, along with the two other mistresses of Malcolm's. They want to do a fashion retrospective and talk about how we are all uniquely different. I've always avoided things like that, but I think using the media now to show that I'm not a victim might be a good idea."

Amelia wasn't sure what to say. "I've always thought of the media as working for me. I try to get them to picture me the way I want them to. If I were you, I'd do it, but I'd do it on my own terms."

Louisa nodded. "I have been thinking I should do it because I believe I'm the only holdout. They'd probably paint me in a very unflattering light."

Amelia shook her head. "How could anyone do that to you? Everyone knows how much work you do with charities, and how you took your deceased husband's fortune and used it to fund an organization that helps unwed mothers."

She flushed. "That's only money. I have a lot of that, and a lot of time to give."

Before she could say anything else, Paul, Caro and Gemma walked into the backyard. Paul had a football in his hands and the girls were both laughing at something he'd said. Robert and Geoff were right behind them, carrying trays of food and drinks.

"Want to play a game of kick around?" Paul asked.

"Louisa, Caro told me you taught her to play when she was little."

"I did indeed. I taught Geoff and Gemma as well. I was an accomplished player when I was younger."

"After we eat, you can show us if you still have it, Mum," Gemma said.

Everyone worked together to get the meal ready and they had nice luncheon. Then it was time for "kick around," as Paul called it. Amelia wasn't very athletic, something that everyone noticed the first time she tried to kick the ball and missed.

Geoff came over to her and wrapped his arms around her from behind. "Do you need some lessons?"

"Yes," she said. "I'm afraid soccer isn't my sport."

"Maybe that's the problem, you Yank. We call it football over here."

He put his hands on her waist and bent his legs behind hers, pulling her fully against him. She forgot all about the ball. Geoff was saying something to her, but all she could think about was how good he felt.

"Ready?" he asked.

She shook her head.

He tipped her head back and kissed her quick. "Just try to keep your body limber."

She nodded and the ball came careening toward her again across the very green lawn. She caught it, dropped it and kicked it to Caro.

"I got it."

"You cheated," Gemma said. "You can't use your hands! I've seen five-year-olds with better skills than you."

Amelia smiled at her. "I'm not very athletic."

"No, you're not," Geoff said. "But I wouldn't change a thing about you."

His words warmed her. For a few minutes, she had that floating feeling that came when everything was right in her world. Though she felt accepted by Geoff's mother and sisters and finally admitted to herself that she loved him, she knew that things weren't resolved between them. Geoff was keeping something from her. And she knew that it had to be something big, because he'd tried to talk to her twice and each time he'd been pulled away she saw a look in his eyes that told her time was running out.

Twelve

Amelia sat on the balcony watching the sun set over the city of Bath while Geoff was downstairs dealing with business. Malcolm's attorney had mysteriously arrived ten minutes after his family had left. She knew Edmond through Cecelia, but the man barely even glanced at her when he arrived. Geoff looked angry, so she'd excused herself before he could ask her to.

She was tired, but it wasn't a bad feeling. She really felt like the weekend had changed her perspective on life. Louisa had been a breath of fresh air and a solid example that loving and losing didn't mean giving up on life. The woman might avoid the spotlight, but she vibrated with a joie de vivre that Amelia hoped she still had when she was in her fifties.

She'd brought the pitcher of Pimms mixed with fizzy lemonade and cut-up fruit out on the balcony with her.

She was reclining on one of the solid wood loungers with a thick, red-striped cushion and a soft down pillow at the top.

She was a little chilly as the sun set but wrapped a cashmere scarf around her shoulders. The lights of the city started to come on and she thought that she could be happy in this quiet, small town.

Though Bath wasn't a tiny little burg, it was removed from the hustle and bustle of London and though she knew there were paparazzi in the area since many Hollywood celebrities had houses here, they seemed to steer clear of Geoff's estate.

"Sorry about that," Geoff said, stepping out onto the balcony. "I wasn't expecting that to take as long as it did." He looked strange, as though his mind were still on whatever business he'd been discussing.

"I didn't mind sitting here. I was enjoying the quiet tonight."

"Was it too loud today with everyone?"

"Not at all. I really like your family. They are exactly what I always dreamed I'd have when I was visiting someone else's house. For a few moments today, it felt like your family was mine, too."

"I loved sharing my family with you."

"Thank you, Geoff." She waited for him to continue, but he was quiet. She was tempted to ask him what he'd been about to tell her earlier, but she couldn't bring herself to do it.

Geoff sat down on her lounger by her legs, facing her. He lifted her legs over his lap.

"Amelia, we have a good thing. I only know that right now this is working and I don't want it to end."

"Neither do I. You have become important to me. I'm not sure how that happened because I vowed to myself that you weren't going to get the better of me."

Geoff smiled down at her and it was easy for her to see the caring in his eyes. She felt lit from within when he looked at her like that.

"I think I've had the very best of you," he said.

"You have," she said as he leaned in to kiss her.

"We'd better pack up and get going. I have a pretty busy week," Geoff said.

Her mellow feeling started to wane. She knew this was just the reality of two very busy people getting together. She had her life and he had his.

"I guess I should get my things together," she said, starting to rise. He stopped her, and her breath caught.

"Amelia?"

"Yes?" she said.

"Will you live with me?" he asked.

Live with him? She wasn't sure she was ready for that. But at the same time she was entranced with the idea. She wanted to spend more time with him and this might be the right move. Except that she wasn't sure.

"Can I think about it for a few days?"

"What's to think about, Amelia?"

"I'm just not sure. I'm not trying to be difficult," she said.

He leaned in closer to her. "What are you afraid of?"

"Needing you," she said.

"You'll have me. I'm not going anywhere."

"For now," she said, studying his expression.

"If I made you a promise, would you believe me?" he asked.

"I don't know," she admitted quietly.

"Let's give it a try. We'll spend a few nights at each other's places first and see what happens."

She wanted to say yes, realizing that if she were going to let fear motivate her, then she wasn't going to have a very good life.

"Okay. But you'll have to stay with me. I have my dog."

He let out a laugh, and for a moment the concern behind his eyes vanished. "No problem. Do you want to set up specific days?"

"Not if you're going to laugh at me."

"I'm not, I swear. Monday, Wednesday and Friday?"

"Next weekend I'm scheduled to fly to Paris to speak at a conference."

"I'll check my schedule. If I'm free I'll come to Paris with you. Unless you'd rather be alone."

"No, I'd love to have you with me," she said.

Planning for the future made her feel like they were a real couple. She was scared to trust in that but she decided that for right now, she was going to. There was no other solution that was going to work.

She was already in love with Geoff. Now she'd be able to figure out if she could live with him. She'd just have to trust that whatever was bothering him would come out sooner or later. If he was asking to live with her, then it probably had nothing to do with her, she told herself.

* * *

Geoff wasn't the kind of man who liked to leave loose ends and "living" with Amelia felt like a loose end. He had met with both her and Auggie earlier in the day and he'd wanted to make their arrangement official, but she'd been cool and businesslike, probably because her board didn't want to see any untoward behavior from her.

Edmond had left another warning message on his voice mail and frankly, Geoff was sick of the older gentleman. There was no contest in his mind between Amelia and Everest Air. He'd always pick Amelia.

Edmond had not been too pleased with that but Geoff didn't back down and he knew the profit he was increasing at the airline had helped to sway the older gentleman. Geoff wasn't Malcolm and Amelia hadn't made him lose interest in his business. It had in fact made him even more determined to succeed so that their joint venture would be profitable and help her out as well.

His secretary reminded him that he had the fund-raising dinner that night with Mary Werner. He called Mary to confirm that they were still on and then called Amelia to let her know he'd be home late.

"This is Amelia," she said by way of greeting.

"It's Geoff."

"Hey there, sexy."

"Hello back," he said. "I have to attend the breast cancer function tonight, so I'm going to get to your place late."

He heard the sound of rustling papers on her end. "I think I have something…yes, a dinner party. Do you want me to stop by the event on my way home? We are one of the corporate sponsors of the event—Munroe Foundation, I mean."

"No, that's fine. I'll just look forward to seeing you when I'm home."

"That will be better. Then I can have you all to myself," she said.

"I like the sound of that," Geoff replied.

"Do you?" she asked.

"Yes, I do. I am going to like seeing you almost every day," he admitted.

"I'll be home by ten."

"I'll try to get there then as well."

"That's my other line. I have to go." She hung up before he could say another word.

When he picked Mary up at her place for their evening, he wished he were picking up Amelia instead. As he rang her bell, he thought he saw someone behind him, but when he glanced up and down the street, he saw nothing.

"Hello, Geoff," Mary said when she opened the door to her Notting Hill town house. She looked nice in her pink dress. He leaned in to give her a kiss and thought he heard a click behind him. When he turned around, all he saw was a man walking his dog at the end of the street.

He shook his head. He was getting paranoid because of the photographers who always followed Amelia around. "Are you ready to go?"

"Let me grab my purse," she said.

A few minutes later they were seated in his Audi, driving toward the event, which was being held at the Munroe Hotel. He pulled up and tossed his keys to the valet. Then he gave Mary his arm as they walked into the hotel. There was a red carpet leading to the ballroom and lots of people taking pictures as they entered.

"Thank you for escorting me tonight, Geoff."

"No problem. This event is important."

Mary nodded. "This is one of your mother's causes, isn't it?"

"I think it is every woman's cause. Since I have a mother and two sisters, it is important to me."

Mary smiled over at him. "Shall we get a drink and hit the dance floor?"

Geoff didn't want to hold any woman other than Amelia, but one dance with Mary didn't seem like it was too much to ask.

"Okay, let's go."

"To this song?" she said with a bit of surprise in her voice. The song was Pink's "Who Knew."

"I'm not much of a fast dancer," Mary said.

"Let's give it a try. I bet you'll be pretty good at it," he said, realizing that with Mary she just needed some gentle encouragement.

She gave him an excited grin and stood up. "Okay. Let's do it."

They hit the dance floor as the music changed to another upbeat number, this one by Steph Cordo, an act his half brother Henry was producing for Everest Records. They danced to her song, and at the end they transitioned into the new John Mayer song.

"Yes, a slow dance," Mary said giving him a very hopeful look.

"Okay, one dance," he said.

She stepped closer to him and he put one hand on her

waist and held her hand in his other one. They danced well together, which surprised him. On the dance floor, he saw another side to Mary. After several songs, he paid her compliment.

"You should dance more often, Mary. It brings out another side to your personality."

"You think so?"

"Definitely," he said.

"Devonshire," someone called. He glanced over to see a rather shabby-looking photographer with an expensive, professional camera around his neck.

The man snapped a picture of Geoff and Mary, and then disappeared into the crowd. Geoff went after him, but by the time he got through the crowd, the man was gone. This would be fodder for Edmond and Malcolm and the papers, but he'd handle it.

He tried to tell himself the photo was nothing and he wasn't going to worry about it, but he feared that Amelia might see things differently. When he got back to the table, Mary was acting like a gracious hostess to the others there.

"I have to go," he said.

"I understand. I'm going to stay a bit longer and I'll catch a cab home," Mary said.

He nodded and left the hotel, intent on getting to Amelia before any more damage was done.

Amelia was having a good night out. Bebe was a guest at Dominic Regenti's dinner party as well, so she'd been hanging out with her friend, drinking lovely fruity cocktails and talking about Geoff all evening.

"He sent me flowers today at my office. Did I tell you that?"

"About a dozen times," Bebe said.

"That was really sweet. They are the same flowers that are hanging from baskets on the streets of Bath. We walked all over the city and no one paid any attention to us. It was so nice," Amelia said.

Bebe put her arm though Amelia's and said, "I know, I know. It was an enchanted weekend, something that didn't even feel real."

"Am I babbling?" Amelia asked her friend.

"Only the slightest bit and I don't mind at all. I think you are in love."

"I think I am, too," Amelia said.

Dominic sat down next to her. "You are what?"

Dominic was one of her dearest friends. His party was small and intimate—just her and Bebe, and Dominic and Lucinda, his wife. Dominic and Amelia had met years earlier at one of Amelia's mother's fashion shows. He was fifteen years older than Amelia, and he'd been there with one of his mistresses. That was aeons before he'd met Lucinda and settled down.

"Don't say anything until I'm back in the room," Lucinda called from the kitchen. She was bringing dessert into the sitting room.

Lucinda was a celebrity chef who had gotten her start working in Gordon Ramsay's kitchen. On one of his early shows her charisma and beauty had been spotted by one of the producers and she'd been offered her own show. That was when Dominic had started courting her.

"Okay, here I am," she said, carrying a tray with champagne Jell-O and whipped cream.

Dominic stood up, took the tray from his wife and gave her a kiss on the cheek. "Let me take that."

"You guys are so sweet," Amelia said.

"We are," Lucinda agreed. "So what about your man? We want to hear about Geoff."

"I'm not sure what to say. He's…" She trailed off, realizing she didn't know how to talk about him without revealing how she felt. Or sounding foolish. She was still afraid of being hurt.

"He sent her flowers at her office today. The same ones that were hanging in baskets in Bath," Bebe said, "which is where they were this weekend."

"He wanted to remind you of the time you spent together," Lucinda said. "Why don't you do that, Dominic?"

He tugged Lucinda down on his lap as she handed the last dessert out. "Because you are allergic to flowers, my love."

She kissed him on the cheek. "That is right."

"He also sent me a mask from Botswana, which is where we first met. He'd noticed that I'd admired it, I think," Amelia said.

"That is good. What else does he notice?" Lucinda asked.

"Everything. When I'm with him, I feel like I'm the only woman on the planet."

Dominic smiled at her and she saw that he was happy for her. "It's about time you found a man like that. Why didn't you bring him with you tonight?"

"He had a function to attend. He's as busy as I am

but I think we are starting to merge our calendars and spend more time together."

"That is the hard part," Lucinda said. "Dominic travels a lot and that was a big struggle in the beginning of our relationship."

"Yes, it was, because she was stubborn and wouldn't quit her job to go with me."

"I'm glad she didn't. That was not nice of you to ask her to give up her career for you," Bebe said.

"Hey, I offered her a lot of money to be my personal chef."

"I hope you said no, Lucinda," Bebe said.

"She did, of course. But eventually I brought her around to my way of thinking."

Amelia laughed at her friends. As they bantered and had their dessert, she realized that she missed Geoff. She missed having him at her side, enjoying the evening with her.

Being in love was more than just a feeling, she thought. It was also the fact that she wanted to spend every moment of the day with him. And of course the nights. If he'd been here, he would have fit in well with Dominic and Lucinda. She wanted him to become integrated completely into her life and she wasn't going to be happy until he was.

Happy, she thought. She'd never gotten to the point where she felt safe being happy. She was afraid to trust that what she had with Geoff was going to last, and that wasn't fair, she thought. Not to herself, and not to Geoff. She couldn't wait to get home and tell him.

She wasn't going to hide the fact that she loved him anymore. She wanted the life that Dominic and Lucinda had together and running away from love wasn't the key to that kind of deep-seated happiness.

She left Dominic's a little after ten, which was later than she'd thought she'd be. She and Bebe shared a cab. When Bebe got out of the car, she gave Amelia a hug and Amelia sat back in the seat as the cabbie took her home. She had a bubble of excitement in the pit of her stomach as she got closer to her house where she hoped Geoff was waiting for her.

Thirteen

Amelia got out of the cab and walked toward the entrance of her apartment building. She noticed that Tommy had company this evening and she smiled at the men as she walked past them. She heard them calling her name and asking about Geoff, but she didn't pay the least bit of attention to them.

Taking a page from Geoff's family's book, she'd decided to start ignoring them and it felt good. The bellman held the door for her and she thanked him as she walked by.

The elevator was empty when she swiped her key card and took it up to her penthouse. And as she walked into her apartment, she felt a thrill to see Geoff standing in the living area on his cell phone.

He hung up when he saw her and turned to face her. She saw that look again—something was wrong.

"How was your evening?" he asked.

"Fun, but I missed you, Geoff," she said. "I didn't realize until tonight just how much a part of my life you've become." She wanted to know what he had to say, but not before he knew exactly how she felt.

"You've become very important to me as well," he said.

She dropped her purse on the floor and Godiva trotted out to sniff it. Amelia bent down and petted her adorable little dog before sending her back to her padded bed.

Then she walked over to Geoff. She wrapped her arms around him, resting her head on his chest. Geoff's arms came around her and he held her very tightly to him.

"We need to talk."

She tipped her head back, panic settling in her throat. "Right now? I was hoping that you'd scoop me up and take me to bed. I want you to make love to me."

His pupils dilated and she felt his erection stir against her belly. "I'd like nothing more, but—"

She silenced him with the most passionate kiss she could muster. Finally, he lifted her into his arms and carried her down the hall to her bedroom. He set her on her feet next to the bed. With Geoff she felt exotic in a good way.

She wrapped her arms around his neck and pulled his mouth down to hers, kissing him with all the love she'd kept bottled inside. His mouth opened over hers and she couldn't get enough of him.

She pulled him closer to her and reached for the tie around his neck. For a moment, it seemed like he would try to stop her, but she loosened the knot and pulled it free. She felt his hands on her back and soon he was whispering in her ear, which inflamed her even more.

He found the zipper in the side of her blouse and undid it. She whipped the silk fabric over her head and tossed it on the floor. Reaching for his buttons and undoing them as quickly as her fingers would allow, she fumbled over the middle button.

"Get naked," he said, his voice ragged and almost harsh.

She took off her bra and then unzipped her skirt and pushed it down her legs, along with her panties. She stepped out of her heels and turned to drop her clothing on the floor. Geoff came up behind her.

His naked body pressed all along her back. His hands came up to cup her breasts and tweak her nipples. His hard manhood pressed into her butt and she moved her hips, stroking him with her backside.

He dropped kisses along the length of her neck and she felt his teeth against her skin. She wanted more.

"I need you."

"Amelia," he said. "I need you, too."

He bent her forward and she braced her arms against the bed as he widened his stance behind her. She felt him at the entrance to her body and she tightened and pulsed in anticipation. He cupped her breasts in both his hands and then entered her slowly from behind.

When he was fully seated she almost came. He was so deep and as he thrust in and out of her, she felt everything so much more intensely than she ever had before.

He slid one hand down her body though the thin curls between her legs and stroked the center of her pleasure as he continued to thrust in and out of her.

He leaned in low over her and she felt him pressed all along her back, his hands between her legs and on her breasts. She was completely surrounded by him. Her world narrowed and focused until it was only Geoff.

She felt everything in her body tightening and she called his name as her orgasm rolled through her. A minute later Geoff cried out as he came, filling her with his essence. He fell down on the bed, keeping them connected and holding her close to him. Sweat dried on their bodies as their breathing slowed.

"I love you," she said before she could stop herself.

Geoff's eyes widened. He pulled her back into his arms and made love to her again until they were both exhausted. As they fell asleep, she couldn't shake the thought that Geoff hadn't said he loved her back.

Geoff woke to the sun shining and the smell of coffee from the kitchen. He was in the bed of a woman who'd confessed to loving him last night. He took a moment to savor this before a sick feeling settled in the pit of his stomach as he realized he'd left loose ends last night. Someone had taken a photo of him with Mary and he needed to tell Amelia before she saw it. And that wasn't all he needed to tell her.

He heard her phone ring. A minute later, his mobile phone started ringing. He glanced at the caller ID and saw that it was Edmond. He jumped out of bed, grabbed his pants and yanked them on as he tried to run into the kitchen.

Amelia was standing in the doorway with her little dog dancing at her feet. She was pale and she stared hard at him. She held a copy of *The Sun* in one hand and as he walked toward her she shook her head.

"How could you do this?"

"I can explain," he started to say as his eyes fell on the front page.

There was a photo of him kissing Amelia on the streets of Bath with a caption that read "Sunday?" Next to that was a photo of him kissing Mary hello at her door, and one of them dancing. The caption read "Monday?" The headline read, "Devonshire Playboy Bests Trashy Heiress at Her Own Game."

"What is this, Geoff?"

He took the paper from her and sat down, running his hand through his hair. "I should have told you right away."

"Told me what?"

"That Mary was my date last night."

Amelia had tears in her eyes. He wanted to take back what he had just said. He hurt her, and that wasn't his intent.

"It's was nothing with Mary. She and I had plans to attend the function before I even knew you, but of course the media is trying to make it into something it's not."

"I'm not jealous of Mary Werner," Amelia said. "If you want to spend your time with her, that's fine with me. But do me the courtesy of at least letting me know that you have a date with another woman."

"I—"

"Don't! Please don't try to justify this or explain it to me. I'm not…"

"Not what?"

"Not some party girl you can have an exotic thrill with and then cast aside. I asked you about Mary, remember?"

Geoff shook his head. "I'm not casting you aside. I asked you to move in with me."

"It's not enough. Now I know why you couldn't tell me you loved me last night… I thought the words might be hard for you to say, but now I know this is just a game to you."

"That is not true. Don't let your temper get the better of you."

"Stop trying to calm me down," she said, sparks in her eyes. "I'm so mad at you right now."

"I'm sorry."

She shook her head. "That's not enough. I need you to leave. I don't want to lay eyes on you ever again."

"Too bad…I'm not walking away that easily," he said.

"Your life—our life is not a crazy circus. This is a sensationalized story to try to sell papers. You know that I wouldn't go from one woman's bed to yours."

She started to argue, but then stopped. "You're right. I do know that. But I'm not sure I can hold my head up while the rest of the city believes I'm part of the Devonshire legacy."

"No one believes this crap."

"Yes, they do," she said. Her phone rang again. "We can't keep seeing each other."

"Why not?"

"Because I love you, you idiot, and I can't stand to see a photo of you with another woman. And this won't be the last one. No matter what you do or where you go someone will always be following you trying to find the evidence that you are just like Malcolm."

He was starting to get angry with her. "I'm not Malcolm. And I've never treated you with anything but respect."

"You look like Malcolm," she said. "And you're the

star of the gossip rags this morning with two different women. Are the comparisons starting to add up in your mind?"

"You aren't being rational," he said.

"I am. I'm just not saying anything that you want to hear. But it makes sense. You know as well as I do that ignoring this isn't going to make it go away."

"I don't know that and neither do you. What I know, Amelia, is that you don't even want to try. That you are letting fear guide this decision."

"Fear? Of what?"

"Of finally being with a man who isn't going to let you scare him off with your 'outrageous' behavior. I think you're afraid to live a normal, quiet life. You were probably waiting for this to happen so you could use it as an excuse to cut me out of your life."

His mobile was ringing nonstop; he ignored the calls from his sisters, but his mother wasn't someone he could send to voice mail. When Amelia picked up her dog and walked out of the room, he answered the call from his mother.

"Mum, this is Geoff."

"I'm…I don't know what to say to you. How could you do that to Amelia?"

"It's not what it looks like," he said, trying to defend himself.

"I'm sure in your eyes it isn't. But this behavior is unacceptable and I have no choice but to disown you."

"Mother, don't be dramatic."

"I'm not. You have sisters, Geoff. I raised you to be a gentleman—"

"I *am* a gentleman, Mum. I will fix this."

"You had better. I'm going to call Amelia later. This is…I'm so upset with you, Geoff."

"I know."

He hung up the phone and it rang again, this time it was Edmond.

"Devonshire."

"I guess you've seen the papers this morning."

"Indeed. Did you do this?"

"No. You were managing the heiress and your line of business very well. Why did you add another woman to the mix?"

Geoff realized that what Amelia had said was true. Everyone was going to believe he was simply another Devonshire male who couldn't be satisfied with one woman.

"I didn't. Listen, I need to sort this out with Amelia. She is more important to me than you or Malcolm."

"Is she?" Edmond asked.

"She is. And I have to figure out how to handle this."

"Good luck, sir. I think you will need it."

Geoff knew he wasn't going to be able to fix things right away, and he frankly had no idea what to do. He left her apartment and walked through a flurry of paparazzi—and the idea came to him.

He drew Tommy aside and asked the man to take a picture of him later that day. Then he went home and called his half brothers so they would know what he planned to do.

"I think you're a nutter," Henry said. "But love does that to the best of us."

Love. He'd never thought he'd admit to it, but losing

Amelia made him desperate and he knew that he'd loved her since he'd first clapped eyes on her. "Love will."

"I hate to say it but I agree," Steven said. "I flew to New York when I could have sent my VP and suffered through jet lag just to have a drink with Ainsley."

Geoff laughed and was glad he'd found these brothers. "Are you sure the publicity will be okay?"

"Definitely," Henry said.

"Of course," Steven chimed in. "We need to right the wrongs that Malcolm perpetrated when he abandoned our mothers. Show the world that Devonshire men know how to treat ladies."

"I agree."

He ended the call with his brothers. Now it felt good to call them that. He looked at the sign he'd made and went downstairs and drove his Veyron across town to her apartment building.

Good to his word, Tommy waited out front. Geoff knew this could all backfire, but he also knew that if he didn't take a chance on love with Amelia he'd miss out on the greatest adventure of his life.

He got out of the car and left his suit jacket behind. He held the poster board with the message he'd written on it. Tommy snapped pictures as he walked to the building. And Geoff held up his sign.

"Make sure this gets in *The Sun* tomorrow," Geoff said, handing the man some folded bills.

"I will."

Geoff didn't like the thought of leaving, but he knew that now was the time to wait. So he got in his Veyron and left, hoping tomorrow Amelia would see the papers and put him out of his misery.

* * *

Bebe had arrived shortly after Geoff had left and she stayed the night. They'd drank martinis and talked and cried. Amelia took comfort from her but Bebe couldn't stop the hurt.

Amelia's mobile rang and she glanced at the caller ID. "Hey, Auggie."

"Lia, are you okay? I saw this morning's paper and I'm not sure what to say. I'm ready to end the deal with Everest Air. I mean, no one treats you like he did."

"Thank you, Auggie, but business comes first. This could be your last chance with the board."

"No, sis, you come first. I know I haven't been a great big brother but I'm ready to make up for lost time."

"Auggie, that's so sweet."

"I mean it," he said. "But seeing *The Sun* this morning made me hesitate to call and cancel the deal. Have you seen it?"

"No," she said. She turned to Bebe. "Will you run to the corner kiosk and get *The Sun?*"

"I will."

Bebe left and Auggie hung up. Amelia sat on her couch with her little dog, holding her close and wondering why it was that she kept going after the one thing that she knew she couldn't have. She should have kept her feelings to herself.

But not saying she loved Geoff out loud wouldn't have made the emotions not exist. She did love him and she missed him.

"Oh, my God," Bebe said as she came back into the apartment fifteen minutes later. "Look at this."

Bebe brought the paper to Amelia and she glanced at the photo there. It was Geoff and he held a sign in his hand...*Sunday, Monday and every other day of the week, I love Amelia Munroe.*

She put her hand to her mouth, afraid to believe what she was seeing.

"He's downstairs," Bebe said.

"Who is?"

"Geoff. He told me he wants to see you. Will you let him up?"

"I don't know. What should I do?"

Bebe hugged her close and then stood up. "Listen to the man. You fell in love with him, so he must be something special."

Bebe left and a few minutes later the doorbell rang. She put Godiva down and walked over to answer it. Geoff stood in the doorway, looking as if he hadn't slept a wink all night.

"Can I come in?"

She nodded and stepped back.

"Did you see the paper?" he asked.

"Yes. But that doesn't change anything."

"I love you, Amelia. That changes everything."

She wanted to believe him but her heart was still vulnerable after yesterday, and she was afraid to trust him. "As long as we are together the paps are going to be parked downstairs. They are going to keep on waiting to see what we do next. To try to find some story—because to the world, we don't make sense."

"You make sense to me," he said.

"It's not enough."

Geoff started to sweat. He knew that writing his feelings on a sign for the world to see was one thing, telling Amelia how he felt was another thing entirely. He wasn't sure he wanted her to know that he was vulnerable where she was concerned. That she was the weakness he'd hoped to keep the world from seeing.

He hadn't realized he could love someone the way he loved Amelia. And that scared him.

"I care about you."

The words came out in a rush and weren't at all rehearsed. He was a man who always knew what to say and when to say it, but now, faced with losing the one woman he didn't want to let go of, he couldn't string together a decent sentence.

"I know you do, but that's not enough."

Geoff shook his head. "You are bold and brash and you live your life by your own standards. And…I love you."

"What?"

"You heard me. And I'm not walking out of your door this morning to leave you alone. We are going to spend the rest of our lives together."

"Do you mean that, Geoff?"

"Yes," he said. He walked across the room and pulled her into his arms. "I'm not about to let you go, Amelia Munroe. You are the best thing that has ever happened to me."

She hugged him close. Not saying a word as he held her, he rocked them back and forth. He knew he had a lot of things to get sorted but he was determined to keep Amelia Munroe and make her his wife.

They spent the next month planning their wedding. Geoff attended every public event that she did and was always at her side, touching her and kissing her. And without their releasing a statement or saying a word to the media, the stories started to change. Soon they were called the most romantic couple of the year.

Amelia's mother designed her wedding dress and the invitations were sent out. Bebe was to be the maid of honor and Geoff decided to ask Paul to be his best man. He knew that Caro and Paul were a serious item.

Geoff, Steven and Henry all received a telegram two days before Geoff's wedding that Malcolm had died.

Geoff didn't know how the other men felt, but he had a moment of sadness that he'd never had the chance to really get to know Malcolm.

Steven was declared the winner of the competition that Malcolm had laid for his three heirs. And Geoff and Henry were both given the option of staying on as the CEOs of their business units, something they both accepted.

The morning of the wedding dawned clear and sunny, and Geoff woke his bride by making love to her. Eight hours later she was still glowing as she walked down the aisle toward him.

Choppers flew over the country estate where they were being married and a famous photographer took pictures of them, but Geoff and Amelia both knew that they wouldn't need pictures to remember this moment or this day.

As they shared their first dance together, Amelia looked up at Geoff and reminded him of the promises he'd made to her.

"I would never break a promise to you, Amelia," he said. "I love you too much."

* * * * *

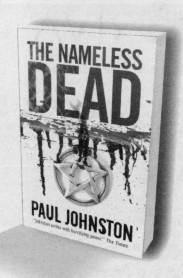

ONE WOMAN'S PRIVATE WAR…

1940, and Vivienne de la Mare waits nervously. The island trembles to the sound of bombs on the French mainland. It will be Guernsey next. And everyone knows that the Nazis are monsters…

Except Captain Lehmann is different…and the reality of war cannot touch the world they have built together. Until Vivienne witnesses the casual, brutal murder of a slave-worker in a Guernsey prison camp… And her choice to help will have terrifying consequences.

Available 20th May 2011
www.mirabooks.co.uk

Kaylee has one addiction: her boyfriend, Nash.

A banshee like Kaylee, Nash understands her like no one else. Nothing can come between them. Until something does.

Demon breath—a super-addictive paranormal drug that can kill. Kaylee and Nash need to cut off the source and protect their human friends—one of whom is already hooked.

But then Kaylee uncovers another demon breath addict. *Nash.*

Book three in the unmissable Soul Screamers *series.*

www.miraink.co.uk

Join us at facebook.com/miraink

Love and betrayal.
A Faery world gone mad.

Deserted by the Winter prince she thought loved
her, half-Summer faery princess, half-human
Meghan is prisoner to the Winter faery queen.
But the real danger comes from the Iron fey—
ironbound faeries only she and her absent
prince have seen.

With Meghan's fey powers cut off, she's stuck in
Faery with only her wits for help. And trusting a
seeming traitor could be deadly.

mira
Ink

"To say that I met Nicholas Brisbane over my husband's dead body is not entirely accurate. Edward, it should be noted, was still twitching upon the floor..."

London, 1886

For Lady Julia Grey, her husband's sudden death at a dinner party is extremely inconvenient. However, things worsen when inscrutable private investigator Nicholas Brisbane reveals that the death was not due to natural causes.

Drawn away from her comfortable, conventional life, Julia is exposed to threatening notes, secret societies and gypsy curses, not to mention Nicholas's charismatic unpredictability.

www.mirabooks.co.uk

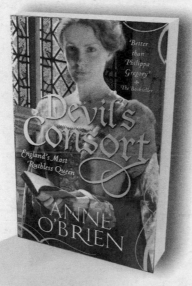

What would you do if your son was accused of murder?

High-powered lawyer Danielle's sixteen-year-old autistic son Max has always been a handful. And when he's discovered, unconscious and bloody, beside a fellow psychiatric patient who's been brutally stabbed to death, it's hard not to question his innocence.

But Danielle swears to save her son from being destroyed by a system that's all too eager to convict him—no matter what the consequences.

On sale 18th February 2011

www.mirabooks.co.uk

Sometimes love is stronger than death…

For Agent Dante Moran, finding Tessa Westbrook's missing daughter becomes personal when he sees the teenager's resemblance to his murdered girlfriend.

Tessa needs to know who told her daughter the terrifying story of her conception. And it soon becomes clear to Dante that the truth is dangerous—but is it worth dying for?

www.mirabooks.co.uk

MIRA

Her only hope of survival was her worst enemy

Private security agent Lucie Evans jumps at the offer of escape to South America to become a billionaire heiress's bodyguard. Then her nightmare begins.

With Lucie's life at stake, her ex-boss Sawyer has to ignore their rocky past and forget his contempt for her before it's too late. Lucie's captor will not rest until she is silenced…once and for all.

www.mirabooks.co.uk

MIRA

FREE BOOK
AND A SURPRISE GIFT

We would like to take this opportunity to thank you for reading this Mills & Boon® book by offering you the chance to take a specially selected book from the Desire™ 2-in-1 series absolutely FREE! We're also making this offer to introduce you to the benefits of the Mills & Boon® Book Club™—

- **FREE home delivery**
- **FREE gifts and competitions**
- **FREE monthly Newsletter**
- **Exclusive Mills & Boon Book Club offers**
- **Books available before they're in the shops**

Accepting this FREE book and gift places you under no obligation to buy, you may cancel at any time, even after receiving your free book. Simply complete your details below and return the entire page to the address below. You don't even need a stamp!

YES Please send me a free Desire 2-in-1 book and a surprise gift. I understand that unless you hear from me, I will receive 2 superb new 2-in-1 books every month for just £5.30 each, postage and packing free. I am under no obligation to purchase any books and may cancel my subscription at any time. The free book and gift will be mine to keep in any case.

Ms/Mrs/Miss/Mr _____ Initials _____

_____

Surname _____

Address _____

_____

_____ Postcode _____

E-mail _____

Send this whole page to: Mills & Boon Book Club, Free Book Offer, FREEPOST NAT 10298, Richmond, TW9 1BR